"Are you in you   "
asked.

"Uh-huh. Down the end of the hallway."

"I know."

Carly twisted her head to peer at him. "How d'you know?"

"I used to watch your lit window on summer nights." He'd ridden his bike across town, from his family's small home in a poor neighborhood to this heritage home on South Hill—which his mom called Snob Hill. Except that Irene was no snob and Carly...well, she'd never once made him feel lesser because of where he lived or who he was. But her father was an investment banker and Carly seemed to have inherited his drive to succeed in business. Finn had no problem with a good work ethic; he had one himself. But what had Irene said? Carly was pushing herself too hard, working all the time. What did she have to prove?

Carly's face lit with a delighted grin. "You couldn't have seen anything. I always drew the curtains."

"Your silhouette was very sexy."

"Liar. I was a beanpole."

Not anymore, he thought. She was shapely in all the right places.

Dear Reader,

Writing this final letter to you is bittersweet—my first published romance novel was a Superromance and the line will always hold a special place in my heart.

It's only fitting that my final Superromance, *Meant to Be Hers*, is a book of my heart. In my twenties I lived in a series of group houses where friends, friends of friends and strangers who became friends created a kind of family. We lived together, ate together, drank together, shared the rent and the chores and the ups and downs of everyone's lives. Just as in *Meant to Be Hers*, a lot of the socializing took place in the kitchen and around the dining table. In the last group house I lived in I met my husband-to-be. We went from housemates to falling in love to getting married and starting our own family.

Meant to Be Hers is about other things, too—rediscovering a career passion, dealing with loss, navigating a path to happiness and, of course, finding that special person, the one you're meant to be with.

Thank you from the bottom of my heart for sharing the journey with me.

Joan Kilby

PS: This isn't goodbye. I'm still writing, with many more stories to tell. Look for them at joankilby.com.

JOAN KILBY

Meant to Be Hers

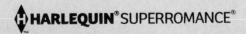

Recycling programs
for this product may
not exist in your area.

ISBN-13: 978-1-335-44925-2

Meant to Be Hers

Copyright © 2018 by Joan Kilby

Printed in U.S.A.

When **Joan Kilby** isn't writing her next Harlequin Superromance title, she loves to travel, often to Asia, which is right on Australia's doorstep, so to speak. Now that her three children are grown, she and her husband enjoy the role reversal of taking off and leaving the kids to take care of the house and pets.

Books by Joan Kilby

HARLEQUIN SUPERROMANCE

Home to Hope Mountain
Maybe This Time
To Be a Family
Protecting Her Son
Two Against the Odds
In His Good Hands
Her Great Expectations
How to Trap a Parent

Visit the Author Profile page at Harlequin.com for more titles.

This book is for all my readers, everywhere. Because of you, I've spent my life doing what I love—telling stories.

CHAPTER ONE

WHERE WAS FINN? Carly Maxwell scanned the funeral guests clustered around her late aunt Irene's living room for the tall, dark-haired musical prodigy. Finn Farrell had been Irene's star pupil, his family's greatest hope and Carly's teenage crush. He should be here. He'd disappointed her aunt enough during her lifetime. Did he have to add to it after her death?

Carly moved among the guests, pouring tea from a huge earthenware teapot, trying to hold herself together when all she wanted to do was curl up under the covers and bawl her eyes out. It didn't help that she was still on New York time and jet-lagged.

"More tea, Brenda?" Carly paused before her cousin, a comfortably plump blonde in her early forties who had sunk deep into soft sofa cushions.

"Yes, please." Brenda's blue eyes were sympathetic as Carly poured unsteadily into a hand-thrown pottery mug. "You've been on your feet since early this morning. Can I take the tea around for you?"

"Thanks, but no," Carly said. "If I stop moving I might never get going again."

In fact, she hadn't stopped the entire week, from the moment she'd heard about Irene's death. Finn's Facebook message had popped into her work inbox like a Molotov cocktail, exploding her crammed diary into shards of missed meetings, unreturned phone calls and hurried apologies. Rushing back to her apartment, she'd listened to voice mail messages from her aunt's neighbor, Frankie, who was worried about Irene's dog, and Irene's lawyer, Peter King, who said her aunt had listed Carly as next of kin.

Carly had caught the red-eye from New York to Seattle, rented a car, and driven up to Fairhaven, Washington, an historic district at the south end of Bellingham. Grief-stricken and in a daze, she'd arranged for a celebrant, put notices in the newspapers and on Irene's social media, organized the funeral home and the caterers. After the service Carly had invited everyone to Irene's three-story Queen Anne home on South Hill for the reception.

Now here they all were. With barely a moment yet to shed a tear she had a feeling she would look back and think the organizing and activity was the easy part. Dealing with her grief was going to be harder.

"Sit down a moment, at least." Brenda patted the taupe cushion next to her. "We haven't had a chance to talk."

Carly sank onto the couch, cradling the warm teapot against her navy suit jacket. "Could you hear me okay when I was giving the eulogy? I wasn't sure if I spoke loudly enough." She'd choked up, every painful pause thick with sorrow. Several of Irene's friends and music students had also spoken. One young girl broke down completely and had to be led off by her mother.

"You were great." Brenda clutched a damp, shredded tissue. "I couldn't have done it."

Carly blinked away the salty moisture burning her eyes. "I can't believe she's gone. Only fifty-eight."

"Fifty-eight going on eighteen," Brenda said with a watery smile. "She was so much fun."

"Thank God she isn't alive to witness her own funeral." Carly glanced around at the somber faces. A girl drooped over the keyboard of the Steinway grand piano, softly picking out minor chords. The gloomy atmosphere was at odds with Irene's uproarious house parties in happier days. "She would have hated all this weeping into hankies."

"Everyone's shell-shocked," Brenda said. "Irene was so full of life, it's hard to believe she could die so quickly. I guess that's what can happen with a brain aneurysm."

"Is it?" Carly asked dully. "I have no idea."

"I Googled it," Brenda said. "Sometimes people survive but have brain damage. Sometimes they go like that." She clicked her fingers.

"Don't, please," Carly begged. "I can't help thinking that if someone had been with her, she might have survived." And not just anyone— her. If she'd accepted Irene's invitation to go on the Alaska cruise, her aunt might be alive today.

"You shouldn't torture yourself. That's an impossible question to answer." Brenda sighed and patted Carly's arm. "It's good to see you, even under the circumstances."

"Are you staying in town long?"

"I have to go back to Portland tomorrow. Work."

"I should be going back to work, too, but there's too much to do here." Carly chewed the inside of her cheek, tasting blood. The timing of Irene's death couldn't have been worse from her perspective. Her high-pressure job as a recruitment consultant for executives had started only a few months ago and already she'd had to ask for time off.

But she wouldn't have had it any other way.

Irene had been like a mother to Carly after her own mom died when Carly was nine years old. An only child, she'd spent every summer after that, and sometimes Christmas, with her aunt. At any rate, there was no one else to organize the funeral. Irene had never married and had no children. Her brother, Brenda's dad, was on a sailboat somewhere in the South Pacific. He'd been notified by ham radio but it would be weeks before he could get back. Carly's father, who might have helped, or at least been a support, was in London on business.

Where was Finn? If anyone should pay his respects to Irene, it was him. As far as Carly knew he hadn't set foot in Fairhaven for twelve years, not since he'd fled town after his disastrous performance at that year-end concert. But she and Finn had been friends, good friends, or so she'd thought. Although what kind of friend ran off to Los Angeles and never contacted a person again?

She roused herself to put an arm around her cousin's shoulders in a quick hug. "We should stay in touch. Come and visit me in Manhattan sometime."

"I will," Brenda promised. "And you're always welcome in Portland."

Rising, Carly glanced out the bay window overlooking the quiet residential street. A vintage red Mustang had just pulled in to the curb. Her heart leaped as a man, easily six foot three, unfolded himself from behind the wheel. He ran a hand quickly through his wild dark hair and straightened the long black waistcoat beneath the slim-cut, asymmetrical suit jacket in ebony satin.

Finn Farrell, at last. Carly saw him glance at the house and his mouth drew down, tight and sad. She could feel his grief from here and her own chest grew heavy. Then he took a deep breath, unclenched his hands and started purposefully up the front path. He was almost at the steps when around the side of the house, a dog barked. Rufus, Irene's ditzy Irish setter. Finn changed direction and headed for the side gate, disappearing from view behind a camellia bush in bloom.

Carly carried on dispensing tea but her gaze kept drifting to the hall from which Finn would appear if he entered by the back door. She accepted condolences and offered hers in return. Her generous, loving aunt had touched so many lives.

A warm, furry body nudged the back of Carly's thigh. Rufus had been distressed all week, restlessly searching the house for Irene and whimpering outside his mistress's closed bedroom door at night. Now he bumped Carly's hand, his red, silky body wriggling for attention, already forgiving her for banishing him to the backyard during the reception.

"Where did you come from?" she said, even though she knew Finn must have let him in. "I'm sorry but you have to go—Rufus, no!" The dog rose on his hind legs and planted his front paws on her chest. Tea jostled out of the pot onto her silk blouse. "Rufus, get off! Help, someone!"

"Down, Rufus. Sit." Finn grabbed Rufus's collar and hauled the dog off. He looked at Carly, his dark eyes connecting with hers. The years apart dissolved in a moment of shared grief. Then his gaze turned curious as he took her in, cataloging the changes, no doubt. Her blond hair a shade darker, and shorter, just brushing her shoulders. A few extra pounds. Fine lines at the corners of her eyes. He had those, too, as well as laugh lines around his mouth.

Coming as she did from Manhattan's Upper East Side, Carly had once thought of the poor-but-talented Finn as a modern-day combination of Byron and James Dean—sexy, poetic and tragic. Naturally, she'd grown out of that silly fantasy. Poetic and sexy he might be but he wasn't tragic, just unreliable.

"Take him out." She dabbed at the wet splotch on her blouse. "Please."

"Sorry I missed the service." Still holding Rufus's collar, Finn leaned in to kiss her cheek. His warm breath stirred old memories, which she ruthlessly shoved away. "I wasn't thinking. As soon as I heard, I just got in the car and drove. Should have taken a plane."

"Irene would have understood." No matter how badly Finn had let Irene down, she'd always forgiven him. Carly wasn't quite so generous. She didn't mind for herself, but her aunt deserved better treatment. She forgot now why she'd wanted him here so badly. He caused ripples, disturbed the equilibrium. People were glancing over at the dog, at the larger-than-life figure Finn cut, shaken out of somnolence.

"How've you been?" Finn's gaze searched hers, oblivious to everyone but her. "You look terrific."

"Good. Well, not so wonderful at the moment obviously." She felt her cheeks heat, and she couldn't take her eyes off his face, drinking in the thick straight slashes of eyebrows, the curling bow of his upper lip, the sexy mole on his right cheek. The eyes that saw everything. Despite his trendy suit, he had a slightly disreputable air about him. How could she possibly feel a tug of attraction after all this time, and everything that had happened between them? Or rather, hadn't happened.

"Help yourself to food." She gestured to the dining room through the arched doorway where the table groaned with sandwiches and cakes. "Do you want tea? Or there's coffee."

"Yeah...no." Finn's gaze skimmed her classic dark suit and discreet heels. "You've gone all corporate. When did that happen?"

"When I grew up and got a real job." The day she'd signed her current work contract she'd gone on a shopping spree to upgrade her wardrobe and was still paying off the resulting credit card bill. She gave him the same once-over. "You've gone all Hollywood."

"Camouflage. It helps to look the part." He swiveled to survey the clusters of dispirited guests. "Irene would have hated this. So hoity-toity, so stuffy."

Even though he echoed her earlier comment, she was irked. Was that a judgment on her? "It is a funeral."

"It should be a celebration of her life. She found something positive in every situation, no matter how dire. She brought people joy." Finn's eyes narrowed a moment and then he snapped his fingers. "I know. We'll have a wake. A good old-fashioned Irish knees up. I know where she kept her good whisky."

A trio of Irene's women friends standing nearby—an older woman in a long skirt, a well-dressed businesswoman and a grandmotherly type—turned, their faces brightening.

Finn winked at them. "These gals are up for it."

"Behave yourself," Carly protested, biting back a smile. Typical Finn, he managed to fluster, annoy and amuse her all at the same time. "For Irene's sake."

"This is for Irene's sake." He removed the teapot from her hands and passed it to the woman with the expensive haircut. "Take care of that, please. We'll be back."

With one arm around Carly's waist and the other hand in a firm grip on Rufus's collar, he steered them out of the living room, across the entrance hall and down the corridor into the kitchen. Deciding it was useless to protest, Carly allowed herself to be led. It was a relief to get out of the gloom.

Finn shooed Rufus into the yard. "Sorry, boy. It's only for a couple of hours." Then he put his hands on Carly's shoulders and gently pushed her into a chair at the long oak table in the middle of the country-style kitchen. "Sit down before you fall down. You look as if you're about to break into a million pieces."

"I'm fine," she insisted. She wasn't, of course, far from it, but she wasn't going to spill her guts to Finn. They'd been too long apart. She didn't know him anymore.

"Now let's see what we've got." He rummaged

through the cupboard above the fridge and took down a bottle of Glenmorangie. Grabbing a pair of water glasses he poured triple shots. Handing one to Carly, he raised his glass. "To Irene."

Carly swirled her glass. She didn't usually drink hard liquor but the smoky amber liquid beckoned. Still, she hesitated. "The guests…"

"We'll get them a drink in a minute."

"That's not what I meant." She took a tentative sip. Silky smooth and fiery, the scotch burned her throat and set up a warm glow in her empty stomach. As if by magic, her frayed nerves calmed. She took another swig. And another. Then wiped her mouth with the back of her hand and thrust her glass forward.

Finn poured another two fingers of scotch. "Careful, don't get plastered. This is sipping whisky. Have respect." He gazed into his glass, a thumb rubbing the rim thoughtfully. "Did my parents come to the funeral?"

"No. I invited them, of course, but they couldn't make it." Carly paused, having gathered from Irene that this was a delicate subject. "Have you seen your mom lately?"

He drained his glass and reached for the bottle. "Not in twelve years."

Carly sipped her scotch, grateful for the numbing haze as questions tumbled around in her head. How could he have stayed estranged from his mother for so long? What had he been doing all these years? Why had he stood her up?

She settled for the more immediate question. "How did you hear about Irene?"

Finn took off his jacket and slung it over the back of a chair. "I Skyped with her last week. She told me about her hiking expedition to Mount Baker."

Carly passed a hand over her eyes. "I still can't believe she went by herself."

"She was very fit, why shouldn't she?" Finn said. "But I asked her to email me when she got back so I would know she'd gotten home safely. When I didn't hear from her, and she didn't respond to my phone calls, I asked Dingo to check on her."

"Dingo? Is he your Aussie friend from high school?"

"Yeah, the ne'er-do-well who introduced me to rock music." Finn's grin flashed and then he sobered. "He told me Irene's death had been reported in the local news that night. She was found on the trail by another hiker."

Until this moment Carly had avoided forming a mental image of Irene at the scene of her death. Now she staggered to her feet and across the tiled floor to lean over the sink, her stomach contracting convulsively. It was wrong that her aunt should have died alone, possibly in pain, without anyone to even hold her hand. Wrong, wrong, wrong.

Finn was instantly at her side. "I had no idea you were such a lightweight drinker, Maxwell. Do I need to take you to the bathroom and hold your hair?" He spoke lightly but his hand on her back was steady and comforting.

"No." She swallowed, willing the wave of nausea to subside. Then she splashed cold water over her face. Finn handed her a towel to dry herself. When she'd recovered, she said, "Irene asked me to go on an Alaskan cruise with her this month. If I'd said yes she might still be alive. She and I could be watching humpback whales together right now. If something went wrong I would have been with her."

Finn took her by the shoulders, forcing her to focus on him. "You couldn't have known she was going to have a brain aneurysm. Her death wasn't your fault."

Maybe not. But she wished she'd made time for her aunt instead of chasing that Wallis Group account. An account she still desperately wanted. Carly dragged her sleeve across her damp eyes. "Did she know anything was wrong with her health? She didn't say anything to me."

"Nor to me." He rubbed Carly's arm. "Don't beat yourself up. She had lots of friends. She could have asked someone else to go on the cruise. Or to go hiking with her. Even then there's no guarantee she would have survived."

"I know." Carly filled her glass with water from the tap. Through the window she could see the backyard and the new leaves on the trees. A pile of tomato stakes rested against the fence next to the shed. April was the month Irene started to dig the garden beds for planting vegetables. Carly could picture her getting tools from the garden shed in the corner of the yard. Trundling wheelbarrow loads of compost over to the beds. Instead, the garden was overgrown with weeds and the grass needed cutting.

"Carly?" Finn said. "Are you okay?"

"I haven't eaten much today." She pressed a hand to her stomach. "The scotch is hitting me hard."

"I meant, in general." He paused, his gaze searching. "I got the impression Irene was worried about you. If there's anything I can do, let me know."

Carly closed her eyes at the rough caring in his voice. She'd had a massive crush on him for years when she was a teenager, but though he'd been friendly and teasing, he hadn't seemed to notice her in "that way" until the summer after he'd graduated high school.

He'd invited her to the year-end concert put on by Irene's students and to the party afterward.

That night he was to perform part of the repertoire he was using for his live audition for the Juilliard School of Music the following week. She'd bought a new dress and sat in the first row next to Irene, her palms damp and heart racing, not sure if she was more excited about his first major public performance, or what might happen afterward.

The concert was held in the high school auditorium and was open to the public. All his schoolteachers and classmates, his friends and their parents, and all of Irene's other students' families had been in the audience. Everyone knew of his talent and was rooting for him to be awarded a scholarship to the prestigious music school. The anticipation had been building for weeks and was a fever pitch by the night of the concert.

And then, disaster. Finn's performance was a shambles. His fingers stumbled over the keys, he forgot whole passages, he stopped midbar and skipped notes. It was so unlike him. Then someone in the back booed and Finn stalked offstage without finishing. Irene had been gray-faced, speechless. His parents, Nora and Ron, had hurried out, their heads hanging. Every single person in the audience had felt some combination of shock, betrayal and disappointment. What should have been a jubilant celebration had turned into a debacle. Finn hadn't gone to New York for his Juilliard audition, nor did he pursue what should have been a stunning classical career. A week after the concert he left town, never to return. He'd not only stood Carly up for the party, he hadn't contacted her or answered her calls. She'd never seen him again until today.

"Why was Aunt Irene worried about me?" Carly asked. One more thing she would never be able to ask her aunt. It was hard to comprehend the fact that she was gone. That Carly could never again pick up the phone and hear her voice.

"Just that you were working too much," Finn said. "I could have misinterpreted. Aren't you a high school guidance counselor?"

"That was years ago," she said. "I switched to human resources. Recently I got a job with an international head hunting firm." She had loved counseling teenagers but one day she'd looked around and realized that her friends were leapfrogging to the top in their various professions whereas she was stagnating. Now or never, she'd told herself, and started applying for jobs that would make use of her dual major in business and psychology. She'd worked her way up the ladder and had recently landed a plum position at a prestigious company.

"Sounds like a big change," Finn said. "Do you like it?"

"Love it." Mostly. Irene was right about working hard. Most weeks she logged upwards of sixty hours. Kind of put a cramp in anything else she might want to do, like have a life. But the payoff would be worth it when one day she got that corner office and the word *partner* after her name.

"Irene told me you live in Los Angeles," she said, changing the subject. "What do you do there?"

"Drink too much," he said cheerfully and raised his glass.

"She had such high hopes for you." The words fell out of her mouth and hung in the air between them.

"My life isn't over yet." Their eyes met and his smile faded at the reminder that Irene's was.

Cursing her lack of tact, she touched his arm. "Sorry." She couldn't begin to understand what had been going through his head at that concert or why he'd blown off a chance for a place at Juilliard. Such a waste of talent.

Finn poured himself another shot. Seeing his long, tapering fingers on the bottle—a pianist's hands—brought back the memory of their first, and only, kiss. The stuffy heat in the third-floor turret of this house, his hands anchoring her hips, the slide of his tongue against hers.

Remembering, a pooling warmth settled in her belly that had nothing to do with the scotch.

He raised the bottle. "Hit you again?"

She pushed her glass closer. He held her wrist to keep the glass steady and sloshed in another two fingers' worth. Then he clinked glasses. "Here's to you, Carly Maxwell. Long time, no see."

This time when she looked into his eyes, a rush of boozy affection washed over her. With his black hair brushed back from a high tanned forehead and his rakish grin, he looked like a pirate in a designer suit. "To the good old days."

He smiled and gave her a wink that made her heart skip. "What might have been may still be yet."

Peter, Irene's attorney, entered the kitchen looking for someplace to put his empty coffee cup. He set it next to the sink. "Carly, while I'm thinking of it, come see me at my office next week for the reading of Irene's will. I'm her executor."

Carly had been so busy organizing the funeral and calling people that she hadn't had time to think about what was going to happen with Irene's property and personal effects. She hoped Irene had remembered how much she loved the seascape that hung in the dining room. It reminded her of their beachcombing expeditions. "I'll call first thing Monday to make an appointment."

Peter spied the bottle of scotch. "Is that alcohol? I sure could use a drink."

"What'll you have?" Finn went to the cupboard over the fridge and started pulling down liquor bottles. "There's also bourbon, gin, vodka and brandy." He handed the bottles to Peter, who lined them up on the table. "Carly, are you okay with dipping into Irene's stock of liquor?"

"Of course," Carly said. "She liked her guests to enjoy themselves."

"To Irene." Finn raised his glass. "An awesome teacher and a good friend."

"To Irene," Carly and Peter chorused.

"Now," Finn said. "It's time to pay tribute to the lady." He headed back to the living room. Carly heard him announce, "Booze in the kitchen, folks. Help yourselves. Then come and sing."

People began to stream into the kitchen. Carly helped them find glasses and ice then left them to it. She wandered back to the living room and stood against the wall between the fireplace and the bay window. Outside, the sun was setting spectacularly over Bellingham Bay.

Finn organized Irene's music students, past and present, coaxing a red-haired man to pick up a guitar from the stand in the corner of the dining room. A fortysomething woman in sleek black pants and a pullover took the cello from the same stand. A teenage boy produced a tenor saxophone and a twentysomething woman a clarinet. The rest Finn arranged into a choir circling the piano where so many of them had honed their singing skills.

He sifted through bundles of sheet music and selected a piece. Then he sat on the bench seat. The instrument was a full concert grand in a richly gleaming mahogany. He ran his long fingers softly over the ivories. Around the room, heads turned and conversation hushed. Carly held her breath, hoping he wouldn't play anything sad that would make her cry.

With a ripple of notes and a flourish of his hands, Finn launched into a popular Gershwin show tune, one of Irene's favorites. Startled, her aunt's former students glanced at each other, then smiled. One woman began to sing, then another. One by one, the other instruments joined in and soon the pickup orchestra and choir were in full swing.

Carly kicked off her high heels and took off her suit jacket, relaxing for the first time in days. The other guests drew closer, their gloomy expressions turning to smiles. Others hurried back out from the kitchen with drinks in their hands. Before long, the whole room was rocking, just as it used to when Irene threw a party. When the first song was over, Finn quickly got them started on another, pounding out the notes, embellishing with his own improvisations. Voices lifted in a rousing tribute to the woman they'd all loved. Music had been Irene's life and Carly was grateful to Finn for transforming the tragic occasion into one of celebration.

Bottles collected on the coffee table. Booze was poured directly into teacups.

Carly drifted back to the kitchen. There the non-singers had gathered to drink shots and exchange anecdotes about their absent friend. The somber mood had evaporated and laughter outweighed the tears. Carly learned tidbits about her aunt that she'd never known as a youngster only coming for summer visits. About how Irene had been a breath of fresh air in the stuffy garden club, how she'd baked dozens of loaves of her special sourdough bread at Christmas for the homeless, how she'd done the limbo at the animal shelter fund-raising party.

"Remember when she got Rufus?" Frankie, the next-door neighbor, had spiky black hair and an impish grin. "He was from a pet hoarder's home and was skinny and mangy. He had so many issues no one wanted him. But she took him and worked with him and now he's a beautiful dog."

Rufus. Carly squinted at her watch. Nearly 7:00 p.m. and the dog hadn't had any dinner. She got to her feet, grabbed for the back of the chair and ended up clutching Frankie's shoulder. *Whoa. Getting a bit tipsy.* The room swayed as she crossed to the laundry room where her aunt kept a big plastic bin of kibble. Carly scraped the bottom with the plastic scoop and got only half a cup. That didn't seem like enough. She added a couple of egg salad sandwiches from the platter on the counter and carried his bowl outside.

Dusk was falling. The sky glowed with the last light of day but the long backyard was full of shadows and the cedar trees along the back fence were a blur of black.

"Dinner, Rufus. Here, boy." She set his bowl onto the concrete patio.

The dog didn't come bounding up as she'd expected. Maybe he was patrolling the back fence, saying hello to the neighboring spaniel. Or digging in the soft dirt beneath the cedars. He was probably fine but she should check. Now where had she put her shoes? Her stockings were already ruined but even so, she didn't fancy crossing the darkened lawn in what amounted to bare feet.

"Carly?" Beneath the patio light, Brenda's cheeks were rosy and her blond hair ruffled.

"D'you know if Irene has more mixer anywhere? I couldn't see any in the pantry."

"I'll have a look." Carly took one last quick scan of the yard, saw no sign of Rufus, and went inside.

She found more tonic water and cola. Then the opening bars of "Happy Talk" from the musical *South Pacific* drew her back to the living room where the singers stood four and five deep around the piano. At the town's summer solstice party every year Irene led the Fairhaven choir in this upbeat song. Carly had no musical talent herself but she knew all the words to all the tunes in her aunt's record collection. She belted out the song, secure in the knowledge that her flat notes would be drowned out by the well-trained voices.

Finn caught her eye and a moment of wordless joy passed between them. Maybe alcohol was making her brain fuzzy but it was wonderful to see him again. For years she'd put him to the back of her mind, never quite forgiving him for that summer. Whatever friction remained between them, he was probably the only other person in the world who had known her aunt as well as she did—and would miss her as much. Tears welling in her eyes, she smiled as she sang.

CHAPTER TWO

"THAT'S THE WAY, one foot in front of the other." Finn put his arm around Carly's waist to guide her up the staircase, no easy task given she wasn't in full control of her limbs. He pretended he didn't notice her left breast moving against his rib cage.

Outside a taxi sounded its horn, ready to take another group of guests home or to their hotel. When Finn had realized the party was getting out of hand he'd insisted drivers hand over their car keys. Brenda had purred at him as she put her keys in the bowl, evidently under the mistaken impression she was participating in a seventies-style, sexy free-for-all. He hadn't seen her for a while and assumed she'd found a bedroom upstairs and was sleeping it off.

As he paused at the landing, Carly slithered out of his grasp and sat abruptly. She gazed blearily up at him, her blond hair mussed and her sky-blue eyes smudged with mascara. The top three buttons of her tailored white blouse were undone, exposing the curve of a creamy breast.

"Ya know," she said, slurring her words and stabbing a finger at him. "Ya might be a screwup but you're awesome. You turned a stuffy funeral into a f-fiesta. Irene woulda been proud."

"She deserved a good send-off." A screwup? Was that how Carly thought of him? True, he'd passed up a chance at a music scholarship after working his ass off for years. But at eighteen he'd changed his mind about wanting to be a classical pianist so it was no loss.

"How come you're not drunk?" Hiccupping, Carly lolled against his leg, stroking the fabric of his suit.

"Didn't feel like it." He'd restrained himself when he realized Carly was going on a bender. Partly because he owed it to Irene to watch out for her. But also because his own emotions—grief over Irene's death, his feelings for Carly, plus ambivalence about being back in Fairhaven—were too big and complicated to drown and too scary to unleash.

Tonight Carly had been like a tightly coiled spring with the pressure released, springing in every direction, out of control. Something was up with her, as Irene had alluded to in their last conversation. He'd like to know more, but he wasn't going to get a meaningful answer in her present condition.

He grabbed her under her arms and tugged her gently to a standing position. "Ready to go?"

She swayed into him, draping her arms around his neck and plastering herself against his body, meltingly soft and warm. "Man, I am so ready."

Her breath held a not unpleasant aroma of aged scotch and her hair gave off a perfumed scent he wanted to bury his nose in. His hands slid of their own accord down her back and settled on the flare of her hips. His gaze dropped to her full, pink mouth. Did she taste as good as he remembered from that time in the tower?

A few years ago he'd looked her up on social media, but she didn't share anything publicly except a few photos of herself with work colleagues, and cute animal videos. His finger had hovered over the Add Friend button then he'd decided that even if she wasn't still pissed off at him, he couldn't bear to field questions about "what are you doing these days?" Followed by polite silences when she found out. Although he didn't know why he thought that way. Everyone he knew in Los Angeles thought he was doing pretty darn good. And he was, only not in the way folks in Fairhaven had expected.

Her eyes drifted closed and she tilted her face as if expecting a kiss. Not being the kind of guy who took advantage of inebriated women, he wasn't going there. Instead, he unhooked her arms from around his neck, faced her forward, and readjusted his grip. "Gee up, little pony."

"Aw, I'm not a pony." She clutched the banister and staggered up another step. "Maybe a Lipizzaner. They're beeyootiful."

"They're stallions."

"Stallions, really? All of them?"

"The ones that perform are. Almost there." He coaxed Carly down the hallway. Judging from the snores emanating from behind closed doors, at least three of the five bedrooms were occupied. "Are you in your old room?"

"Uh-huh. Down th'end."

"I know."

She twisted her head to peer at him. "How d'you know?"

"I used to watch your lighted window on summer nights." He'd ridden his bike across town, from his family's small home in a poor neighborhood to this heritage home on South Hill—which his mom called Snob Hill. Except that Irene was no snob and Carly...well, she'd never once made him feel any less than an equal because of where he lived, even though her father was an investment banker and Carly seemed to have inherited his drive to succeed in business. Finn had no problem with a good work ethic, he had one himself. But what had Irene said? Carly was pushing herself too hard, working all the time. What did she have to prove?

Her face lit with a delighted grin. "You couldn't have seen anything. I always drew the curtains."

"Your silhouette was very sexy."

"Liar, I was a beanpole."

Not any more, he thought. She was shapely in all the right places.

He opened her bedroom door and maneuvered her inside. The single bed was unmade and clothes were piled on an open suitcase balanced on a chair. He got her a big glass of water and stayed beside her while she drank it. "Do you need anything else?"

She splayed her fingers over his chest and looked up at him. "You."

It was the alcohol talking. "Not tonight."

Regret stabbed him for what else he'd thrown away besides the scholarship. Carly? No, that was making too much of their friendship. Her New York family came from old money, and her future was blue chip. She might have a fling with a guy like him but when the crunch came, she would run back to her own kind.

"Come on, Finn." Her finger slid up to rest on the pulse beating in the base of his neck. "Why don't you finish what you started back when we were teenagers?"

For a moment he was tempted despite everything. Maybe it wasn't too late. Maybe he could still have a shot at finding out if that spark they'd had could burst into flame.

Yeah…no. Better not make this any more complicated or difficult than it already was. In a day or two he'd be heading back to LA, and out of her life. Anyway, he wasn't the guy she used to know, the talented pianist with a bright future. Back then he'd been a big fish in the small pond of Fairhaven. Now he was a guy who played on studio recordings for other artists and wrote songs at night. True, one of his songs had become an indie hit, even though Screaming Reindeer had messed around with the tempo. Ruined it, in his opinion. That aside, all his demons were here in Fairhaven, writhing and wailing, buried just out of sight. He didn't want to drag Carly down into his personal hell.

"In you go." He gently pushed her into bed and pretended he hadn't heard her proposition him.

She seemed to have already forgotten anyway, flopping onto the crumpled covers still in her dress. Her stockings were full of runs and one big toe poked through a hole. Not quite as well turned out as earlier in the evening but she was softer, more vulnerable.

Yawning, she punched the feather pillow. "Where are you bunking?"

"Downstairs on the sofa." He thought about helping her out of her clothes and then decided against it. He was going to have a hard enough time sleeping as it was. "I planned to stay at Dingo's but it's late and I don't want to wake him and Marla—"

"Rufus." Carly suddenly bolted upright in bed, eyes wide. "I didn't see him when I went out to give him his dinner."

"He'll be all right."

"I should let him in." She started to get out of bed.

"Stay put. I'll get him."

"But…"

"Go to bed. That's an order."

"Well, okay. Thanks." She subsided onto the pillow and closed her eyes. He was about to turn out the light when she spoke. "Why'd you give it up? Music, I mean. You're good. Professionally-speaking." She slurred the word *professionally* almost to the point of nonrecognition.

Finn's hand tightened on the doorknob. "Who says I gave it up?"

"You used to be brilliant. You could have smashed that concert," she said. "Could've had a scholarship. Could've played Lincoln Center by now if you'd kept at it."

"Yes, I probably could have." He didn't bother defending himself. Carly was in no condition to take in his version of events. Maybe he'd tell her later but this wasn't the moment. "I didn't want to go to Juilliard."

Carly's forehead scrunched in a deep frown as if she was trying hard to concentrate. "So you aren't playing with a symphony orchestra now?"

"No," he said patiently. Had Irene never talked about him to Carly?

"But you're still a musician?"

"Once a musician, always a musician." He could tell her about the studio sessions but no doubt she'd find that incomprehensible, as well. Why would he settle for that when he could have been a concert pianist? A spurt of anger flashed through him that she thought he was a no-hoper for abandoning a promising career. Well, that was her problem, not his.

"Whatever." She gave up and snuggled deeper into the pillow. "'Night."

He refilled her water glass, turned out the light and closed the door. Years ago she'd sat on the window seat in the living room and read while he'd had lessons with Irene. He'd played to her even if she hadn't known it, showing off, perfecting the pieces so she would be impressed. Was it any wonder that she didn't understand why he gave it all up?

He paused outside Irene's bedroom where Carly had posted a Private sign. He'd never been in here and he didn't know what made him open the door now. Looking for absolution? He scoffed at himself. There was none to be found, not here, not anywhere.

Moonlight cast a silver glow over the room, illuminating a white-painted iron bed frame covered with a handmade quilt. An armchair with a floor lamp sat next to the window, a low bookshelf on the other side stacked high with music books. A guitar was propped in the corner and a flute case lay on the dresser.

But it was the sight of Irene's worn Birkenstock sandals next to the bed that clutched at his chest. They looked so empty. He understood Carly's guilt, her sense of regret. Life was short. If he'd known Irene would pass, he would have accompanied her on the Alaskan cruise himself. She'd been like a second mother to him, like his *only* mother given he hadn't spoken to his mom in over a decade. He'd let people down, especially Irene. But he was damned if he would apologize, even now. He'd done what he had to do to survive. Even so, his heart was heavy as he closed the door.

Going downstairs, he walked through the darkened kitchen to open the back door and flip on a patio light. There was a clatter of metal on concrete and a pair of raccoons scattered, retreating a few paces. They'd been eating food set out for the dog, abandoning a sandwich in the water bowl.

"Scat!" He stepped forward onto the grass and clapped his hands to shoo them away. "Rufus! Here boy."

The yard was quiet. Finn waited a few minutes then refilled the food bowl and carried out the dog bed from the kitchen and placed it against the outside wall. Not much more he could do tonight.

He went back inside and through to the living room. The sofa was wide and long enough to be comfortable and the cashmere throw would keep him warm. He started to pull the curtains when his gaze fell on the piano, the richly polished surface gleaming softly in the glow of the moon.

Seating himself he ran his fingers softly over the keys. No one was around to hear. He began to sing a song he'd composed but hadn't offered for sale because he couldn't bear to give *all* his songs to other musicians.

Turning thirty earlier this year had felt like a big deal, as if he'd arrived at adulthood. He'd just sold a couple of songs to a famous artist and to celebrate he'd thrown a huge party, rocking on into the night. Now, only a few months later, that success felt hollow. Being estranged from his family, especially his mother whom he'd been so close to, was hard. And since Irene died, he'd been waking in the small hours, staring up at the dark ceiling wondering, what had he done with his life? Where was he going? Was this all there was, writing songs for other people to sing?

Maybe his indie hit would turn out to be a fluke. More singers were writing their own material these days. Anyway, songwriting was an up-and-down business at best.

Even though Irene had never said so, he knew she'd been disappointed in him, not for messing up at the concert but for giving up performing. She'd been his conscience, and though he'd deliberately ignored her advice at times, he would never forget all she meant to him and had done for him. And while she might be gone, there was no escaping himself. Or the fact that his mother, equally devoted to his musical education, was still around but might as well be dead for all the contact he had with her.

He switched to a lighter piece, trying to shake off the negative vibe that had stolen over him. He was doing what he loved, that was the main thing, right? He missed that connection to an audience but he had a life that many musicians would kill for. He wasn't making a fortune but he had enough to live comfortably. He had friends and a career that was challenging and satisfying. Wanting more would just be greedy.

Accolades didn't mean much to him, anyway. And he knew he would hate the media attention that came with fame. He was happiest like this, the words and music pouring out of him, gritty and real, but hopeful. Moments of feeling down aside, he'd never lost his core optimism, and he clung to it harder than ever now. If he only ever sang his songs for himself it would be enough. It had to be.

CARLY'S EYES OPENED in the dark. Faint sounds came from downstairs. Head spinning, she sat up and listened. Piano music. Finn singing. Stumbling out of bed, she crept out of her room and down the stairs to peer around the doorway into the living room. One look at his face and she changed her mind about going into the room. His eyebrows were pulled together, his expression intensely focused. She knew instinctively that he wouldn't want to be disturbed.

Nor did she want to cause him to stop. The piano notes were riffs upon riffs, complicated and mesmerizing. The words were tender, coaxing, laughing. His husky voice held a yearning tremor that hit her right in her gut. And her heart. The music was powerful in a way she'd never heard from him before. She tiptoed back to the landing and sat on the step, shivering, not with cold but with the force of his voice.

Yes, he was still a musician. The question was, why was he keeping such a treasure hidden?

CHAPTER THREE

CARLY BURROWED DEEPER beneath the covers, trying to shut out the noise of a bird cheeping one note over and over, like a tiny jackhammer to her frontal lobe. Giving up, she pulled down the blanket and squinted into morning sun streaming through the undrawn curtains. Full consciousness hit her like a smack in the face as the previous day came back to her. Irene's funeral, drinking way too much, singing, and talking till she was hoarse. Finn practically carrying her upstairs.

She gulped water from a glass beside the bed that she didn't recall putting there.

Finn must have done it. Finn… Had she really put her arms around his neck and rubbed her body against his, inviting him to finish what he'd started as a teenager? Groaning, she pulled the covers over her head again. She would never have done that in her right mind. Sex with Finn wouldn't be finishing something they'd started. It would be starting something they could never continue. She was going back to New York and he'd return to Los Angeles and never the twain shall meet.

Suddenly she remembered hearing him singing in the middle of the night. Had she dreamed that? He'd sounded unbelievably good. Was that real or had she still been tipsy?

Her phone rang. She scrabbled for it on the bedside table. "'Lo?" she rasped.

"Carly? Are you sick? You don't sound well."

Oh no. Leanne, her boss Herb's personal assistant. Leanne was only twenty-two and looked like a *Vogue* model if models were five foot nothing. She was terrifyingly efficient. Just plain terrifying, really. How did she get her makeup that perfect?

"I'm just…" Hungover. Nope, couldn't say that when it could get back to Herb. Carly struggled to a sitting position. "The funeral was more… intense than I'd expected."

"Oh, yes, I'm sorry about your aunt." Leanne's voice softened and there was a brief pause before she went on. "I hate to bother you at such a sensitive time but there are a couple of things I need to take action on."

Carly gulped more water. "Fire away."

"The senior partners are expecting you for their annual forward planning meeting on May eighth," Leanne said. "I've been asked to confirm your presence."

"Oh, I'll be there." She had to if she wanted to be included when the partners were divvying up the big accounts. She'd been courting the Wallis Group, trying to bring the large financial investment company into the fold for weeks. They had offices on three continents and getting their recruitment business would be a coup, both for the firm and for her, personally. After she'd done all the legwork she was damned if she was going to let another consultant snag the account out from under her.

Carly flipped through her phone for the calendar app. May eighth was two weeks away. She only had a few more days' leave anyway. Since Peter was executor there was nothing left for her to do in Fairhaven now that the funeral was over. "No problem. Lock it in."

"Excellent," Leanne said. "Second item. I'm writing up a furniture order. Do you want a credenza or a bookshelf? You can't have both." There was a touch of the field marshal in her tone, as if Carly had asked for an entire suite of furniture.

"Um…" Carly tried to picture how best to fit her books and personal things into her new office but her brain was too fuzzy to think. "It's Sunday, Leanne. You shouldn't be working."

"Well, I did try to get these things cleared up

on Friday before end of working hours but you weren't answering your phone."

"Sorry. I was busy with funeral arrangements." In between crying jags and looking through albums for photos of Irene to put on display.

"So…?" Leanne prompted.

Carly massaged her throbbing forehead. "Could you repeat the question?"

"Bookshelf or credenza."

"Bookshelf."

"Most of the other recruitment consultants chose a credenza."

"All the more reason to take a bookshelf," she said with a weak laugh. Silence. Carly scrunched her eyes shut as her stab at humor fell like a lead balloon.

"If you say so." Keyboard clicks came down the line. "One final thing. Everyone's getting new business cards. Do you want a serif or sans serif font on your cards?"

"Whatever is the house style will be fine."

"The basic format is the same for everyone but Hamlin and Brand allow their employees small touches of individuality."

Very small touches, Carly thought drily. "I honestly have no opinion on fonts. I'll be happy with whatever you choose."

"It should be your decision," Leanne insisted.

"I'll give you a couple of days to think about it. Get back to me by Wednesday."

Carly bit down on her fist to suppress a groan. "Serif," she blurted.

"No, don't choose like that. You want to project the right image. I'll send you some examples to look at."

"All right. Fine. Goodbye, Leanne." Carly clicked off her phone before the PA could say anything else.

She flung herself back on the bed, an arm across her eyes. Everything would be better when she felt stronger and more in control. Picturing her own office with a bookshelf and a new box of business cards on her desk made her feel a little better. In future she would be very firm with Leanne and not allow the woman to bully her. The Wallis Group account—if she got it—would represent another quantum leap on her trajectory from high school counselor to human resources officer and now international recruiting consultant with her own accounts. The prestige, the salary package, the boost to her curriculum vitae, all a huge step up. She'd better not blow this opportunity.

Until then, she had guests in the house and she needed to make sure Rufus was okay. Ignoring the lurch of her stomach, she swung her legs over the side of the bed, taking half the covers with her. Disentangling her feet from the bedding, she went to her suitcase for clean clothes but found only dress slacks, work skirts and silk blouses. Clearly she hadn't been thinking about comfort when she'd packed. Turning to the closet she dug through her old things until she found a pair of leggings and a flannel shirt. Clutching the clothes, she stumbled down the hall to the bathroom.

Having a shower made her feel marginally better. The non-seductive clothing would send a distinct message to Finn. She had a suspicion she'd cried on his shoulder, too. That was acceptable though, right? After all, she'd just lost her aunt.

Finn had loved Irene, too. He would understand that Carly had been grief-stricken and prone to doing and saying things that she couldn't be held accountable for the next day. When she saw him she would be friendly and polite, like the old buddies they were. Should she apologize for her behavior, or would that give it too much importance? Maybe he'd forgotten or it hadn't even registered. The guy was seriously hot. Women must come on to him all the time.

What*ever*. She didn't have time to obsess over Finn. She had to find Rufus.

All the bedroom doors were shut as she walked down the hall to the staircase. How many people had stayed over? During the university school year Irene rented one or two rooms, mostly to music students but now and then to someone from another faculty. Luckily, the last group of tenants had already moved out for the summer and Carly didn't have to deal with strangers.

In the kitchen, bottles and empty plates littered the counters and the terra-cotta tiled floor had sticky patches. The smell of stale beer made her stomach rumble queasily.

Ignoring the mess, she went outside, her bare toes curling against the cold concrete of the patio. "Rufus?"

"He's missing." Finn came around the side of the house looking disgustingly alert despite his worried frown. This morning he was wearing jeans and a brown leather bomber jacket over a dark green sweater. "I couldn't find him last night and this morning the side gate was open. Hard to tell how long he's been gone."

Carly dragged her hands through her hair, pushing it off her face. "I should never have made him go outside. Irene loved that dog so much. If anything's happened to him I'll never forgive myself."

"It's not your fault. The latch was loose."

"I shouldn't have gone to bed without making sure he was here."

"It's my fault, too," Finn said. "I didn't search because it was late and dark."

Carly sank onto a cedar planter at the edge of the patio. "Rufus is sweet but he has no street smarts. What if he's been hit by a car?"

"We'll find him." Finn touched her shoulder then quickly withdrew his hand.

Too quickly. How hard had she come on to him? Was he wary of getting too close now? Perfect. Her first encounter with the crush of her life in twelve years and she'd made a complete idiot of herself.

"Maybe one of Irene's friends knew he would need a home and took him," she suggested hopefully.

Finn shook his head. "No one takes a dog and doesn't mention it."

"If they were drunk, they might."

"Let's go for a walk and look for him. For all we know he's mooching around somewhere close by."

"Let me grab something quick to eat first."

Back inside she checked the fridge but nothing new had appeared overnight. Same old half-empty jars of marmalade and pickles, out-of-date yogurt and Irene's sourdough starter.

She opened the jar of starter and sniffed the contents. It smelled fruity and yeasty, a bit over-ripe. "I think it's gone off."

Finn took the jar from her. "That's the way it's supposed to smell. But you probably need to feed it."

"Feed it what?" Carly said. "Dead mice?"

"Flour and water," he replied. "It's a bit like a pet, one you knead but you don't have to walk."

Carly bit back a smile at his lame joke and moved to the leftover platters of food on the kitchen table. The past week had been a blur of funeral arrangements. Mundane activities like grocery shopping had gone by the wayside. Irene, who was renowned for her hospitality, would be spinning in her grave—that is, if she'd been buried instead of cremated.

Carly peeled back the plastic wrap on one of the plates and sniffed the stale sandwiches then chose a couple of the least squashed.

"Sure you want to eat those?" Finn asked. "They've been sitting out all night."

"Salmonella poisoning couldn't be worse than I feel right now." She took a bite and offered the other sandwich to Finn.

"Pass." He let a beat go by, then one dark eyebrow cocked. "I don't like to start something I can't finish."

She choked on chicken and cucumber. "About that."

"About what?" he asked innocently.

She'd forgotten how he liked teasing her. And

how she always fell for it. Forget apologizing. Her minor indiscretion was no big deal. "Funny. But I'm not going to bite."

He looked at the sandwich in her hand. "Are you making pun of me?"

Carly rolled her eyes. "Let's go find Rufus."

She grabbed a leash from the hook in the back porch then slipped on a pair of old tennis shoes and a hoodie and they set off down the block.

It was a typical Sunday morning in the small, Pacific northwest town. Many of the houses in this neighborhood were, like Irene's, beautifully maintained period homes. Dads mowed manicured lawns and kids rode bikes. Cherry trees burst with pink blossoms and overhead, the sky was a deep clear blue. Off to the west, the bay was calm with white sails scudding past and a ferry in the distance.

Her gaze drifted to the top of the hill. Not five blocks away was a narrow strip of woods and beyond that, the highway. Six lanes of speeding traffic which might not stop in time for a goofy red dog. "He'll never survive out in the wild on his own."

"South Hill is hardly the wild," Finn said. "He's probably in some little old lady's kitchen right now, chowing down on pork chops."

He sounded so certain she was tempted to believe him. Casting him a sidelong glance she was struck by how good he looked. Today his clothes were casual but stylish, his black hair clean and shiny. "You said you're still a musician. That's pretty vague. What do you do exactly?"

"I'm a studio musician. I play backup on albums."

"I heard you singing last night."

He froze midstride, just for a split second, then resumed walking. "I thought you were asleep. Sorry to disturb you."

"Don't apologize. You were amazing." Just because she hadn't heard of him didn't mean he wasn't a big deal in California. "Have you recorded anything?"

"Did Irene never mention my studio work and that I also write songs for a living?" he said, mildly aggrieved.

"No." Carly didn't want to tell him that she'd always been the one to cut short any conversation about Finn. Mention of him shouldn't hurt so much after so many years…but it did. "Don't you perform?"

"Those days are behind me," Finn said shortly. Then he cupped his hands around his mouth and called, "Ru-fus."

There was no answering *woof.*

"He doesn't know either of us very well," Carly said. "He might not come to us even if we find him."

At the corner they turned to the right and trudged to the top of the hill before making their way down, back and forth along the streets, calling and peering into yards.

"Have you written any songs that I would recognize?" Carly asked.

"One or two, maybe."

Was it her imagination or did he sound a tad touchy? She peered into a hedge but there was no Rufus hiding beneath the dark green foliage.

"So, your parents…" Carly began cautiously. "What happened? I gathered from Irene that you're estranged from them, but she didn't go into detail."

"My mother wanted me to be a classical concert pianist," Finn said. "Juilliard was her idea and she put a lot of pressure on me to go there. She's never forgiven me for the wrecked concert or for bailing on the audition and pursuing my own music in Los Angeles."

"Twelve years is a long time for her to stay mad at you," Carly said. "Maybe while you're here you could reconcile."

"I'm mad, too." Finn stopped, hands on hips. "I called her once or twice over the years but she wasn't cordial. She's blown this whole feud up."

"Someone has to make the first move," Carly said. "Just saying."

"Not going to happen, at least not on my end,"

he said with finality. After a moment's silence he changed the subject. "When I was a kid my dog Prince got lost."

Carly sighed and went with it. She didn't have the energy to pursue the conversation about his mother anyway. "I remember him. He used to follow when you came to Irene's for your music lesson. He was a German shepherd, right?"

"That's right. He was actually a she but Princess didn't seem to suit. She got scared during the fireworks on the Fourth of July, jumped the fence and ran away. We never found her. She probably got run over but I told myself that she ended up in the yard of another little boy and had a great home, even if it wasn't with me."

"That's so sad," Carly said. "I guess they didn't put microchips in dogs' ears back then. Didn't she have a registration tag?"

"Registration costs money." Finn kicked a pebble off the sidewalk. "Any spare cash was spent on my music lessons."

"Oh." His talent had been worth the sacrifices, but Carly could only imagine the stress on the rest of the family. Even the dog had missed out. How betrayed they must have felt when Finn chucked it all in and ran off to Los Angeles, especially his mother, who'd devoted herself to his classical music studies. It must have killed her when he'd thrown away his chance at attending Juilliard.

"This is hopeless." She pressed a hand to her stomach, which had begun to churn again. "Let's go back before I throw up in someone's flower bed."

"What you need is Rhonda's 'Morning After' brunch special," Finn said.

"I don't know what that is, but I'm game for anything that will neutralize the toxins."

Rhonda's turned out to be a trendy corner café in the heart of the old town. The aroma of freshly roasted coffee drew Carly into a light-filled room where potted plants nestled between comfy couches and restored wooden furniture. Plum-colored walls were crowded with original local artwork. The Sunday café crowd was seriously chill with a fair sprinkling of kids. The buzz of genial conversation mingling with recorded jazz in the background was warm and welcoming. In one corner stood a raised platform with a microphone stand and a stool. Overhead, wooden ceiling fans whirred lazily.

"Find a table and I'll order," Finn said. "The works?"

"Yes, please. And a very large coffee. Black. Hot. Strong."

She secured a table and tried to put Rufus and her abandoned funeral guests out of her mind to relax for a few minutes. Her gaze followed Finn as he wove his way to the counter. She wasn't the only one watching. Women's heads turned like dominos.

At the counter, the young waitress, a rounded girl with mousy hair, gazed at Finn with huge, adoring eyes. When he moved to the cash register to pay, she scurried over to ring up his order. He chatted to her, making her laugh. Good thing he wasn't the cocky type or all that female attention would make him unbearable. But aside from his annoying habit of teasing Carly, he was genuinely kind, and his thoughtfulness and quiet strength had helped her through Irene's wake. In fact, she thought drowsily, lulled by the warm atmosphere, she was very grateful for Finn's presence in her life right now.

Carly shifted her gaze to the hand-chalked menu board on the wall behind the coffee machine. Real java done in any style with multiple choices of beans roasted on the premises. If New York wasn't home, she would love living in Fairhaven.

"I waited while the barista made your coffee," Finn said, setting a steaming mug in front of her. "Figured this was an emergency."

"Thanks." She took a sip and moaned in pleasure. "Ah, black, hot and strong. Just what I wanted."

"Black and bitter, she said," Finn murmured, his gaze cast up to the ceiling. "Bitter as the life she once led."

Carly's fingers tightened on the mug. Teasing was one thing but mocking her? "My life is not bitter, okay? Rather sad at the moment but not bitter."

"No need to be defensive. I wasn't talking about you." Finn pulled a battered notebook from his jacket pocket and scribbled with the stub of a very sharp pencil. A silver ring etched with black runes circled his left index finger.

"I'm not defensive. Just setting the record straight." She tried to read upside down but his hand covered the words. "I hope you're not writing a song about my alleged bitterness."

He ripped out the page and showed her. LOST: IRISH SETTER, answers to RUFUS. South Hill area. "Rhonda has a notice board. We can post this on our way out. What's your cell number?"

She told him, thankful that his brain cells were working even if hers weren't.

Flipping the notebook shut, he leaned back in his chair, one side of his mouth curling up. "So, would you like me to write a song about you?"

"No! I wouldn't want my intimate secrets aired in public."

Finn leaned forward. "Tell me more about these secrets. They sound interesting."

"I hardly know you now," she said primly. "Why would I tell you secrets?"

He grinned. "Last night you were ready to haul me off to bed."

"You had your chance and muffed it," she countered with a dismissive flip of her hand. "Too late."

The waitress arrived just then with their breakfast. Chorizo, spinach and feta frittata with fried potatoes, mushrooms and roasted tomatoes. Healthy-ish, but with enough carbs and grease to soak up the lingering alcohol in her system.

The waitress lingered, pulling at her brown ponytail, as Finn took his first bite. "Is it okay?"

Finn smiled at her. "Delicious, thanks…" He read her name tag. "Annie."

Annie broke into a wide smile that transformed her face. "I'll be right back with your freshly squeezed orange juice." With a little skip, she hurried back to the kitchen.

Carly stuffed a forkful of frittata into her mouth. "This is genius. And a lot of food."

"Remember…" Finn gave her a wink. "If you can't finish what you start, I'm your go-to man."

"Stop that, right now." She pointed her fork at him. "I know what you're doing so don't pull those innocent eyes on me. I've known you since you were a pimply-faced adolescent."

"Ouch. So cruel." He sipped his coffee. "Why did you think I could write a song about your bitterness? Alleged bitterness," he amended when she bristled. "You have this perfect life in New York complete with a fabulous new job. What could be wrong?"

"Nothing is wrong. My life is great." She pushed a piece of chorizo around the plate. Yeah, the competitive culture at Hamlin and Brand was tough but she could handle it. In this dog-eat-dog world she needed to be a Rottweiler not a Shih Tzu.

"Glad to hear it," Finn said. "Irene must have been worrying needlessly. She sometimes did."

"I know, right? For someone so laid-back, she could stress out." But Irene's intuition was part of what had made her such a great teacher and musician in her own right. What did she know about Carly that Carly didn't know herself?

Finn was still studying her face intently. Was he thinking about a song he was writing…or about kissing her? Goodness, why had that popped into her mind? Now she could barely breathe. Feeling heat creep up her neck, she dropped her gaze and concentrated on spearing a mushroom.

A buzz of static from the stage heralded the arrival of a man in jeans and a gray T-shirt with a sun-streaked brown ponytail. He bent to speak into the microphone.

"Welcome to open mike," he said with an Australian drawl. "My name's Dingo and I'll be MC today. If anyone wants to add their name to the list of performers, we have a few slots free."

"Is that your friend?" Carly asked, interested.

"Yep. He has a cover band that plays mostly sixties rock but he does this on Sundays." Finn waved to Dingo. A pretty brunette sat at the table next to the stage, a sturdy blond toddler on her knee. When the little boy saw Finn he tried to launch himself across the café. "That's his wife, Marla, and their ankle biter, Tyler."

"We have a local hero in the audience today," Dingo announced. "Finn Farrell, how about singing us your hit song?"

The crowd began to clap, encouraging Finn to play.

"What does he mean, your hit?" Carly asked.

"Just a song I wrote." Finn shook his head at the stage, mouthing, "No."

"Ah, right, sorry." Dingo's face twisted into an apologetic grimace as if he'd just remembered about Irene and was mentally kicking himself. "No worries, mate."

The café crowd didn't seem to notice this exchange. Dingo's apology was drowned out by whistling and applauding. The clapping became rhythmic. Finn half rose and made a small bow with his hands palm out in gracious refusal.

Still, the audience kept clapping and calling out. Finn sank lower in his seat. Carly frowned. Couldn't they see that he didn't want to play? Unable to stand it another second, she moved her elbow and knocked over her glass of juice. It rolled off the table and clattered to the floor. Juice splashed everywhere.

"I'm so clumsy." She leaped up and dabbed ineffectually at the mess. "Can't take me anywhere."

All eyes had now turned to her but the clapping stopped, thank goodness. Annie brought over a cloth and mopped up, retrieving the fallen glass. Meanwhile, Dingo strummed his guitar, bringing attention back to the stage. A murmur of approval rose from the audience.

Carly recognized a recent indie chart-topper. "I love this song." She glanced at Finn, thinking he'd be pleased no one was looking at him anymore, and was surprised to see he was still tense.

He tapped out the beat with long fingers on his knee. Now and then he grimaced painfully. Before the song was even finished, he was on his feet. "Let's get out of here."

He lifted a hand in Dingo's direction and headed for the exit. Dingo sang the last bars but his worried gaze followed Finn across the café.

Carly grabbed her hoodie. She was almost out the door before she remembered the community noticeboard and quickly tacked up the notice Finn had composed.

"Slow down," she called, running after him. He strode ahead, his long legs encased in skinny jeans, his broad shoulders hunched. Catching up, she grabbed his jacket sleeve, forcing him to look at her. His face was white and dotted with perspiration.

Shocked, she let go of his sleeve. "What's wrong?"

CHAPTER FOUR

FINN PULLED ON the neck of his sweater, sucking in air as Carly stared at him, eyes wide. Inside his tight chest his heart thudded like a drum solo. If he'd known Dingo was going to blindside him like that he would never have set foot in Rhonda's café.

"What's going on, Finn?" Carly said. "What happened back there?"

"You wanted to know if you'd ever heard a song I wrote?" he said. "That was my song. I wrote it."

"Are you kidding me?" Her eyes popped. "I had no idea you were famous."

"I'm not," he said flatly. "The band who sang it is."

"Why didn't you sing?" she asked. "Why let Dingo do your song?"

"I don't perform anymore." He hated the way Carly was looking at him, all worried and wanting an explanation. He'd enjoyed hanging with her and hoped they could spend a day or two together before he went on his way. Not going to happen now.

He resumed stalking up the hill. It galled him that fans loved the Screaming Reindeer's version, and today, Dingo's. They were all fine musicians, no offense, but no one had ever heard the song the way he'd intended it to be played. The familiar dilemma stuck in Finn's craw. He couldn't have it both ways, simultaneously wanting anonymity and recognition. Craving the applause but not willing to risk making a fool of himself by choking onstage.

"Finn, wait," Carly persisted, hurrying after him. "Why did you run out? Why do you look like you're having a heart attack? And why are you scowling? Aren't you pleased that people like your music?"

"I should be, shouldn't I?" Finn strode briskly up South Hill toward Irene's house.

Carly jogged behind, trying to keep up. "So what's the problem?"

He threw her a black look. "Forget it. It's no concern of yours."

"You were my aunt's favorite student," she said. "Her concern is my concern."

"I'm not a lost dog," he growled. "You're not responsible for me."

"I care about you! You and I go back a long

way. I thought we were friends." She stopped and pressed a hand to her stomach.

Finn circled back and put a hand under her elbow. "Are you all right? You look sick."

"I think I really am going to throw up this time." Beads of sweat broke out on her forehead. "I am never drinking scotch again."

"Sit down." He led her to a stone retaining wall and made her sit, gently pressing her head forward with a hand on her back. "Head between the legs. Never would have pegged you as being so high maintenance."

"I'm not. Usually I'm the one looking after other people." Her voice was muffled by the messy honey-blond hair falling over either side of her face.

Her slender nape looked so pretty and feminine. Finn blew on her damp skin and massaged circles on her back. Soothing Carly took his mind off himself and helped him calm down. There were better things to expend his emotional energy on than flogging himself for not being the man everyone had expected him to be.

Her breathing slowed and after a moment she sat up. "Thanks. I was afraid for a moment I was going to lose the hangover cure."

He brushed the hair out of her eyes. Soft and silky, it slipped through his fingers as he tucked it behind her ears. "Sit here. I'll go get my car."

"No, just give me a minute. I'll be all right." She straightened and pushed his hands away. "I still don't get why you walked out of the café."

Finn's sigh was more like a groan and came from someplace deep and dark. He wasn't ready to spill his guts to Carly, not even after she'd witnessed his anxiety, so he continued talking about the side issue. "This is going to sound egotistical but I can't stand hearing my music played by other people. Not the artists I sold it to, not even my friends."

"Why not?" she asked. "It's such a compliment. Aren't you proud?"

"No one ever plays my music the way I hear it in my head." His hands clenched. "It…grates. I try not to make a thing of it, but that's the way it is."

"That's not egotistical," she said. "That's wanting to express your vision. You should play your music yourself, show the world how it's supposed to sound and what it means to you. Why didn't you take the opportunity today?"

"I wasn't prepared." But it was more than that, of course. Even now he could feel the band tighten around his chest and he struggled for breath. "After that failed concert I never performed before an audience again." Not successfully, that is.

Carly lifted her head, eyes wide. "But…that's totally messed up."

"That's me, messed up."

"Wait, I'm confused," Carly said. "The difficulty breathing, the perspiration on your forehead. That looks like anxiety to me. Are you saying you don't want to perform, or that you can't?"

"Can't, don't want to, what's the difference?"

"Big difference. Huge."

"It comes to the same thing."

A crease appeared between Carly's eyebrows as she tried to puzzle him out. "You played last night at Irene's wake. You were right into it, enjoying yourself."

True, but there hadn't been an audience per se. He'd been surrounded by other musicians all singing or playing. He hadn't even thought about it, just headed for the piano and tried to conjure Irene from the keys. Put him in front of a room of people watching and he would have frozen, as he knew from painful experience the few times he'd attempted it in Los Angeles bars.

"Well?" Carly was eyeing him like a therapist trying to bring her patient to the brink of a breakthrough.

"Don't go getting any ideas that you can help me, or change me," he said. "Your aunt tried to do that. It didn't work. And I owed her a whole lot more than I owe you."

"You don't owe me anything." Carly touched his chest with her fingertips. "Irene didn't believe you owed her anything, either." Sadly, she added, "She loved you."

"I loved her, too," Finn said quietly. He hated that he'd hurt her. And he hated that he'd let his mother down. But he'd also vowed that he wasn't going to try to live up to anyone's expectations but his own.

As if she'd read his mind, Carly said, "It's yourself you're hurting by not fulfilling your potential."

Not fulfilling his potential. How many times had he heard that? Way too many. His life was not a tragedy.

"I'm better off than a lot of people." And he was grateful for it every single day. Rising, he said, "Ready to go?"

They trudged up the steep hill, Carly half a step behind, silent, no doubt still taking in everything he'd said. Finn walked faster, his shoulders bowed by the weight of everyone's unfulfilled dreams for him. Ahead, his Mustang beckoned. He longed to sink into the soft black leather, turn the music up real loud, and head on down the road. Out on the highway, all by himself, his problems wouldn't exist. But he couldn't leave town so soon after the funeral when Carly was still bereft over Irene and she hadn't found Rufus.

He slowed as he approached the car, reaching into his pocket to jingle his keys. "Do you want to drive around, look for Rufus some more?"

Carly hesitated, glancing toward the house. "I should probably go inside, see if anyone's still there."

"Okay, well, I'll cruise around for a bit before I go over to Dingo and Marla's."

"They'll be worried about you," Carly said.

"They're cool." But he felt bad about the way things had played out. Dingo would never deliberately make Finn feel uncomfortable. He'd only played the song as a nod to him. It was Finn's fault for not confiding fully in his friend. He'd told Carly more in the past five minutes than he'd told Dingo in twelve years. How had she managed that?

"How will I get in touch with you?" she asked. "You know, if Rufus comes home."

"Give me your phone." When she fished it out of her pocket, he programmed in his cell number. "I'll be in town for a few days. I'll touch base later tonight, see how you're doing. Call me if you need anything."

"Thanks for helping me search, and for well,

everything." Her smile came and went quickly. "I wouldn't have survived last night if not for you."

"You were doing just fine."

"No, I was floundering."

"All you needed was a stiff drink."

"Or five." She made a face that was half grimace, half grin. "Thanks for the hangover, too. It's a doozy."

"Hey, I poured you two glasses. You did the rest." She rolled her eyes but there was a sparkle there. *Always leave 'em laughing.* He opened his arms. "Come here, Maxwell."

After a moment's hesitation, she stepped into his embrace. He folded his arms around her. With her head tucked beneath his chin and her cheek pressed to his chest, she fit just right.

"Everything's going to be okay." The words came out more gruffly than he'd intended. Truth was, he needed her emotional support as much as she needed his. Now he didn't want to go but it was too late to make an excuse to stay.

"I know." She hugged him hard, then kissed him briefly on the cheek before easing away, hands jammed in the front pocket of her hoodie. Her face worked and moisture filled her eyes. He was about to reach for her again when with a wave of her hand, she turned and walked swiftly up the steps. The front door opened and shut with finality.

He took a step toward the house then stopped. She'd said she was okay. Don't push it. Things were better off uncomplicated. And the last thing he wanted was for her, or anyone, to try to fix him. His career and his relationship with his parents might be broken but he wasn't.

CARLY CLIMBED THE front steps as the Mustang's engine growled to life. From the porch she watched Finn do a U-turn and roar off. Here and gone, kind of like her whole experience of him. In the twenty or so years that she'd known him, she'd only seen snapshots of his life. Childhood and long summer days when the sweetest music was the jingle of the ice cream truck. Then came the teenage years and the excitement of a new awareness. She'd eyed him covertly, managed the odd fumbling touch of hands, then that kiss in the tower...

She'd known nothing of the trials he went through during the rest of the year when she wasn't around. He must have grappled with schoolwork that took a back seat to music, parental pressure and expectations, his family struggling to make ends meet.

In her limited viewpoint, his musical progress had come in spurts. One year he was a boy tenor playing simple pieces on the concert grand. The next summer his voice had broken and he'd graduated to longer, more complex music. She still couldn't wrap her head around the fact that he no longer performed. At the café he'd shown the classic symptoms of an anxiety attack. Maybe it wasn't surprising considering how that concert had ended. It was a crime that his talent was lost to the world, whether he would have gone on to play his own music or classical.

Nor could she understand how he could have stayed estranged from his parents for so long. He and his mom had been so close. Did that conflict have anything to do with Finn's inability to play in front of an audience?

She hated that he seemed to have settled into an obscure career. No doubt he enjoyed writing songs but once upon a time he'd wanted so much more. She was convinced he still did. He'd tacitly admitted as much by wanting to hear his music played the way he'd envisioned it.

With a sigh, she went inside the house. Lead-lights spilled a jeweled glow on the polished wood floor of the foyer. Moving through the jungle of potted ferns, she entered the living room, an eclectic collection of antique and modern furniture, Persian carpets and avant-garde sculpture. Her aunt had talked of updating the house while retaining the period features but had never got around to renovating. Now that would never happen. Carly went around the room looking for stray cups and plates. There weren't any. Someone must have already cleaned up.

Her heart hurt for Finn but it was no use trying to analyze him. Even as a teenager, he'd been a complicated character. Aside from any romantic or sexual fantasies she used to have about him—and they were just that, fantasies—she had no illusions she could help him. If he, with all his passion and drive for music, had given it up, how could she change his mind? Anyway, he'd made it very clear he didn't want her to interfere in his life.

Before Rufus had run away, she'd been half hoping Finn would take the dog. Now she wondered what kind of a life he led in Los Angeles. Did he have a girlfriend or a long-term partner, or even a dog already? Maybe the place he lived in LA didn't allow dogs. Although if he wrote top-ten songs he probably wasn't hurting for money.

Carly carried the dishes along the passage and heard women's voices in the kitchen. Brenda was at the sink, washing crystal glasses that couldn't go in the dishwasher. Blond curls were stuck to her temples and she had an apron tied around her ample waist. Frankie from next door had put her hair up in a spiky black knot and was mopping the floor. The leftover food had been put away and the empty liquor bottles moved to the recycling box.

"You didn't need to do this, but thank you. I can't tell you how much I appreciate you both being here." Carly hugged Frankie, leaning over the mop to squeeze the shorter woman's narrow shoulders. Then she stepped carefully across the damp tiles to embrace Brenda.

Her cousin's wet hands were warm on her back. "How are you feeling this morning?" Brenda said. "You looked as if you were having a good time last night. Irene would have been proud of the way you sang."

Carly winced at the memory of belting out "Oklahoma." "Someone should have reminded me that I can't carry a tune in the proverbial bucket."

"No one cares. What mattered was that we honored Irene with a fitting send-off." Frankie nodded at a plate of blueberry muffins on the counter. "Hungry?"

"I had a huge breakfast at Rhonda's café with Finn." Carly drifted to the counter anyway, irresistibly drawn by the warm scent of fruit and vanilla.

"I made them this morning," Frankie said. "Think of them as breakfast dessert."

"Is that a thing?" Carly took a muffin and bit

into a moist crumb bursting with blueberries. "Mmm. If it's not, it should be."

"That Finn sure can play the piano," Brenda said.

"Not a bad looker, either," Frankie said, winking. "If I wasn't happily married…"

"Didn't you and he go together years ago?" Brenda asked Carly.

"No." There was only that one kiss. Things might have progressed if they'd gone to the party afterward instead of him running out of the concert. But that was water under the bridge. And she didn't want Brenda and Frankie jumping to false conclusions. Her thoughts about Finn were jumbled enough as it was.

"Where is he, anyway?" Brenda asked.

"He had things to do." Carly turned to Frankie. "Irene told me how you and she used to exchange recipes."

"Yep, we bonded over baking." Frankie slid the bucket along the floor and mopped under the table. She'd stacked the chairs on top for easy access.

"Would you like to have Irene's sourdough starter?" Carly asked. "She's kept it going for decades. I hate to throw it away."

"Oh, honey, she gave me some long ago." Frankie blew a wisp of damp hair off her forehead. "All her friends have a bit. I tried making bread but sourdough is an art and keeping the starter alive takes commitment. I've got three kids and a husband plus I work part-time at an aged care center." She smiled cheerfully. "If I had to nurture one more thing I'd probably sit and cry."

Carly turned to her cousin. "Brenda?"

"I can't keep a cactus alive." Brenda pulled the plug to empty the sink then grabbed a towel to dry her hands. "Throw it away and don't look back. It's not like you're putting down a sentient creature."

"I know but…" Carly licked blueberry off her finger. "It meant so much to Irene."

"You can't keep her alive by holding on to her stuff." Brenda's blue eyes turned gentle. "Dad and I went through this when my mom passed two years ago. The sourdough is only the beginning. You're going to have a difficult enough job clearing out her things. You have to learn to be ruthless."

"But… Irene's estate will pass to your father, won't it?" Carly said. "As her brother, he's her closest relative."

She would be happy to help her uncle Larry dispose of Irene's personal effects but didn't relish deciding the fate of her aunt's collection of art objects and furniture.

"I don't know." Brenda shrugged. "It's not like

he needs it. He made a pile of dough when he sold his tech company."

"The reading of the will is next week," Carly said. "Maybe you should be there since your father can't."

"Sorry, I really do need to get back to Portland," Brenda said. "Let me know what happens and I'll pass it on to Dad."

"Sure." Carly nodded. "Have either of you seen Rufus? He went missing last night. Finn and I searched the whole neighborhood this morning."

"No, I was wondering where he'd got to," Brenda said. "That's terrible."

"I haven't seen him, either." Frankie straightened to wring out the mop. "Have you called the animal shelter?"

"Not yet. I'll do that." Carly pulled her phone out of her hoodie pocket and flicked it on to find a dozen messages. Her father; Althea, a friend in New York; Herb, her boss; a celebrant she'd contacted but not used in the end. She would reply to those TEXTS later. Finn's message she opened and read aloud, "Checked the animal shelter. Rufus hasn't been brought in."

"I'm sure he'll turn up. Never knew that dog to miss a meal." Frankie took the bucket and mop out to the laundry room. When she returned she glanced around the clean kitchen and nodded, satisfied. "I've got to take my son to soccer. 'Bye, Brenda. Nice to meet you."

"Likewise. I wish it had been under different circumstances." Brenda turned to Carly. "I'm going, too. Sorry I can't stay and help some more."

"It's fine. Thanks again."

Carly walked them out, leading the way down the hall to the foyer. While Brenda ran upstairs to get her suitcase, Carly gave Frankie another hug. "I'm glad I got to talk to you last night. Now I know why my aunt liked you so much."

Frankie squeezed her shoulders. "Come over any time for coffee. How long are you staying in town?"

"Not long," Carly said. "A few more days."

"With Irene's passing I don't suppose you'll come west as often." Frankie started down the steps. At the bottom she turned and looked up at the house, a wistful expression softening her pointed features. "I'll miss hearing the music. In the evening, after her students had gone, she would play the piano for hours."

"I remember." Carly leaned on a post, smiling. "When I was young and had to go to bed early, I would lie awake, listening."

"Mom!" A boy of about nine in a soccer uniform of a white jersey with green shorts and socks ran out of the house next door. "I'm going to be late."

"Coming!" Frankie waved goodbye to Carly and hurried down the sidewalk.

Brenda bustled out, wheeling an overnight bag. "Take care and keep in touch, okay? You have my email. My cell number is in Irene's address book next to the phone. Call me any time."

"I will." Carly hugged her and waited until Brenda had driven off in her rental car. Before she could head inside, a red Mini packed to the roof with overflowing boxes pulled out of the parking spot Brenda had vacated.

The door opened and a tall young man unfolded his thin limbs and emerged. In his midtwenties, he had dark blond hair neatly combed from a side part and wore thick glasses. His blue cardigan looked hand-knit and the pocket protector in his cotton shirt bulged with pens, a small ruler and a calculator.

He pulled a piece of paper from his back pocket and consulted it, looking up at the house.

"Can I help you?" Carly asked.

He wiped his palms on his pants and approached the open gate in the picket fence. "I'm Taylor Greene. It's April 30. I'm a day early. I hope that's okay."

"I'm sorry, I don't understand what you're talking about."

He adjusted his glasses and squinted at her. "Are you Irene Grant?"

"No, I'm her niece, Carly. Irene passed last week."

"Oh, I'm sorry. I didn't know." He made as if to drag his hand through his hair then carefully patted it instead. "The thing is, I rented a room in her house." He gestured to his car. "I've brought all my stuff, ready to move in."

Carly's headache returned, tiny hammer blows to her right temple. "I'm afraid that's not possible. I had no idea she'd rented out a room or I would have contacted you to let you know it's no longer available."

Behind his thick lenses panic flashed in his eyes. "You don't understand. I really need this."

"The room isn't available," Carly repeated. "I don't know what's happening to the house but I imagine it will be sold."

"I have a rental agreement," he insisted. "I viewed the listing online and deposited the first month's rent directly into her bank account."

How could he not understand? Her aunt was dead. "I'll return your money, of course." Carly turned her palms out. "I wish I could help you but—"

"She was so kind and welcoming." Taylor's tone hovered between hope and despair. Behind his thick glasses his eyes beseeched. "Breakfast and dinner were included."

"I'll talk to her bank manager tomorrow and arrange a repayment," Carly said. "You must see it's impossible."

"Please don't say that. I'm doing my PhD and starting a new phase of my research tomorrow. I've booked the telescope. If I miss my slot I won't get another chance for months. I don't have time to look for another place to rent." He swallowed, his Adam's apple bobbing. "Anyway, I can't go back."

"Back where?"

"H-home." His voice cracked.

Carly had a strong urge to run inside and lock the door. She didn't want to know, didn't want to feel sympathy for him. All too easily she got entangled in people's lives and tried to help them.

"Did your marriage end?" she asked reluctantly. "Did you break up with your girlfriend?"

His fair skin suffused with color from his collar to his hairline. "I still live at home. My father left my mother for another woman last year. Since then I've been all my mom's got." He broke off to take an asthma puffer from his pocket, sucking in a couple of deep pulls. "If I go back now I may not have the guts to leave again." He stood there, arms slack at his side, resignedly awaiting her verdict.

Carly sighed. "You'd better come inside and we'll talk about it."

Taylor followed her into the house, craning his neck to glance around as she led him straight to the kitchen. "It's even nicer than it looked on-line."

"Have a seat," Carly said. "Do you want a cup of coffee, or a beer?"

"A beer sounds great." He sat at the table. "That's something I should buy for myself, though, right?"

"If you were staying, yes." She handed him a beer from the fridge and crossed her arms. "You say you're doing a PhD. What's your thesis topic?"

"Astrophysics," Taylor said, "Pulsar activity."

"Pulsars. What are those exactly?"

Behind his glasses, Taylor's eyes glowed. "When a star explodes it leaves behind pieces no bigger than a grain of salt. Yet each grain weighs more than the sum total of every human being on Earth."

"I didn't know that." Drawn in despite herself, Carly sank into a chair.

"The tiny grains emit pulses of light that travel clear across the universe." Taylor waved raw-boned, big-knuckled hands as he warmed to his subject. "I'm hoping to pick up pulsars from trillions of light-years away."

The scientific details meant little to Carly but she was impressed with the way Taylor lit up like a supernova when he spoke of his research. If only the clients she dealt with had that kind of excitement for their profession, her job would be so much more rewarding. Most of the people she interviewed had pat answers to standard questions. Many claimed to have passion, but it was clear they only said that because they thought it was expected. Taylor was the real deal.

"Can you show me the agreement between you and my aunt?" she asked Taylor.

"Sure." He pulled out his phone and scrolled through emails until he came to the simple contract. It was as he'd said. Irene had agreed to give him room and board for the summer term. "I have a copy printed out and signed by both parties in my files but that's in the car. Do you want to see that, too?"

"Yes," Carly said. "I'll have to show it to my aunt's lawyer when I meet with him this week, see what he says."

"Does that mean I can stay?" he asked hopefully.

Carly hesitated. Everything in her screamed that she was making a mistake not turning him away now but he seemed so needy and she was a sucker for strays, always had been.

"For now," she said. "I don't know what the

lawyer will say but it's quite possible that who- ever inherits this house will sell it. You'd better prepare yourself to find other accommodation as soon as possible."

"Okay." He shook her hand with big pumps. When he smiled, he was quite good-looking in a geeky sort of way. "Thanks, thanks very much. I'll bring my stuff in."

Carly watched his loping stride as he eagerly headed back to his car. Great. This was all she needed on top of everything else.

CHAPTER FIVE

FINN DROVE SLOWLY down the main drag of
Fairhaven, keeping his eye out for Rufus's red-
gold coat and the fringed tail that waved like
a flag. The town had changed since he'd lived
here. The Mexican restaurant was still there and
the secondhand bookstore. But alongside the historic buildings there were trendy stores selling
eco-this and organic that. The Alaska ferry and
a cruise ship were in port and shoals of tourists
roamed the streets.

It took all of three minutes to drive through
town and then he was heading south on Chuckanut Drive. Now that his pulse had finally slowed
and his breathing was even, he tried to put the
incident at the café into perspective. Maybe sixty
people witnessed today. What exactly had they
seen? A guy declining an invitation to get onstage. Big deal. They didn't know he'd broken
out in a cold sweat or that his heart rate had shot
to two hundred plus beats per minute.

Get over yourself, Farrell. Nobody ever died
from embarrassment. He might be well known

in songwriting circles but hardly anyone outside that world had heard of him. And that was just fine.

But it bothered him that Carly had witnessed his humiliation—again. He cared about what she thought of him. Twelve years on the shame of that concert still burned hot and bright, the pain still raw.

He slowed as he passed the mudflats at the mouth of Chuckanut Creek and came to Teddy Bear Cove. Irene used to walk Rufus here but the pebbled shoreline was empty. It didn't seem likely the dog would have gone this far overnight. At the end of Chuckanut he looped back to Fairhaven along the freeway.

Taking the off-ramp back into town, Finn turned down a side road where the houses were smaller and the cars older. The Mustang's engine rumbled as he cruised through the quiet, familiar streets. Slowing, he pulled to a stop outside the house where he'd grown up, gray stucco with an asphalt tile roof. The trim had been painted a cream color and the gravel driveway was paved. His parents were doing better since he'd left. Well, sure, they had more money to spend now that they weren't paying for his musical tuition.

He saw the house as if with X-ray vision. The small bedroom he and his big brother Joe had shared, their walls covered with posters of rock

bands and hot cars. The living room and the upright piano his mom had bought secondhand.
She'd been his first teacher, showing him the
scales and how to play simple tunes. There was
the kitchen where the family had sat around the
table playing board games in the evenings. And
the backyard, scene of extended family gather-
ings with aunts, uncles and a mess of younger
cousins.

A man with close-cropped gray hair and
glasses, dressed in jeans and an old sweatshirt,
came through the carport pushing a lawn mower.
It took Finn a moment to recognize with shock
that it was his dad, Ron Farrell. Twelve years
had wrought big changes—the gray hair, creased
forehead, a mouth bracketed by deep grooves.
The signs of aging brought home just how long
Finn had been away and how much of his parents' lives he'd missed. He knew some things
from talking to his brother but that wasn't the
same as spending time together, or hearing about
the day-to-day stuff. He ached for that lost time.

His father was about to start the mower when
he noticed the Mustang idling at his curb. "Can
I help you?" Then his head jerked as he recognized his son. "Finn."

Finn turned off the engine and got out of the
car, searching his father's face for signs of welcome but finding only a wariness that increased

his sense of isolation. Awkwardly, he went in for a brief man hug. "Good to see you, Dad. It's been so long."

"I guess you're in Fairhaven for Irene's funeral." Pain flashed in Bob's eyes as if at the thought Finn wouldn't have come to town to visit them. "Your mom and I were both working and couldn't make it."

"I missed it too but went to the reception." Had he subconsciously skipped the funeral to avoid possibly running into his parents? He glanced at the house. "Is Mom home?"

"She's at the store. Won't be long." Bob hesitated. "Can you stay? I'll put a pot of coffee on."

For a moment Finn imagined setting aside the past and making a fresh start. And then he remembered the last time he'd spoken to his mother, Nora, on her sixtieth birthday. Her stilted surprise that he'd called, her terse, cool replies to his queries about the family. He'd heard the party going on in the background and cut the call short to let her get back to her guests. What if when she saw him, she rejected him in person, told him she wasn't interested in reconciling?

"Sorry, Dad, I can't." He slid back into the car. "I was just passing."

Bob's mouth drew down and he took off his glasses to rub them on the hem of his sweatshirt. "Your mom will be disappointed."

"Will she?" Finn asked. When his father didn't reply, he started the engine. "Thought so."

Estrangement was better than another fight. Nora hadn't cared about what he wanted, only about raising a prodigy. The bitter accusations and recriminations that had flown between the two of them in the weeks before the concert had escalated into a massive fight just before he'd walked onstage. He'd sat down at the piano shaken and scattered, not focused the way he needed to be. No wonder he hadn't been able to play or even remember the piece. His brain had been a seething mess of fury and righteous indignation. The emotional repercussions stayed with him for days and weeks—years—afterward.

She'd never forgiven him for making a fool out of himself and her. It was as if she thought he'd choked on purpose to thwart her ambitions for him. As for him, his anger and resentment simmered undiluted. If he was stubbornly unforgiving it was because he'd gotten that trait from her.

Coming by the house had been a mistake. Nostalgia was insidious. It sucked you in and wrapped its tentacles around you, trapping you in a rose-tinted past colored by wishful thinking and stained with broken dreams.

Finn drove to Dingo and Marla's house a few blocks away. They weren't back yet from the café so he grabbed his guitar from the backseat and sat on their front steps. A couple of little girls played hopscotch on the driveway of the house next door, their high-pitched laughter carrying in the still spring air.

Finn strummed a chord and then picked out notes, pausing now and then to write down the melody in his notebook. When Dingo's van pulled into the driveway some time later Finn stood and stretched, surprised to see by his watch that he'd whiled away nearly two hours.

Marla emerged from the van and went to the backseat to bring Tyler out. The little boy's head flopped on her shoulder, his eyes shut and his small fingers curled into a fist. She walked carefully up the steps with him in her arms. "This is going to ruin his night's sleep but we'll have a quiet dinner hour."

Dingo transferred his guitar case to his other hand and clapped Finn on the shoulder. "Beer?"

"Sure." He followed his friend into the kitchen. "Uh, sorry about earlier at the café."

"No, that was my bad," Dingo said. "I was so stoked to see you that I completely forgot about Irene for a moment." He grabbed a couple of bottles of craft brew from the fridge and handed one to Finn. "Are you okay? Marla and I were worried."

"I'm fine." Finn said. "It's good to see you again. Been too long as usual." In leaving town he'd also lost the tight friendship he'd shared with Dingo. They kept in touch and Dingo had visited him in LA a couple of times but it wasn't the same. Dingo didn't even know about Finn's "problem."

"Marla would have come after you but we could see you were with someone," Dingo said.

Finn twisted off the cap on his beer. "Irene's niece, Carly."

"Ah, I thought she looked familiar." He winked at Finn. "Hot."

Finn shook his head. "Don't even go there."

Dingo got out a large pot and filled it with water. Then he pulled a package of pasta from the cupboard and a container from the fridge. "Chicken cacciatore leftovers. Hope that's okay."

"Better than okay. Marla's a great cook." Finn tossed his beer cap in the bin. "Anything I can do?"

Dingo squinted at him over the neck of the bottle. "You could fill in with the band next Saturday night at the bar."

Finn laughed uneasily. "I meant, like set the table."

"I'm serious," Dingo said. "We're short a lead singer. Rudy had to pull out because he took a job on night shift. We've got gigs lined up."

Finn walked over to the sliding doors that opened onto wooden decking and the backyard with a toddler pool and sandpit. "I'll probably have left town by then."

Dingo dumped the penne into the pot of boiling water. He went quiet a moment, stirring with a wooden spoon. "I was actually hoping you would join the band for a while. We landed a gig as a warm-up act at the RockAround in Seattle."

Finn turned around, eyebrows raised. "Congratulations, that's awesome. You're hitting the big time."

Dingo didn't smile. "It's taken us a lot of years to get this far. We're lucky to have the opportunity but we'll blow it without a good lead."

"Can't Rudy hang in there?" Finn said. "This could be the start of better times."

"They've got a baby on the way and his wife has preeclampsia," Dingo explained. "She's confined to bed and can't work. No one is more bummed than he is."

Finn felt like the biggest jerk on the planet but there was nothing he could do. He couldn't get anywhere near a stage without feeling anxious. A gig at the RockAround would probably bring on a full-blown panic attack. That wouldn't do Dingo and his band any good at all.

"Sixties rock isn't my shtick anyway," he said. "It wouldn't work out."

"You love sixties music and you know it." Dingo pointed the spoon at him. "Not only do you rock the keyboard, you've got a voice, man. A once-in-a-generation voice."

Finn went to the cupboard and took down bowls. Dingo had worked hard for years with his band, playing high school reunions, weddings, any venue they could get. They were good. They deserved the opportunity to be heard on a bigger stage.

"Don't say no before you've had a chance to think about it," Dingo said. "Do me that much of a favor, please."

No amount of thinking would make a difference. Even with the best will in the world he wasn't capable of getting on a stage and singing in front of hundreds of people. The last time he'd tried to perform he'd frozen in front of a packed house at a bar in West Hollywood.

"The truth is," Finn said, "I have performance anxiety."

Dingo laughed knowingly. "Give me a break."

Finn rolled his eyes. "Not that kind."

"You mean singing, playing? Are you kidding me?" Dingo frowned, his head tilted. "Mate, I had no idea. We've jammed together."

"Yeah, but I don't play in public," Finn said. "Not even in a café."

People didn't get it. They heard him play among friends and didn't understand that it wasn't the same as performing in public. Even if he could rehearse with Dingo's band he would still choke up on the big stage. He couldn't risk messing up Dingo's big chance.

"Wow." Dingo scratched his beard scruff. "Have you, I don't know, seen anyone about this?"

"Years ago." Finn shrugged. "Didn't do any good."

"But…" Dingo couldn't seem to wrap his head around it. "It's a colossal waste of talent for you not to perform. You were on track to become a classical pianist but you could have been a rocker…" A light went on in his eyes. "That concert here in Fairhaven when you crashed and burned? Was that…?"

"When the anxiety started? Yes."

"So that's why you hightailed it out of town. You never said a word and I always wondered." Dingo's eyes were warm with compassion. "Never mind about playing then. My band isn't your problem."

Finn felt in his pocket for his keys and clenched them till the sharp edges dug into his palm. This was why he didn't tell people. Dingo meant well, but his sympathy made Finn feel less than equal.

"Tell you what I can do," Finn said. "I'll talk to my agent. Tom's bound to know of some talented rocker who could fill in for Rudy. What do you say?"

"If we can afford him," Dingo said doubtfully.

"I'll make sure you can." Even if he had to subsidize the fill-in himself on the QT. "Problem solved."

Dingo smiled wistfully. "Would have been cool, though. Remember how we used to dream about our band becoming famous?"

"Yeah, we had some great times." Back in high school he'd recruited Dingo to his garage band and they'd played at Dingo's house, keeping it a secret from Finn's parents. Dingo had later formed a cover band and played regular gigs as a sideline to his job in construction.

"It wasn't the same after you left town," Dingo went on. "You had the charisma to be the front man. Without you, the rest of us weren't ever going to be more than a garage band."

"Sorry, man." He'd let Dingo down, too, when he'd fled Fairhaven. Another promise broken, another expectation unfulfilled.

"Ah, forget it. It's just good to see you." Dingo took a swig of beer. "Got any plans while you're in town?"

"I'm helping Carly out for a few days. Irene's dog is missing. I don't want to leave before he's found."

"I'll get the band together tomorrow afternoon

so you can hear them play," Dingo said. "That way you can tell your agent what kind of musician we need."

"That would be great." Finn mustered a smile.

"I appreciate this, mate, I really do. This gig means the world to us and to have your help in any way is a godsend."

"It's nothing." Finn set the bowls around the table. And he was telling the truth. Such a paltry contribution really wasn't much at all.

"SHE LEFT THE house to me?" Carly rocked back in the guest chair in Peter King's office, trying to absorb what the lawyer had just read to her from Irene's will. She'd expected to be left something but the house and all the contents? "What about my uncle Larry, Irene's brother? I assumed he would inherit the bulk of her estate."

"Irene rewrote her will just before Christmas last year. These are her wishes." Peter passed over the slim document on his desk so she could read for herself.

To my dear brother, Larry, I leave our father's World War II mementoes, our mother's collection of antique clocks and the photo albums passed down from our childhood.
To my niece, Brenda, I leave my collection of bone china which I know she loves.

Carly smiled through her tears. She could almost hear Irene's voice.

To my niece, Carly...dear, dear, Carly... I leave my beloved house and all its contents. There are no stipulations about occupancy attached to this bequest but I pray that she will choose to live there and someday raise a family to fill those old rooms with love and laughter. I know she doesn't always share my taste in decor so she's free to give away, sell, or do whatever she wants with the furniture and artwork. To Carly I also entrust my dog, Rufus, if he's still alive at the time of my passing.

Carly's eyes blurred and she grabbed for a handful of tissues from the box on Peter's desk. *No, Irene. Don't, please don't make me feel... Feel what? Bad. Guilty. Pressured. Heartbroken. Don't make me feel, period. Because as much as I love the house I can't feel happy about the way I've acquired it.* Blindly she pushed the will back to Peter. "Is there anything else in there?"

Peter read, *"To Finn Farrell, I leave my Steinway grand piano in the hopes that he'll play the damn thing and be inspired to share his talent with the world. If not, at least he'll appreciate it more than anyone else possibly could."* Peter looked up from the document. "There are also numerous small bequests to other family members, friends and charities."

Carly blew her nose and dabbed at her eyes then straightened her shoulders. Knowing Irene, she wouldn't want Carly to be sad but to enjoy the gifts she'd given her. But although Carly wouldn't mind keeping a few treasured items she didn't have space for all of Irene's things. As for making her home in Fairhaven, while she loved the town, that was simply out of the question.

"I live in New York. I have a job I need to get back to." She crumpled the tissue into a ball. "I'll have to think about what I'm going to do."

"That is entirely up to you," Peter said. "In spite of her stated wishes, there's no legal requirement for you to live in the house. You can sell it, keep it and rent it out." Peter paused, then added, "However, there is the matter of mortgage payments. Those have to be kept up."

"Oh." Carly couldn't afford to make payments on two properties. "As I say, I'll have to think about it."

For now, though, the most pressing problem was to find Rufus. If she couldn't fulfil her aunt's wish for her to live in the house, the least she could do was take care of the dog. An Irish setter in Manhattan wasn't the best fit but she would make it work somehow.

"When you're ready, you can go next door to the bank and sign the papers transferring ownership of the house over to you," Peter said. "I took the liberty of making you an appointment with the manager. He'll advise you on taking over the monthly payments and if you wish, to renegotiate the mortgage. But if you're not up to it now, we can reschedule."

"No, I'm fine." Carly blinked and mustered a wan smile. *"Andiamo."*

Peter rose from his desk and gathered up the folder containing the will. "I beg your pardon?"

"It's Italian for 'let's go,'" Carly said. "Irene used to say it all the time."

"I don't know that I ever heard that," Peter said. "Was she Italian?"

"No, but she studied the language so she could interpret opera librettos."

"Well, well." Peter ushered her through the door. "Even after her death, your aunt continues to surprise."

CHAPTER SIX

FINN LAY ON the couch, eyes closed, pretending to be asleep. Tyler ran in and out of the living room, carrying armloads of Matchbox cars and trucks and arranging them in rows on the coffee table. Finn cracked an eyelid. The rug rat was awful cute.

Dingo had left for work hours ago. Marla was getting ready to go out, too. When Tyler disappeared again, Finn checked his phone. There was a message from Carly.

Need to speak to you. Meet at Rhonda's at noon?

He sent her a thumbs-up to signal he'd received the text and shut his eyes again as Tyler settled in between the coffee table and the couch to play.

"Vroom. Vroom." Tyler accelerated his toy SUV across the pine coffee table and leaped, Evel Knievel-style, onto the couch. He took the truck off-road up Finn's arm, tracking over his shoulder and into the no-man's-land of his head. The wheels got caught in Finn's hair but Tyler kept pushing, his own cherubic curls bouncing.

"Ouch." Finn's eyes shot open. A belly button peeked out between Tyler's striped T-shirt and his red pajama bottoms. "You're stuck, man."

"Thtuck," Tyler lisped, spraying Finn in the face.

"Here, let me." Finn swung his legs over the side of the couch and felt around in his hair, pulling gently. The toy got even more tangled. "I'm going to need a mirror, kiddo."

"Baffroom." Tyler led the way at a trot, down the hall.

"Tyler, what's going on?" Marla, dressed in skirt and blouse and carrying her purse, came out of her bedroom. "Finn, why do you have a truck in your hair?"

"Thtuck," Tyler explained.

"Thtuck," Finn confirmed.

"Here, let me." Swiftly, she untangled the wheels and handed the toy back to Tyler. "Dingo asked me to tell you the band will be over around five o'clock."

"Okay." He ran a hand through his hair, feeling for knots. Nothing a good brush wouldn't cure.

"Did you eat your breakfast?" Marla asked her

son. "You're going to stay with Grandma for a couple of hours while I go to a job interview."

"I wanna stay with Finn." Tyler looked up at her earnestly. "Me and him are playing."

"He and I are playing," Marla corrected automatically. "You're not dressed. Besides, I'm sure Finn has other things to do."

"Not till lunchtime." Finn ruffled Tyler's blond curls. "You can leave the little dude with me while you go out. We'll go to the beach and look for crabs."

"The beach, yay!" Tyler shouted, jumping up and down.

"Are you sure?" Marla said. "I'll be two to three hours."

"No problem," Finn replied. "Go, and good luck."

"There's a spare key on the kitchen windowsill," Marla said. "I'll get his car seat out of my car before I leave." She bent to hug Tyler. "See you later, honey. Be good for Finn."

If good meant amiable, then Tyler was very good but the ordeal of trying to clothe a rambunctious toddler gave Finn a newfound respect for parents. Finally he got the boy strapped into the back of the Mustang. As they drove to Teddy Bear Cove Finn told Tyler about the times he'd spent there as a kid, combing the drifts of washed-up seaweed for Japanese fishing floats and shells. And how his friend Irene used to walk along the shore with her dog.

The Alaska ferry was steaming past as he and Tyler scrambled down a path overgrown with thimbleberry bushes and over the railroad tracks down onto the pebbly beach.

"Big boat," Tyler said, pointing.

"Very big boat. It's going to Alaska." If things had turned out differently he might have been standing at the rail with Irene, searching out the gray slate-roofed turret of her house on the hill.

"What's 'Laska?" Tyler put his hand in Finn's as if it was the most natural thing in the world. Maybe for a tiny kid it was but Finn was charmed.

"A faraway place up north." They crunched over the sloping beach, rounded stones sliding beneath their running shoes, heading away from town toward the point where the rock pools were. Even he knew better than to take a kid to the mudflats.

Tyler's brows scrunched together. "Is it where Santa Claus lives?" Tyler exclaimed.

"Not quite, but close. Polar bears live there, too."

"Pole bears swim under the ice," Tyler informed him. "Like seals."

"Polar bears," Finn corrected. "You know a

lot for a little kid. Do you know how to skip stones?" He found a smooth, flat, round stone, showed it to Tyler, then threw it with a sideways motion into the choppy waves. "Can you count the jumps?"

Tyler concentrated hard. "One, two, forty hundred, nine..."

Smiling, Finn handed the boy another stone. "You try."

The kid was too little but he enjoyed chucking rocks in the water. Well, who didn't? Finn bent over to search for another suitable stone.

"Doggy," Tyler announced.

Finn looked down the beach. A large reddish-brown dog was sniffing a pile of washed-up seaweed. Rufus? This dog's fur was matted and muddy, unlike Rufus's silky, groomed coat, but twenty-four hours in the bushes and on the mudflats could account for that.

He dropped the stone in his hand and whistled. "Rufus, here boy."

The dog stopped and cocked his head.

Tyler patted his thighs. "Here, doggy."

Rufus, if it was him, trotted away from them, up the beach toward the bushes.

"I think this dog belongs to a friend of mine." Finn spoke in a low voice to Tyler. "We're going to go after him. Don't run, okay? We don't want to scare him."

Eyes shining, Tyler put his hand in Finn's. "Okay."

SHE OWNED A HOUSE. Still dazed by the news, Carly carried her date scone and latte to a window table in Rhonda's café. She'd expected a small bequest from her aunt but nothing like this. She was grateful, certainly, but she didn't know whether to be glad or not. The house was worth quite a lot, but there was also a substantial amount left owing on it. Money Carly would have to repay.

Irene had never been a thrifty type. She enjoyed spending her money on concerts, antiques and trips. Carly had felt slightly ill at signing her name to take over the mortgage. The bank would be checking on her finances but barring any unforeseen circumstances she was now the proud owner, and responsible for, a three-story Queen Anne home on the opposite side of the country from where she lived.

Money and practical considerations aside, Carly loved the house. It represented so many happy memories of her summers with Irene. And yes, sad memories of her aunt's death, but overall, the good memories far outweighed the bad. Should she sell, or try to hang on to it for sentimental reasons?

She'd always been a practical person. If she sold, she could afford to buy an apartment in New York. It would be easier to house Rufus if she owned rather than rented. Except that Rufus would be happier staying here, in his own home.

The dog's ownership was the only thing that Irene hadn't said Carly could do as she pleased about. Irene had worshipped her fur baby. Poor Rufus. Wherever he was, he must be pining for his mommy. But it was crazy to make major decisions like keeping or selling Irene's house based solely on what Rufus would like best. Wasn't it?

Carly picked at her scone. She wished Finn would come. She needed to talk to him. Firstly to tell him about the piano, but also she simply needed to talk to someone who was rational because she was feeling very confused right now. So many things pulled her to Fairhaven—Rufus, the house, the town itself. Every time she was here, she was reminded how much like home it felt. But her life was in Manhattan. Her father, her friends, her favorite deli, the theater. Most of all, her new job with her own office complete with bookshelf and business cards.

Oh, she'd almost forgotten to include her lodger Taylor in the equation. What was she going to do about him?

Finn was twenty minutes late. She swiped her phone open to call him. Just as she did, it rang. "Where are you?" she asked.

"Teddy Bear Cove." He was speaking in an excited whisper. "I found Rufus."

"Are you sure?" she said, hardly daring to hope.

"Pretty sure. Although he won't come when I call. And he runs off every time we get near. We've been stalking him for the past forty minutes."

"We?"

"I've got Tyler with me."

"Rufus has a white spot on his chest," Carly said. "It's why Irene couldn't show him."

"It's hard to tell if there's a spot under to all the mud," Finn said. "Can you get down here right away? Bring food. He's got to be starving. Oh, and a collar and leash."

Carly was already standing up, pushing her chair back. "I'll be there in ten."

"Carly's coming," Finn told Tyler as he put his phone away. He glanced around. "Where's Rufus?"

"Doggy go dat way." Tyler pointed to the train track. Thirty yards away Rufus was nosing his way along the ties.

"Good spotting." Finn gave him a high five but his heart sank.

On one side of the railway track lay the beach. On the other side, the road and beyond that, dense forest. If Rufus went into the woods, he would be harder to track. Or he might run onto Chuckanut Drive and get hit by a car. Even as they watched, Rufus left the train tracks and trotted into the woods.

Finn grabbed Tyler's hand. "Let's go. Quiet now."

They crept closer and crouched below the siding. Finn peered over, mentally marking the location the dog had entered the forest between a dead pine and an alder sapling. A moment later he glimpsed the dog moving parallel to the shore. He and Tyler followed on the beach side of the tracks.

Carly arrived, stumbling down the trail in a skirt that rode above her knees, and patent leather shoes smeared with dirt. She carried a leash over her shoulder with the price tag still on it and a plastic shopping bag. Finn went to meet her. The scent of her citrusy perfume was like a waft of fresh air above the earthy smells of pine and seaweed and mudflat.

Finn relieved her of the shopping bag and took her hand to help her down the last bit of the trail. "I see you dressed for the occasion."

"I had an appointment at the bank this morning. I didn't want to take the time to go home and change so I stopped at the supermarket for this stuff." She noticed Tyler. "Hi there, sweetie."

"Ty, this is Carly, the dog's owner." Finn peered into the bag. "Is this the food?"

"Yessiree." She reached over and pulled out a warm rotisserie chicken in a foil bag. "I defy a starving dog not to come to roast chicken."

Finn had been expecting kibble or at the best, canned dog food. "Brilliant."

"I hungry." Tyler edged closer, eyeing the chicken.

"Here you go." Carly ripped off a small wing and handed it to him. "Where is Rufus?"

"He went that way," Finn said, pointing across the tracks to the woods. "We haven't seen him for about five minutes."

"Maybe I should go alone in case too many people scare him," Carly said.

"I'll go, in case a cougar smells that chicken and comes looking for lunch," Finn said.

"Coug'r?" Tyler's eyes rounded with excitement.

Carly looked as if she would faint. "Cougar?"

"No, probably not," Finn said hastily, kicking himself for scaring them. "Let's all go."

Finn hoisted Tyler onto his hip and carried him up the rocky siding. Then he turned to give

Carly a hand but she was already at the top. They pushed their way through the undergrowth between the trees. The dog was nowhere in sight.

Carly stopped in a small clearing and tore open the foil bag. She waved a hunk of chicken in the air. "Ru-fus. Here, boy. Come and eat. Rufus."

For at least sixty seconds, nothing happened. Then a rustling in the bushes. The Irish setter poked his noble, daft head through the bright green fronds of a sword fern. Lifting his muzzle, he scented the air.

Carly handed Finn the chicken and took the collar and leash in both hands. "You lure him and I'll sneak around and collar him," she whispered.

"What I do?" Tyler asked in a stage whisper between greasy bites of chicken.

"Stand by and be ready to give him lots of pats," Carly said.

"Okay," Tyler said, very seriously. He laid his half-eaten wing carefully on a mossy log and licked his fingers. "Ready."

"Here, boy." Finn walked very slowly forward, holding the chicken in front of him. "Come to papa."

Tentatively, the dog put one paw in front of the other. Finn tore off a chunk of meat and threw it on the ground. Carly tiptoed around the dog's flank, gradually closing the distance as Rufus crept toward the meat and gobbled it down in a single gulp.

Finn crouched with another piece of chicken in his hand. This time he held on to it, urging the dog to come closer. Rufus stretched his neck out and nibbled at the meat, trying to tug it free. Carly dropped the leash over his outstretched neck and grabbed the other end. It was then the work of seconds to snap the collar on.

Finn tore off more chunks and threw them to the starving dog, careful not to give him any bones.

Tyler patted the dirty red fur with greasy fingers. "Good doggy. You safe."

Elated and relieved, Finn glanced at Carly to exchange a smile over Tyler's cuteness. "We found him."

"You found him." Her eyes were very blue in the dark of the forest, her expression a confusion of sadness and relief. Her hair was mussed and she had smears of dirt on her clothes.

"You caught him." He'd never seen her look so beautiful and yet so vulnerable. Like she didn't know whether to laugh or to cry.

"We did it together." Her smile flickered and faded.

He wanted to kiss her. Something stopped him, something to do with the inner turmoil she radiated. One crisis was over but he sensed another was brewing. He touched away a drop of moisture at the corner of her eye and let his fingertip linger a moment on the soft skin of her cheek. "What was it you wanted to tell me?"

CARLY DASHED AWAY the welling tears. She'd been fine until she'd seen Rufus looking like a stray dog all filthy and starving. Now the emotions of the past few days were catching up to her. She would figure things out. She had to believe that even if she was struggling to cope right now. "Let's go back to the beach."

Once there she slumped onto a driftwood log and hugged Rufus. The dog put a paw on her knee and licked the moisture off her cheeks with big slurps of his tongue. She laughed through her tears and then cried harder. "You poor sweetheart. You're going to be okay. Everything's going to be okay."

Finn dropped down next to her on the log. Tyler crouched on the other side of Rufus, patting and chatting to him.

"Sorry," she said to Finn, wiping her eyes with her sleeve. "You must think I'm a complete mess. Every time you see me, I'm either drunk, hungover or crying."

"Don't apologize." His arm came around her, warm and solid. "It's okay."

She leaned into him, unable to resist the comfort he offered. "I'm so glad we found Rufus. I remember walking with him and Aunt Irene on this beach."

"I wish I'd kept in touch with her more," Finn said. "We emailed occasionally about musical stuff but I felt as if I'd let her down because I'd given up performing."

"She cared about you, even if you didn't see each other," Carly said. "That's what I wanted to tell you. She left you her piano. It was in her will."

Finn stared, a lock of dark hair falling over his raised eyebrows. "Seriously?"

She nodded, smiling at his surprise and pleasure. "It's a nice piano."

"Nice?" He snorted. "That's like saying a Maserati is a 'nice' car."

"She left me the house and contents. And this guy." Carly leaned down to pat Rufus, now asleep on the smooth stones, his muzzle resting on her foot. "What am I going to do with him."

"He's a great dog," Finn said.

"He's great here in Fairhaven. Not so suitable for Manhattan. I'll be working long hours, living in an apartment…" She shook her head. "I'm not the best person to take care of him. I don't know what Irene was thinking of."

"She gave him to you because she trusted you." He drew a pattern in a patch of sand with a piece of driftwood. "And maybe she didn't think she was going to die so soon."

They fell silent. Gray waves lapped the shiny wet stones at the edge of the water, bringing yellow foam that collected in the crevices. A week ago she was in Manhattan wearing power suits for her high-octane new job and getting a three-hundred-dollar haircut. Now look at her, covered in mud on a Washington state beach with Finn, a runny-nosed toddler and a runaway dog.

She laughed. "Life is so random." Then she sighed. "I might have to ask my father for a loan to carry the house for a few months until it sells."

Finn removed his arm from around her shoulders. "You're not going to get rid of it."

His disapproval immediately put her back up. "What else am I going to do with it? I live in New York."

"People change jobs and move across the country all the time."

"There aren't a lot of jobs at my level here in Fairhaven," she protested.

"Seattle, then."

"I'm in an excellent position where I am. I'd be an idiot to let it go."

"Irene loved that house," Finn argued. "She's been there for… I don't know how many years. But lots."

"Twenty-eight. I found out this morning when

I signed the deed." For a moment she envisaged the future her aunt had hoped for. Moving in, having a family, passing the house down through the future generations. Legacy had meant a lot to Irene. On the other hand, Irene had also believed everyone was in charge of their own destiny. "She said in the will that I could do what I wanted with it. Of course I'd like to keep it but I'm not rich. Why don't you buy it?"

"I already have a house in Los Angeles."

"People move and change jobs all the time," she said, one eyebrow raised. Finn's mouth twisted. Carly found a pebble and turned it over, her fingernail tracing a gray line snaking through the white quartz.

"Being true to ourselves is the best way to honor Irene," Finn said. "You do what you have to do."

"I'm picking up her ashes tomorrow," Carly said.

"Do you want me to come with you?"

"That would be nice," Carly said. "I can't decide whether to keep them or spread them somewhere. Did she ever say anything to you about her wishes?"

"Not that I recall," Finn said. "You don't have to decide right away."

"I can't see taking her back to New York with me. She never liked the east coast."

"How about this beach? She came here a lot."

"That's an idea." Carly tossed away the pebble. "Did you know she'd taken on a new boarder? Taylor Greene, nice guy, total geek."

"No, I didn't. How did you find out?"

"He showed up at the house yesterday afternoon with all his stuff, ready to move in."

"Oh, man. Did you tell him your aunt died?" Finn said.

"I did. He brandished his rental agreement and claimed he had a right. I let him stay—for now."

"I'm no lawyer but I'm pretty sure you're not obligated to honor the agreement under the circumstances."

"I'm not. And I don't want to but he's so…" Carly trailed off, haunted by the look in Taylor's eyes.

"So, what?" Finn prodded.

"It's hard to describe," Carly said. "His reasons for needing the room were pretty compelling—he's doing a PhD in astrophysics and the stars are aligned or something—but it was his personal life that made me cave. He's trying to find his independence and moving into Irene's house is a step along that road. He needs sanctuary."

Finn shook his head. "Carly Maxwell, you're a sucker for a sob story."

"I am not." She sat up straighter. "I'm ruthless. I told him he needed to start looking for another place to live." She didn't know if she'd have the heart to throw him out if he couldn't find one, mind you.

Finn nudged her with his shoulder. "Look at those two." Rufus was flaked out on the sand with Tyler, asleep, draped over him, one chubby arm around the dog's neck. Dog and child were covered in dirt.

"We should put them in the bath together," Carly suggested.

"Okay, but don't let Marla know."

"I'm kidding!"

Finn grinned at her. "I thought it was a good idea."

"Got to admit, they'd be cute." While they'd been talking the clouds had broken up, revealing large patches of blue. Sunlight sparkled on the water. Finn beside her was warm and real and present. She got lost in his dark chocolate eyes.

He looked away first, clearing his throat. "On second thought, I'd better get this little guy back to his mom before she sends out an APB."

Finn bent to scoop up Tyler and lay him over his shoulder. Carly took Rufus's leash and they set off for the path through the woods back to where they'd parked along the highway.

Carly took a breath and let it out. Everything was okay. She was okay. At least for the moment.

CHAPTER SEVEN

FINN LEANED AGAINST the wall in the garage Dingo had converted to a music studio and listened to the band tear through a classic rock-and-roll anthem by sixties legends, The Doors.

Dingo picked out the melody on lead guitar with magic fingers and half-closed eyes, caught up in the trance of the driving beat. Billy, with shaven head and sleeves of tatts, plucked away on bass guitar. Leroy was working the drums.

They were good, damn good. Dingo had filled him in on all their stories. Every single one of them depended on the band's income to supplement whatever they made in their day jobs. They'd been together for four years and the gig at RockAround was the big break they'd been hoping for. All that was missing was a strong lead singer and a decent keyboard player. Rudy's departure had left a hole that needed to be filled before these guys could perform on a big stage.

Finn put a call through to his agent, Tom. Plugging his ear, he shouted into the phone. "Hey, man, how's it going?"

"Where are you?" Tom said.

"Listen to this and tell me what you think." Finn held out his phone toward the band for a minute.

"Tight, with a nice full sound," Tom conceded when Finn came back on. "Retro rock is hot right now. But I don't hear any vocals."

"That's why I'm calling," Finn said. "They need a lead singer who can play keyboard who they can slot in for a big gig coming up in a couple of months. And most likely for the long term if he works out. Have you got anyone on your books that would fit the bill?"

"Yeah, you," Tom said drily.

"I'm serious. Check your list and let me know." Finn paused. "Has Bliss Bombs paid out yet on that song I delivered? It's been a month."

"I talked to them a few days ago," Tom said. "Now they're not sure they're going to use it."

Finn swore under his breath. "They came to me. They're in breach of contract."

"We'll get the money," Tom said. "Just might take a while."

He'd been counting on that money to pay some bills. Oh well, a cash flow problem was nothing new. "Any work come in?"

"As a matter of fact, yes. A big-shot movie

producer called, asking if you would DJ at his son's twenty-first."

"Me, DJ, seriously? I hope you said no."

"I told him you'd think about it," Tom said. "There's a lot of coin in this gig. And it could be a way in to writing music for movies. I advise you to take it."

Tom's advice was usually wise and Finn couldn't afford to turn down a fat paycheck. But a DJ was one step away from being a rock star. Him, standing above the dance floor on a platform, the focus of attention? What if he had an anxiety attack? "It's way out of my field. Turn it down."

As he hung up, a movement at a side door caught his attention. The waitress from the café with the ponytail and the big smile hovered outside. Annie waved and tugged on her straggly hair. He nodded hello.

The song finished. All the guys looked over at Finn. He'd gathered from overhearing snippets of their conversation that Dingo was still hoping he would change his mind about joining the band. But no pressure.

"Well?" Dingo said, propping one knee on the keyboard stool.

"You guys have a great sound," Finn said. "My agent thinks so, too."

Dingo exchanged a glance with Leroy and Billy. "I mean, what about being our lead singer?"

"Tom's going to work on finding you someone."

Bada-ba-boom. Leroy expressed his disappointment with a downbeat riff on drums. "We're wasting our time. Might as well forget about rehearsing until we get someone."

"Come on dudes," Dingo protested. "We've got a lot of work to do. We can't leave learning the new songs till the last minute."

"I'm with Leroy," Billy said. "Anyway, I need to get ready for work at the gas station." He started to unsling his guitar from around his neck.

"One of you can sing lead, can't you?" Finn suggested. "Just for rehearsal."

"Leroy doesn't have the range," Dingo said. "I'm getting a cold and don't want to risk messing up my vocal cords. Billy here…" He directed a fondly exasperated gaze at the youngest member who couldn't be more than twenty-two or twenty-three. "Doesn't know the words."

"Hey, man, this song is like, from the dark ages," Billy protested.

"It's a classic," Finn said. "Every rocker worthy of the name should know it."

"Weren't you a hotshot singer once upon a time?" Billy shot back. "Why don't you take lead?"

Finn shook his head. "My gig is writing songs."

Leroy laid his sticks across the snare. "Sorry, Dingo. I'm outta here."

Dingo swore and shook his head.

Finn rubbed the leather bracelet on his wrist, stretching the ends trailing out of the knot. The success or failure of this concert would impact Dingo's future even more than it affected the other band members. Marla was getting impatient with what she saw as her husband's hobby. It took time away from the family and stopped him from getting a better-paying job that required more hours. Unless they progressed beyond basically being a pub band, these guys had no future as a group. If Finn could perform in public he would help them in a heartbeat, but just the thought was enough to make his vocal cords tighten.

Hovering by the door, Annie cleared her throat. "I can sing."

Leroy rolled his eyes. "Go back to babysitting, kid."

"No need to be rude." Finn turned to Annie and said, "What experience do you have?"

"I was lead in our high school musical last year," she said. "And I love classic rock. I know all the words to those old songs."

"Give her a try?" Finn asked Dingo. Leroy and Billy went about packing up their instruments and wouldn't look at him.

"She's a chick." Dingo stated the obvious. "Jim Morrison was a guy. Nothing personal, Annie."

Finn took Dingo aside and spoke in a low voice. "You don't want her because she's female? She could be a drawcard."

"I only said that so I didn't hurt her feelings," Dingo replied. "It's because she's Annie."

"I don't get it. Why not give her a chance? What have you got to lose?"

"She lives down the street and babysits for us," Dingo said. "She's always hanging around. Harmless enough but it's would-be groupie behavior. None of the guys would even think of going there, of course. She's just a kid and they've got wives and girlfriends. I gather she has a pretty tough home life."

"Does any of that mean she can't sing?" Finn asked. "Maybe she's hanging around because she wants to be in a band."

"She's too young." Dingo waved to Leroy and Billy on their way out.

Finn glanced over his shoulder to see what Annie was making of this conversation but she'd disappeared, too. Shame. She'd put herself out there and been unceremoniously rejected. Although he had to ask himself if maybe he was trying to deflect attention from himself if he was willing to audition every wannabe who raised her hand.

Dingo shut down the amps. "I should call the concert organizers and tell them to get another starting band."

"Give Tom a few days," Finn said. "He'll come up with someone."

"Yeah, sure." Now Dingo wasn't meeting his gaze. "Beer?"

"No, thanks. I'm going to…" Punch a wall in, go on a bender. "I'll go, too, get out of your hair. It's been great hanging with you and Marla, and getting to know Tyler. Thanks for your hospitality."

Dingo put his guitar back on the stand in the corner. "No worries. It's been great seeing you again."

The fact that Dingo wasn't trying to stop him, and wasn't looking him in the eye was telling. Was Finn on the verge of losing his friendship too, the way he'd become estranged from his parents? "Say goodbye to Marla for me."

Dingo glanced out the open garage door at the long shadows stretching across the driveway. "You're not heading out for Los Angeles now, are you?"

"Not tonight," Finn agreed. "Tomorrow."

"Are you staying with us again tonight?"

"Thanks, but I'll get a room at a hotel. I'll be in touch, let you know what Tom comes up with." Finn gave him a man hug and Dingo slapped him on the back. But there was a new coolness, a distance that hadn't been there in the past. It was as if Finn's problem had imposed limitations on their friendship.

How could he have let anxiety rule his life for so long, all the while telling himself he was happy and fulfilled? Worse than not having the solo career he'd dreamed of as a teenager was letting down the people he cared about. About time he called himself on it. He wasn't satisfied with his professional life, not by a long shot, and now his problem was affecting his friendships.

Instead of looking for a motel he pointed the Mustang toward South Hill. Suddenly he needed to see Carly, needed some reassurance that there was at least one person among his old friends that he hadn't let down.

Before he went up the steps to the front door he took a moment to text his mother.

Can we meet for coffee?

Ball was in her court.

"YOU HAD ME WORRIED, RUFUS." Kneeling beside the bathtub, Carly poured warm water over the dog. Rose-scented bubble bath frothed around his ears and his red fur was plastered darkly to his body. "Anything could have happened. You could have been hit by a car, or dognapped, or lost forever in the woods."

Rufus responded by licking her arm.

"To tell you the truth, I feel kind of lost, too," she said, sluicing more water over him. "Irene's passing left a huge hole in my life. You're lucky Finn happened to be in the right place at the right time or who knows what might have become of you. We're both lucky Finn's in Fairhaven right now. I need a friend. So you be nice to him, okay?" Rufus tried to lick her face. "What's that you say? You're my friend, too? Of course you are. Just as I'm yours."

She meant it, too. Last week she'd been too numb and too preoccupied to see Rufus as anything but a nuisance. Finding him bedraggled and starving, she'd realized he was also suffering. If anything, it was worse for the dog. He couldn't understand why Irene had gone away, or that she was never coming back.

Carly drained the water and rubbed him down with a towel before hauling him over the edge of the tub and onto the mat. He did an all-over body shake, sending water droplets flying. She dried him off some more and then got out her hair dryer. "Hold still. I'm going to blow it dry."

As she used the dog brush and the hair dryer to make his coat glossy and smooth, her thoughts drifted back to Finn. He'd looked right at home with Tyler sleeping on his shoulder and seemed comfortable and natural around the boy. From what she recalled, Finn and his brother had a lot of younger cousins. She'd gone to his house once to deliver a package of sheet music from Irene and happened on an extended family gathering with Finn leading the children in a game of softball.

It was such a shame that while he'd achieved success as a songwriter, he seemed content to let his other musical talents go to waste. He clearly had problems he wasn't dealing with. As a former counselor trained in psychology, she knew that attitude led to dead ends. She would happily try to work through whatever was blocking him, even though she didn't need any more problems in her life, but unless she was super tactful he would push away any offer of help.

Carly flicked off the hair dryer. "All done, Rufus, my boy. You may go, but don't forget, you're under house arrest until the gate is fixed."

Rufus trotted out of the bathroom. A moment later she heard him settle with a soft thump on the floor outside Irene's door. His low whine just about broke her heart. Poor Rufus. How would he cope if she left him, too?

Carly scooped up the wet towels and put them in the hamper. Then she cleaned the bathtub and wiped down the wet floor. Time to tackle the next item on her to-do list—write thank-you notes to those who'd donated to the animal shelter in Irene's name in lieu of flowers, as requested.

Carrying a box of note cards she went downstairs to curl up on the cushioned seat built into the bay window in the living room. The table would have been easier to write at but the window seat had been her favorite spot in the house to read when she was a child. It was peaceful, and today it was an anchor to the past, making her feel close to Irene.

While she worked on the notes, her phone chirped, announcing the arrival of a text message. Leanne. Whoops. She'd forgotten all about the business cards and the issue of serif or sans serif. Honestly, she did not care one way or the other but for some reason it was important to Leanne that Carly have an informed opinion. Serif or sans serif, that was the question.

While she pondered, the phone rang. "Hello?"

"Hi," Frankie said. "Thought I'd better mention that garbage cans go out tonight. Pickup is early so it's not a good idea to leave it till morning."

"Thanks for letting me know. Oh, by the way, we found Rufus. He was down at the beach." She chatted for a few more minutes and then Frankie had to go fix dinner for her family.

Carly gathered up her notes, pocketed her phone without sending a message to Leanne and went to the kitchen. If she was putting out the garbage it made sense to clean out the fridge.

With a black garbage bag in hand she turned her ruthless setting to high. Miso paste, out. Dregs of a bottle of oyster sauce, out. Ancient chocolate sauce, out. Rotting lettuce and withered carrots... Irene would have put them in the compost. But who was going to spread compost on the vegetable garden? For that matter, who was going to plant a garden?

Still Carly hesitated. Irene had always been environmentally conscious and didn't like to be wasteful. Muttering under her breath, she put the wilting produce into a bucket to be carried out to the compost bin later. Whoever bought the house might use it. If not, at least the worms wouldn't starve.

She went back to the fridge. Half-empty bottle of ketchup, out. Sourdough starter. Her hand hovered over the jar. Brenda was right, she should throw it out. But this jar contained a culture that Irene had lovingly nurtured over many years. If Carly wanted to feel close to her aunt, there was no better way than to make bread. And wouldn't it be amazing to set a loaf of fresh, homemade bread on the dinner table?

Abandoning the fridge for now, Carly got out her laptop and Googled how to make sourdough bread. Good grief. There were thousands of recipes, hundreds of online clips and whole forums devoted to the art and science of sourdough. She scrolled through pages of description and photos.

When she thought she had the gist of the process, she gathered ingredients and implements together and began to mix the dough. According to what she'd read, she should have fed the starter a couple of times to activate it before attempting to make bread, but she decided to go ahead anyway.

An hour later, flour blanketed the kitchen counter like fresh snowfall. It dusted Carly's navy top and Rufus's russet fur was sprinkled with white as he licked the fine powder off the floor. The wet, sticky blob at the bottom of the mixing bowl didn't look anything like the spongy dough in the video clip. She wished she'd watched Irene more closely when she made bread but Carly had been interested only in the finished product.

Face it, Irene would be horrified if she could see Carly making a mess of her beautiful starter. Instead of feeling spiritually close to her aunt she was cross and tired and felt like a failure. Really, what was the point of keeping the starter going? The closest she got to home baking was eating frozen cookie dough from the roll. And yet, she wasn't ready to admit defeat.

The doorbell rang. She grabbed a tea towel and tried to rub the gooey dough off her fingers on her way to the front door.

"Hey." Finn handed her a bouquet of spring flowers—daffodils, tulips and freesia.

"Thank you. What are these for?" She buried her nose in their fresh, delicate scent and felt her spirits lift. When was the last time a man had brought her flowers when it wasn't her birthday?

"Just because they looked pretty." His wry gaze took in her white-speckled appearance. "I was going to say, pretty like you, but you look like you've been through the mill. A flour mill, that is."

"I'm making sourdough bread." Even his

gently sardonic tone couldn't spoil her pleasure in receiving flowers. "Come on in." She
headed back to the kitchen.

Rufus trotted up to Finn and licked his hand.
"Hey, boy. What happened? He looks as if he
has a severe case of dandruff."

"I know, and I just got him clean." Carly found
a glass vase and filled it with water from the tap.
"But he seems no worse for having spent a night
on the lam." She unwrapped the flowers and arranged them in the vase. "Tea?"

"Have you got a beer?" Finn asked.

She pulled a cold one out of the fridge and
handed it to him. "How was band practice?"

His eyes closed as he took a long pull on the
bottle, draining half in one go. Then he wiped
his mouth with the back of his hand. "The band
is great."

"But...?" Something was wrong.

"They need a lead singer," he said casually.
"The guys can't understand why I couldn't fill
in even for one day."

"Awkward." Carly noted the drawn lines
around his eyes and mouth. He was more upset
about it than he was letting on. "Do you want
to talk about it?"

Instead of answering, he wandered to the
counter. "Is this the offending dough?"

"Yes, look." She tried to pick up the blob. It

stuck to the counter and stretched between her fingers in long sticky strands. "You see what I'm dealing with here?"

"Give it time," he said. "Irene used to leave it overnight and bake it the next day."

"Shoot. I'd hoped to have bread for dinner along with the soup I haven't yet made." Carly glanced at the wall clock. "I've got to feed Taylor something."

"After I fix the gate, I'll give you a hand in the kitchen," Finn said.

"You don't have to do that—" she began.

"We were closest to Irene," Finn cut her off. "We're in this together, for however long it takes. I'll fix the gate and repair whatever else is broken."

"But—"

"Stop." Finn pointed his beer bottle at her. "Don't argue every time I try to help."

"All right, but if you're helping out of guilt or a sense of obligation, it's not necessary," she said. "I could have fixed the gate if I wasn't wrestling sourdough."

"You were brought up in an apartment with a resident handyman," Finn said. "Not a lot of opportunity to learn how to do home repairs."

"I've got YouTube," Carly said. "I can do anything I put my mind to."

"I know you can, Wonder Woman, but you

don't have to. I've got your back." Finn drained his beer and set the bottle on the counter. "I'll get busy on the gate. Are Irene's tools still downstairs?"

"I presume so," Carly said.

Finn went into the laundry room and turned the old-fashioned iron key in the basement door lock. The door creaked open and he descended the wooden steps.

Carly lifted the sticky dough into a plastic container and left it to rise on the kitchen counter. As she scrubbed the residue off her fingers she thought about Finn and his visit to the band. He must have felt humiliated not being able to play. It would do him no good bottling things up. He should talk this out. Maybe he'd come here for that very reason and she'd prattled on about sourdough.

She went to the top of the stairs and peered down into the unfinished basement. "Finn?"

No answer. A bare fifty-watt bulb hung over the staircase and in the dim light, she started down, holding on to the rail. Crap, there were a lot of spiderwebs down here. At the bottom of the stairs she skirted the boiler and followed the glow of a flickering fluorescent strip. Finn stood at a workbench, picking through a jumble of tools. Above the bench was a cobweb-encrusted window that let in a kind of half-light. If he heard her approach, he made no sign.

Carly cleared her throat. "So, do the guys in the band know why you won't sing with them?"

"Dingo knows." Finn studied the blade of a screwdriver and added it to a toolbox. "He probably won't say anything."

"Failing to perform at that concert must have been really traumatic," she said. "All those people expecting something amazing and then you were too rattled to play. I wouldn't blame you for developing anxiety."

Still with his back to her, he said, "I don't talk about it, remember?"

Too blunt. She knew better than to leap straight into things. "You used to love performing," she said, trying another tack. "I remember that time Irene held a recital here at the house. It was mainly other pupils and their parents but even at age fifteen you were quite the showman. I can't believe you don't miss it."

"I'm doing exactly what I want to do," Finn said, sorting screws into a jar.

"I'm sure you do like writing songs but can you honestly say you don't wish you'd given performing a real shot?" Carly asked. "You used to work so hard at your music. It feels to me, and admittedly I don't know what your life is like now, but it feels as if you've, well…"

"As if I've what?" he said sharply. "Given up? Gotten lazy?"

She winced. "Not exactly. But why haven't you tried to overcome whatever is holding you back? It's been twelve years." She paused and added gently, "Isn't it time to move on?"

"I have moved on, hence the songwriting and studio sessions." He shrugged. "I put a few video clips of my music up on YouTube. I get a respectable number of hits but it's a competitive field out there."

"That's why you have to perform live," she said. "It's the way to get noticed."

He added the jar of screws into the toolbox along with a pair of pliers. "Performing isn't that important to me."

She didn't believe that. And they were going around in circles. She hated that when they needed each other the most, there was suddenly a distance between them. "You don't have to admit it to me but you should at least be honest with yourself."

His jaw tightened. "Speaking of being honest… You used to love helping people figure out their problems. Is finding CEOs their next seven-figure job really the kind of work you want to do?"

"It's…rewarding." Maybe not in the way counseling used to be but… "CEOs are people, too, you know." That was weak but they had been talking about him. "I'm good at what I do."

"Being good at a job and enjoying it are two different things," he said.

"What exactly are you getting at?"

"When I knew you, you were everyone's friend," Finn said. "You tried to help the strugglers, the losers and the lost."

His words pushed a button she didn't even know she possessed and she lost her cool. "If I was so good at helping people, why didn't you come to me when you were hurting after that concert?"

His nostrils flared. "Are you saying I'm a loser?"

"You didn't even call to explain why you stood me up for the party."

Wow, she hadn't meant to bring that up, certainly not in that hurt, angry tone of voice. Talk about not moving on.

Finn faced her and stepped in close. "Seems to me you've sold out."

"How dare you talk to me about selling out?" she shot back. "You had all the advantages and training a person could want. What did you do but throw it all away!"

"Why are you here, messing about with sourdough instead of back in Manhattan polishing your name plate?"

"I have to be here. Irene left the house to me. I am going to sell it. Ergo, I need to get it ready and on the market. Honestly, a child could see that."

"Is that so?" Finn said. "Couldn't you simply lock the house up, get the neighbors to keep an eye on it and come back in a couple of months when it's convenient?"

"There's a little matter of the mortgage," she snapped. "I can't afford to pay it and my New York rent. As it is, I'm probably going to have to cover both for a few months."

Finn's eyebrows rose skeptically. "I think you're scared you've made a mistake in your career choice but you need to prove something to yourself so you're pushing yourself hard and it's too late to back out."

Carly was too angry for a moment to speak. Sure she had doubts, didn't everyone? "You talk to me about being scared? You're fixing gates instead of getting back to your wonderful life in Los Angeles as songwriter to the stars. What about your star? You can't even sing in a garage band."

"Dingo's band isn't any old garage band. They would have a recording contract by now if they didn't have to work day jobs and had more time to devote to music." Finn gathered his tools and started back toward the stairs.

"You're evading the issue," she called after him. "Why won't you sing with them? Do you think you're not good enough?"

He stopped suddenly and turned, dark eyes blazing. "I'm more than good enough."

She knew it. She just hadn't been sure till now that he did. "Then why won't you?"

"I'm not talking about this, remember?" he said through gritted teeth.

"You want to change but you can't. Despite all your success and your clients' hits, you think you're a failure. You'll never be happy until you get over this stage fright or whatever it is." She pointed a finger. "Admit it, you're scared."

"I don't need fixing," he growled. "How many times do I have to say it?"

"Counseling could help you figure out what's holding you back," she said. "Just because it didn't work with one therapist doesn't mean it's hopeless. Try someone else."

His face darkened. "I'm warning you. Don't push me on this."

"You're in denial," Carly called after him. "And I don't mean the river in Egypt!"

He took the stairs two at a time. The door at the top of the staircase shut behind him with an angry click.

Carly's lower lip wobbled and she blinked rapidly. She hated fighting and to fight with Finn…

Screw him. She didn't have time to fix him, any-way. He was leaving soon and so was she.

Yes, she liked helping people. But he was wrong about her thinking she'd made a mis-take. She was through being a touchy-feely, nurturing type who took her homemade lunch to work. Bring on the expense account and the fancy apartment. Carly Maxwell knew what she wanted. And it wasn't to hang out in Fairhaven, baking sourdough.

CHAPTER EIGHT

FINN PULLED OFF the twine binding the gate shut and unscrewed the broken latch. *Don't think about it.* Don't think about how angry he'd gotten at Carly, who he counted as one of his closest friends even if he hadn't seen her in more than a decade. Or how badly he felt now because of their argument.

He'd wanted to reassure himself that Carly, at least, thought well of him, and when she'd drilled right down to the bone he'd picked a fight to avoid talking about his problem. She'd been in an edgy mood herself, spoiling for someone to take out her unhappiness and uncertainty on. Didn't mean he should feed that beast. Yesterday at the beach, they'd been so close. Today that had all fallen apart and it sucked.

He tossed the old latch on the ground and picked up the new one he'd bought at the hardware store on the way over. Unlike Carly, he knew his way around tools, thanks to his handyman dad. Not that she was to blame for her lack of experience in that area. And despite her family's wealth, her father had instilled in her a work ethic. Finn respected the fact that she made her own way and didn't rely on daddy's money. Irene, too, deserved credit for keeping Carly grounded and exposing her to a different sort of life here in Fairhaven. The small town had lots going for it—the ocean, the forest, a close-knit community who cared about their neighbors.

It was scary how perceptive Carly was about him. She'd hit the nail on the head earlier. Yes, he was scared. Yes, he felt like a failure. And he hated that she knew it in case she thought him weak. But she was wrong in thinking he didn't want to work at his music. It was just…hard in a way he couldn't deal with. Maybe he was in denial.

He shouldn't have attacked her about her job. Who was he to give career advice? She was smart, she knew what she was doing. And anyway, she was grieving. Actually, they both were. Anger was one of the stages of grief and manifested itself in unexpected ways. For all Carly's inner strength, right now she seemed to be barely holding herself together. Truth was, they were both fragile right now.

He put down the screwdriver and pushed on the post to test how solid it was. Like a rock. Good. Carly wouldn't want to replace the whole fence if she was looking for a quick sale on the property.

He turned to admire the soaring graceful lines of the house. The peacock-blue siding and white trim looked recently painted. But he'd noticed a few loose boards in the porch and the downstairs bathroom sink knocked when water ran. Those would have to be dealt with before the house went on the market.

Thinking of Irene's heritage home going into the hands of strangers made his chest constrict. This house had seen some of his proudest moments. Irene had been the first person outside his family to believe in him and her praise had meant more than any award. She'd been teaching music at his elementary school and had singled him out as having promise. Once she'd convinced his parents he should have private lessons his mother had begun her campaign for him to mine his talent for all it was worth.

He sighed and pushed away from the fence post. All that was a long time ago. He'd put those days firmly behind him—until now. It was no wonder he was feeling churned up. Returning to Fairhaven had brought him face to face with his past, and how he'd crumbled under the weight of expectations when he'd most needed to step up.

Dusk was falling by the time he finished repairing the latch. After making sure the gate was shut tightly he went in through the back door to the kitchen where the rising sourdough gave off a warm, yeasty aroma. Rufus, lying on his bed in the corner, thumped his tail when he saw Finn. Carly was tying up a large black garbage bag. She continued what she was doing without looking at him.

"The gate is fixed. You can let Rufus out." Finn went to the sink to wash his hands. "I'll go to the hardware store again tomorrow to pick up a few other things. Is there anything you need?"

She carried the garbage bag to the back door, still avoiding his gaze. "Packing boxes. Do they carry those at a hardware store?"

"I could try to find a moving and storage company." He paused. "What are you going to do with everything when you've got it all boxed up?"

She pushed strands of hair off her forehead with the back of her hand. "Whatever is left after my uncle and cousin receive their bequests I'll give to whoever wants it."

He nodded, hating the awkward distance between them, wanting to bridge it before it grew. "I, uh, said stuff I shouldn't have earlier. You're going to be awesome in your new job. I hope it turns out well for you."

She turned to him, her expression troubled. "I was out of line, too. I haven't seen you for years. I had no right."

"Yeah, you have a right. You knew the 'other'

me. Few people do nowadays. The only time I get asked hard questions is in Fairhaven." He kept so far below the radar that his LA friends knew little of his past. And that was the way he wanted it. "Must be why I come here so frequently," he added drily.

"You don't have to prove anything to anyone," Carly said.

"Neither do you." He wished he could make her understand he wasn't a failure, that he was still a musical force to be reckoned with, a valued part of the industry. Except that raised the question, was he? "Well, I'd better be going."

"Are you still staying with Dingo and Marla?" she asked.

"They don't have room for a house guest on an extended visit. I'll go to a hotel."

A beat went by. "There's plenty of space here."

He was tempted. But despite their mutual apologies the atmosphere felt too tense. The last thing he wanted was to risk getting into another argument. "I've already booked a room. I'll come by tomorrow."

"Okay."

He nodded at the dough. "I see you wrestled it into submission."

"I'm taking your advice to let it rise overnight," she said. "Anyway, Taylor phoned and he's going to be working in his lab until late.

I'm off the hook for another night as far as dinner goes."

He hesitated. "Do you want to grab a bite to eat with me?"

"Thanks but I'm really tired," she said, subdued. "I need an early night."

"See you tomorrow then." He headed for the back door. "My boots are dirty. I'll leave by the side gate." He hesitated, wanting to reach for her, if only to squeeze her hand. But she was hanging back so he didn't.

Finn fired up the Mustang and flipped throughout the loose CDs in the console for something to listen to. His tiptoeing fingers lingered on an unmarked recording he'd made of himself playing his own music. Not even Tom, who managed his songwriting career, knew about it. The YouTube clips he'd mentioned to Carly were old. This was new, the best work he'd ever done.

If Carly found out, she'd hit him with inspirational talks aimed at helping him reach his "full potential." No doubt in her opinion anyone was capable of scaling Mt. Everest—without oxygen and carrying an extra pack on his back—if only they wanted it badly enough. It would never occur to her that he might already be living up to his potential.

Ah, who needed stardom anyway, with the

pressure and the lack of privacy, the screaming fans? Look what happened to Michael Jackson, Jim Morrison, any number of rock stars dead before their time. Fame had a price. He was happy enough the way he was.

Was he? Or was he still on that river in Egypt?

THE NEXT MORNING when Carly woke, the birdsong in the big maple tree sounded cheerful, like something out of a kids' movie. Good omen. Yesterday was the past. She would put it and the fight with Finn behind her. She swung her legs out of bed and almost tripped over Rufus, lying next to her on the floor. He wagged his tail, wriggling his pleasure at seeing her.

"Good dog!" She stroked his silky ears, pleased that he'd stopped sleeping outside Irene's door. But she hated to think about what would happen if he became too attached to her and she couldn't keep him.

She threw on a light dressing gown over her cami and pajama bottoms and ran downstairs to the kitchen, the Irish setter hot on her heels. Holding her breath, she lifted the lid on the sourdough. The wobbly, bubbly mass half-filled the container.

"It rose, Rufus!" Not as much as she'd hoped, but she hadn't fed the starter. Grinning, she danced on the spot. Rufus woofed and pranced. "Fresh homemade bread tonight."

She put on coffee to brew. Then, following the instructions she'd printed out, she stretched the dough and shaped it into a loaf before placing it into the special mold Irene used. Then she covered it with plastic wrap for another long proofing.

"Good morning." Taylor came into the kitchen, looking bright-eyed and ready for the day. "I'll just grab a drink of water before I go."

"I made coffee," she offered. "If you've got a few minutes I'd like a chat."

Taylor set his briefcase on the floor and sat at the table. "What is it?"

Carly handed him a steaming cup. "I just wanted to confirm what we talked about before. Turns out I inherited the house. I'll be putting it on the market as soon as I've done some basic repairs. So it would be a good idea for you to look for another room so you're not caught short. You don't have to give me any notice and I'll refund any rent paid in advance."

"I appreciate that." Taylor sipped his coffee, frowning. "There weren't a lot of rentals in this area when I was looking."

"Could you go home, just as a stopgap?" Carly asked.

"No, I'll… I'll sleep in my lab before I do that."

Carly's eyebrows rose. Taylor had to be in his midtwenties but he had the air of a much younger guy. She knew it was a mistake to interfere, or even to get to know him, but she couldn't help herself. "I take it you had a difficult time with your mother?"

"Not difficult. I mean, she was good to me." He leaned forward, both hands gripping the coffee mug. "Too good."

From her days counseling high school students, Carly recognized a tortured young man who'd kept his troubles bottled up for too long. A guy who was longing to spill his guts to a sympathetic ear. "Go on."

"She did everything for me," Taylor said. "She was always hovering, asking questions about where I was going and when I'd be home. It was impossible to have…" Red filled his cheeks. "Friends around."

Oh, now she was getting somewhere. "Do you have a girlfriend, Taylor?"

"No."

"Boyfriend?"

"No. I'm not…" He rubbed the large knuckles of one hand. "I had a girlfriend. For a while."

"What happened?"

Taylor gave a diffident shrug of his wide, bony shoulders. "Not much."

Carly bit her lip, fighting her urge to get involved. But if she could draw him out, find out what the problem was, maybe she could give him some useful advice. A parting gift before she evicted him. "Tell me about her."

"Kristin was from my statistics class, really smart and pretty," Taylor said. "Everything was great until I took her home to meet my mom."

"Didn't your mother like her?"

"Mom was fine, welcoming." He sipped at his coffee. "Kristin understood that I was trying to save money by living at home, but when she saw how Mom fussed over me…"

"When you say fussed, what do you mean exactly?" Carly asked.

"She did everything from making my packed lunch to buying my underwear. What was worse in Kristin's eyes was how I allowed it. She told me—pretty darn bluntly—that she was looking for a man, not a boy."

"Ouch." Carly remembered how much she'd loved her mother and how she'd missed her when she'd passed. Her dad was great but he worked a lot and didn't have much time for her. The housekeeper was kind but she wasn't a blood relative. Irene had filled the gap in her life her mother had left. The warmth of their relationship every summer had sustained her through the rest of the year.

"I was so wrapped up in my research that I

didn't see myself until I did through Kristin's eyes," Taylor went on. "After that I tried to do more but somehow Mom always anticipated my needs." He paused, looking miserable. "Anyway, it was too little, too late for Kristin. She's long gone."

"I think you did the right thing by moving out," Carly said.

"I left Mom on her own only a year after she and my dad divorced," Taylor said, clearly wracked with guilt. "I promised I'd look after her and the house."

Instead, his mother was still looking after him. "I assume she's not helpless if she's still doing all that stuff for you," Carly said. "How old are you?"

"Nearly twenty-six." He made an expression of frustration. "I don't want to end up forty years old and be still living at home with my mother doing my laundry and cooking my meals."

Scaring away every woman he brought home. "Was your mom upset when you said you were moving out?"

"Yeah. I explained that I needed to be closer to the university since my research mostly takes place at night." He picked at a hangnail on his thumb. "She thinks that when I'm done I'll move back home. She isn't used to living on her own. I do worry about her."

"I'm sure you're a good son but she needs to make a new life for herself. The longer she's emotionally dependent on you, the harder that will be." Carly thought back to her regular Sunday evening phone calls with Irene, how much they'd meant to both of them. "Call her every now and then, let her know you're thinking of her. Maybe arrange to visit every few weeks."

"You think that will be enough?" Taylor said hopefully.

"Give her credit," Carly said with an encouraging smile. "She'll find the strength. Maybe this is the nudge she needs to forge her own life."

"I hope so." Taylor checked his watch and grabbed his briefcase. "I'd better run. Thanks for the talk."

"No problem." Carly carried the coffee cups to the sink. Finn was right—she had a habit of taking in strays. But when she saw someone in pain or in need, she simply had to help.

Hearing banging out front she went through the house and opened the front door. Finn was tearing up the broken step. Planks of wood lay on the lawn next to a package of sandpaper and tins of paint. A stack of packing cartons sat on the doorstep. She was on the point of telling him again she would hire a handyman to do the repairs when she considered the possibility that he might want to do it for his own sake. It might be his way of repaying Irene for all she'd given him. If it made him feel better, then fine.

Yesterday hadn't been the greatest day for either her or Finn. Even though they'd parted civilly last night their dispute had left behind a new coolness and she still felt bad about the low blows she'd thrown at him. Someone who was hurting needed support, not antagonism.

"Thanks for these," she said, picking up the cartons. Finn glanced up, grunted acknowledgement, and carried on with what he was doing.

She carried the empty cartons into the living room and started to pack books from the bookcase. A music magazine lying atop a stack of industry periodicals caught her eye. She leafed through, curious. There was an article on a famous opera singer, another on a violin maker, one on the interest in ukuleles, a notice about a Steinway piano exhibition. Pages of ads for music suppliers and employment opportunities for musicians.

A half page ad caught her eye. Molto Music, a top recording company, had an opening for a senior staff songwriter. Would Finn have the qualifications? He'd had a hit song recently but a giant firm like Molto would want a proven track record.

She carried the magazine to the kitchen table where her laptop was set up and tapped *Finn*

Farrell into the browser. Two-hundred-thousand-plus results came up, referencing songs he'd written and the artists who'd recorded them. Some she'd never heard of, some she had. Finn was prolific, no doubt about that. Checking the Molto ad again she saw that the return address was in Los Angeles. Perfect.

With Rufus at her heels, she carried the magazine, a cup of coffee and the last of Frankie's blueberry muffins out to the front porch. "Ready for a break?"

"Sure, thanks." Finn put down the hammer and reached for the mug and plate. He leaned against the railing, his long denim-clad legs stretched down the steps.

"There's a songwriter position going that I thought might interest you." Carly handed him the magazine open to the page. "Check out the salary range. Pretty good, huh? I could help you put together an application if you like."

Finn scanned the ad then handed it back. "I appreciate the thought but I freelance. Why would I share my royalties with a big company when I can have the bulk of them for myself?"

She ticked the reasons off on her fingers. "Greater exposure, a wide range of clients, opportunities to write music for movies—"

"I have an agent who can get me all that."

"Security?" she suggested and his gaze sharpened. She added, casually, "There must be lulls where no work is coming in."

"There are periods between contracts," he admitted. "I use that time to write on spec, work on my own stuff. There's never any downtime."

Maybe not, but spec work didn't bring in cash on a regular basis. "Being on staff of a large corporation, you would get a steady paycheck to tide you over the lean times."

Finn brushed the muffin crumbs off his fingers. "Yesterday you wanted me to be a performing musician and fulfil my potential. Today you're trying to make me into a hack. What gives?"

"I saw an opportunity and brought it to your attention, that's all," she said. "It never hurts to keep your options open. Do yourself a favor and think about it."

"Fine. I'll think about it," he said, sounding as if he'd do no such thing. Draining the last of his coffee, he handed her back the cup and plate. "Thanks for the snack. Now I'd better get back to it."

"Me, too." Carly went inside and grabbed a stack of cartons from the hall and headed upstairs, leaving the book packing unfinished. Finn was still a bit touchy after their argument, but then again, so was she. The past twenty-four hours had been a roller coaster of emotions. On the beach she'd accepted the comfort of his arms and a shoulder to lean on, the next day she'd prodded him when she had no business sticking her nose into his affairs. She was still doing it.

But when she thought about yesterday on the beach, it wasn't the comfort she remembered but the play of his back muscles beneath her hands, his thigh pressing against hers and the gust of his warm breath in her hair. Okay, so she was attracted to him. She was a red-blooded woman. Being back in Irene's house where she'd first met him, having him under the same roof, she couldn't help but recall the fantasies she'd had as a teenager—and expand on them now that she'd met Finn, the adult, virile male. Given that they had conflicting agendas, maybe a bit of coolness between them was a good thing. She was in New York, he was Los Angeles-based. She was moving forward, he was happy where he was. Or so he said.

She wandered down the hall deciding where to start. Besides Irene's master bedroom, there were four secondary bedrooms including the one Irene had kept exclusively for Carly's use. Taylor's things were in one of the rental bedrooms but the others were bare of everything but basic furniture.

Dealing with her own stuff would be easiest so that's where she began. Her room was a compilation of the summers she'd spent here. Boy band posters curled off the pale blue walls next to horse pictures from a younger age. A musical jewelry box was wedged between a softball and a shell collection on the dresser. A lifetime of stuff amassed and rarely given another thought.

Ruthless. Everything had to go.

Carly started sorting through the dresser drawers, layered like an archaeological dig. Ancient knee-high socks, bathing suits from when she was fifteen, stretched and faded T-shirts. Neither she nor Irene, it seemed, had ever thrown anything out. She pulled the sock drawer right out of the dresser and tipped it upside down on the bed to figure out what was worth sending to the thrift store and what should be thrown away.

Her fingers encountered a small jewelry box. Inside was an enameled Siamese cat figurine Finn had given her after she'd lamented not having a pet in New York. He'd said her eyes and the cat's were the same turquoise blue. That was the summer he'd kissed her in the tower, a few weeks before the fateful concert. She turned the cat over in her hands. She'd loved it but when September came she'd left it behind, feeling betrayed that he'd left Fairhaven without talking to her. The next year when she'd visited, Finn still hadn't returned.

What might have happened between them if

he'd stayed? She would never know. She set the figurine on the dresser. One or two souvenirs from the past were acceptable.

Several hours later, three full boxes were lined up in the hall outside her room and she was filling a fourth when her phone rang.

"Hey, Taylor," Carly said. "What's up?"

He coughed out a nervous laugh. "I forgot to tell you this morning that I'll be back for dinner tonight."

Dinner. She'd completely forgotten about that. Apart from the sourdough she had nothing in the house to eat. She still hadn't gotten to the grocery store. "How does pizza sound? I'll go shopping soon but I'm not organized yet."

"Pizza would be fine," he said. "When do you plan on eating? I don't want to put you out by being late."

"Let's say, six-ish?"

"Six o'clock. Roger that."

Carly imagined him spinning a dial on his timepiece and lining it up precisely.

Speaking of food, her stomach was feeling empty and it was nearly one o'clock. She went downstairs to find a takeout chicken sandwich from Rhonda's on the counter and a plate empty but for a few crumbs. Finn must have made a run for food.

She padded barefoot to the front door. He was

putting a coat of dark gray paint on the porch. Holding up the sandwich, she said, "Thanks for this." She took a bite and surveyed his work. "Looks good. How long before we can walk on it?"

"Couple of hours. I'll put cardboard down later this afternoon to keep footprints off it."

"You're a handy man to have around, Finn Farrell."

He just nodded and dipped his roller into the shiny paint to apply another layer. But she could tell he was pleased. She watched him from the doorway as she ate, admiring his long back and wide shoulders. His sleeves were rolled up, exposing tanned forearms dusted with black hair and splotched with paint. When he looked up again and raised his eyebrows quizzically, she smiled and backed away. She couldn't keep coming out with flimsy excuses to talk to him.

The afternoon progressed. Carly filled more boxes and cleared out her closet of ancient blouses and worn sneakers. The dust got in her nose and made her sneeze. Through it all, Rufus lay in the middle of the room and watched. When he got tired of that, he slept.

Around five o'clock she heard Taylor and Finn talking downstairs. Then Taylor came up and went into his room and shut the door. Absorbed in her packing she didn't notice anything else until a little while later, she heard a knock at her door.

Finn leaned against the doorjamb, long legs molded by skinny jeans, torso lean and muscular in a tight T-shirt. "Time for a break, babe."

"Don't call me babe." But a break was tempting. Her back ached from hours of bending and lifting and her knees were sore from kneeling on the hardwood.

"Let's go up to the tower and watch the sunset," he said.

"The sun won't set for another three hours," she pointed out.

"So? We've both done enough for today." He held out his hand to help her off the floor and the warmth of his paint-spattered fingers wrapped around hers melted her objections. She followed him down the hall to the spiral staircase to the turret. "Taylor is expecting dinner at six."

"What are you planning to make?"

"I'm ordering pizza and baking the sourdough bread." She snapped her fingers. "I'd better turn on the oven to heat."

"I'll wait for you," he said.

She was back in minutes and they started up the spiral staircase, Finn leading the way. The stuffy heat reminded her of that long-ago summer day when he'd stopped and turned to her, and stepped down onto her step, squashing her against the round wall. Of the feel of his hands on her body and how she'd trembled. How their teeth had bumped and the strangeness of his taste. The dizzying kiss.

She halted, clinging to the iron railing, and realized she was holding her breath. She let it go and sucked in another breath quickly.

"Are you okay?" Finn asked, pausing.

"Fine. Keep going." She fastened her gaze on his boot heels and the supple brown crocodile skin.

A moment later they stepped into the tower, an octagonal room about ten feet in diameter with a love seat in the center and a three-hundred-and-sixty-degree view. It always gave her vertigo to look out to the ocean from so high up. The sky was a vast blue bowl with fluffy white clouds building on the horizon. Far out to sea, a freighter steamed north to Canada.

Finn cracked a side window for fresh air, then pulled her onto the love seat. "Now just breathe. You need to relax."

Carly closed her eyes and slowed her breathing. The ball of tension inside her chest began to ease. Everything would get done that needed to be done. She could only do what she could do. Clichés, sure, but there was truth in those sayings.

She turned to Finn, noting in fine detail how his

dark hair grew in a whorl away from his widow's peak. The thick straight lines of his eyebrows. The straight nose and cupid's bow of a mouth. His smooth olive skin and the sexy mole on his right cheek. "What's your opinion on serif fonts versus sans serif?" she asked.

"Depends. Why?"

"Just answer the question. If you had to choose. If it was a matter of life and death." Because that's what it was starting to feel like.

"Is it printed on paper, or online?"

"Paper."

"Serif, in that case," Finn said. "It's easier to read. Sans serif is clearer online."

She stared at him. "That's so simple, it's brilliant. How do you know these things?"

"I like to investigate obscure and trivial matters."

"Ah, when you're procrastinating?"

"A graphic artist explained it to me once." He leaned back and eyed her with an amused smile. "How do you procrastinate?"

"I don't."

"Bull."

"No lie." She held three fingers to her temple, Girl Scout style. "Not finishing my work makes me more anxious than the thought of doing it."

"And you think I've got problems. You're more uptight than I thought."

"I am not. I'm responsible." And if that sounded boring and mundane, too bad. Pushing the thought away, she focused on the ever-changing shapes of the clouds. So beautiful and so fleeting. They almost made her weepy at their transitory nature. Clouds dissolved and re-formed. The droplets of moisture in them didn't disappear, they rained down on earth and then were evaporated back into the air in an endless cycle. Like life.

"Why do you want to know about fonts?" The gravelly sound of Finn's voice dragged her head back inside the tower. His thigh nudged hers on the love seat.

She explained about the business cards. "My PA has turned this into a huge decision that only I can make. It's like the fate of the free world depends on whether I choose serif or sans serif."

"It'll be worth it," he said. "Imagine handing those babies out to prospective clients."

"Don't mock me." He was teasing but she could imagine handing out her new cards and she loved the idea. Carly Maxwell, international head hunter. Hmm, why stop there? Carly Maxwell, CEO.

"Earth to Carly, come in Carly."

Blinking, she turned to Finn. And immediately got lost in his dark amused eyes that seemed to see right inside her. He really was extraordinarily handsome.

"Look at those kids down there." Finn pointed to a boy and girl, about eleven years old, across the street. The boy was riding a skateboard and showing off to the girl, who walked with her nose in the air. "Does she like him, or not, do you think?"

Carly and Finn had been about that age when she'd first really noticed him. Like the girl below, she'd pretended indifference out of uncertainty and nervousness. She couldn't see the girl's facial expression but the way she glanced over whenever the boy executed a jump or tricky maneuver—and then turned away when he looked at her—was a dead giveaway.

"She likes him. Doesn't want him to know it, though." Carly kept her gaze on the young teens, aware of Finn's knee brushing hers.

"Wonder how he's going to get her attention."

"He should wait for her signal."

"Might never come."

"There may be a reason for that."

"Yeah, she might be afraid."

Carly was drawn back to Finn's searching gaze. Heat filled her cheeks and she glanced away in confusion. "Maybe she doesn't know how she feels."

"He could help her make up her mind." Finn's

hand went to her cheek, his fingertips feather-light. He leaned in and his mouth brushed hers. Warm breath, his nose bumping hers.

He filled her vision and then her eyelids fell shut as she was swept away by a visceral longing. She'd never forgotten him, never gotten over him. And now he was here, his arms coming around her, his lips urgent, ardent. Well, he'd certainly got her attention. And she'd been lying—she did know how she felt. She wanted him even more than when she was younger because now she knew that other men hadn't generated a fraction of what she could feel for him if she let herself.

But Finn was right—she was afraid. He'd dropped out of her life once before. She didn't like it when people did that. It scared her. When she was nine years old her mother had gone away for the weekend with her college girlfriends and hadn't come back. The taxi bringing her home from the airport had been involved in a collision with a truck that ran a red light because the driver hadn't slept in three days.

Life was random like that. Finn had no excuse. He was alive and as far as she could tell, unfazed by breaking all ties with his parents and his hometown and cutting Carly out of his life altogether. Had he ever felt for her as deeply as she'd felt for him?

She could feel for him again, if she let herself…

His hands were moving now, stroking her arms. With every cell in her body aching for him, she broke the kiss and pushed on his chest. "We're not going to do this."

Mirroring her serious expression, he took her hands. "We already are."

"It's not happening, I meant it, Finn." Damned if her lips didn't curl into a smile against her will.

"Tell me you didn't like it just a little bit," he teased.

She regrouped and doubled down on the frown. "I didn't like it, not even a little bit." The smile grew.

"You're a terrible liar, Maxwell."

"You're a terrible kisser, Finn Farrell." Her smile widened. It was like she was freaking Pinocchio.

"Fibbing again," he crowed and tickled her in the ribs.

"Stop it! I hate being tickled." She started to laugh, squirming, her body wriggling beneath his hands, her nose butting his raspy jaw. "Ow."

All at once he stopped and wrapped his arms around her, pulling her tightly to him, kissing the top of her head, her temple, rocking her. Her arms snaked around his lower back and she pressed her cheek to his chest, hearing the quick beat of his heart beneath the damp heat of his shirt.

"Carly," he said, his voice soft and gruff.

Oh, Finn. What are we doing? Where can we go with this?

She'd spent her twenties in and out of relationships that lasted one year, two years, six months, interspersed with stretches of no one when it was almost a relief to be off the roller coaster. She hated the disappointment when her feelings faded, or worse, the crushing sensation of being the one dumped. She was tired of playing the game. What did love even mean in an era when you said, "I love you" to each other and then one day he simply stopped calling and texting? Where was the respect? Where was the romance?

She and Finn had flirted but they'd never crossed the line into a real relationship. There was a reason for that. If she hadn't been so bummed out over his disappearing act she would have swallowed her pride and contacted him. They could have been friends all this time instead of dropping out of each other's lives. She wasn't a social butterfly, she didn't have dozens of close friends. Over the years she'd gathered a handful who'd lasted. True friends, the kind you could count on in a crisis. The kind who would hold you when you were grieving or fix your gate. Who you could pick up with where you left off even when you hadn't seen them for more than a decade. Finn was that kind of friend. Romance would only get in the way.

Easing back, she placed a palm against his cheek and looked into his eyes. The air in the turret was still and hot with just the breath of a cool breeze from the open window. He looked younger, open, vulnerable. Questioning. She was full of questions, too. All unanswerable. Where could they go with an attraction that had no future?

"You're really important to me, Finn. I've missed you." She kissed him lightly, quickly on the lips and nose. "When this is all over, I'd like to stay in touch and stay friends, real friends."

"Why does that sound like a brush-off?" Finn frowned. "What are you saying?"

"The sourdough is ready to bake. I need to go down and put it in the oven. Pizza and bread," she babbled. "Is that too many carbs?"

"Carly, don't you dare leave on that note," Finn said.

She went to the window and pressed her hot cheek to the cool glass. Rising quickly in the stuffy room had made her dizzy. "Why didn't you call me that night to let me know you wouldn't make it? I waited up for hours, wondering if you were going to show. I phoned your house but nobody answered."

There was a long silence.

"My parents and I were still fighting," Finn said finally. "I'm sorry. I should have called you. I thought about it, but frankly, I was in no shape to see anyone. Later, well, I just didn't want to talk about it." He paused. "Still don't."

"Things that aren't talked about fester," she said. "If you'd gone to Juilliard you would have been in New York and we could have seen each other." He didn't reply for so long that she wondered if he'd heard her. "What are you thinking?"

"I texted my mother yesterday," he said. "She didn't reply."

Carly didn't know what to say. "Sorry."

"Do you know what she said when I told her I was taking you to the after-party?" he went on. "That you wouldn't be interested in a poor boy trying to be a rock musician but that you might be interested in a student of classical piano attending Juilliard."

"Pretty sure that back then I would have gone for the rock star from the wrong side of the tracks," Carly said. Probably now, too.

"Mom's comments only made me more determined to follow my own path," he said. "I couldn't make myself into someone I wasn't for the sake of climbing the social ladder."

"Nor should you have." Carly turned back to the window. The girl and boy had made their way to the corner. While she watched, the girl turned to the left and the boy kicked his skateboard straight ahead. For some reason it made her feel sad. "So, can we be friends?"

"That's a given," Finn said.

Carly breathed out in relief. No matter what happened, she didn't want to lose touch with him again.

An older model blue sedan pulled in to the curb. A woman in her fifties with frizzy blond hair that should never have been cut in a bob got out and glanced up at the house.

"Someone's here," Carly said.

Finn came to stand beside her. "Maybe she's going next door."

"Doesn't look like it." The woman, who wore a colorful pullover and carried a casserole dish, climbed the steps to the porch. Faintly, the doorbell rang.

"She must be one of Irene's friends." Carly didn't recognize her from the funeral but there was something familiar about her. "I'd better go down."

CHAPTER NINE

CARLY SWEPT DOWN the spiral stairs, hands skimming the rails, to the second floor.

The doorbell rang again and Taylor poked his head out of his room. "Did you want me to answer that?"

"No, I've got it."

In the foyer, Carly checked herself in the mirror and smoothed down her hair. All she had to do was thank the woman for the casserole, offer a cup of tea and make polite chitchat for twenty minutes.

She opened the door. "Can I help you?"

"I'm Susan Greene, Taylor's mother. Is he here?"

"Oh!" Carly squeaked. She was not prepared for this. "Nice to meet you. Taylor's upstairs."

"Are you Irene Grant?" Susan asked. "I got the impression you were older."

"I'm Carly, Irene's niece." She opened the door wider. "Come in."

She hoped Taylor wouldn't be upset that she'd invited his mom in. After hearing his story she was pretty sure Susan was the last person he would want to see. But how could she turn the woman away without being rude?

Susan held out the casserole dish. "I made pot roast, Taylor's favorite."

"And you brought it all the way from Seattle, wow." Was this stalker behavior or caring maternal instincts? "How kind of you."

"I wanted to see where he was living, make sure the accommodation is as advertised." Susan laughed indulgently. "His head is in the stars in more ways than one, if you know what I mean." She stepped past Carly, her bright hazel gaze darting around the foyer. "The ad said room and board but what some people call dinner these days ought to be against the law. Fast food, frozen food, and goodness knows what."

"Sometimes people get strapped for time." Ordering a pizza didn't make her a bad person. Was it too late to tell Susan that Taylor wasn't there and subtly hint that next time she should call first before showing up on the doorstep?

Before she could, Finn loped gracefully down the stairs. "Hi, I'm Finn. Let me take that for you. Irene would have appreciated your thoughtfulness."

"Why thank you." Taylor's mom might be in her fifties but she succumbed to Finn's charm like a debutante. She handed over the casserole then patted her frizzy hair. "I'm Susan."

Carly watched the exchange with bemusement. Finn might not be a rock star but he had the charm and magnetism of someone able to command attention.

Finn turned to Carly. "Could we offer Susan a drink? Coffee, or something stronger?"

"I'll put a pot of coffee on." Before she could tell him who their guest was Finn adeptly kept the conversational ball rolling.

"How did you know Irene?" Finn asked Susan.

"I don't. I'd like to meet her though." Susan, not picking up on the reference to Irene in the past tense, peered around Carly into the living room.

Carly tried unsuccessfully to block her view. Clearly Taylor hadn't told his mother that his prospective landlady had died. What must Susan be thinking about the house? What with one thing and another, Carly hadn't finished tidying up after the wake. Books were scattered near unfilled empty boxes, a cushion lay on the floor and from here she could see a shoe beneath the couch. No doubt Susan could see it, too, and was passing judgment on what some people called cleanliness these days.

"You don't know Irene?" Finn turned a puzzled gaze to Carly. "Then who?"

"Susan is Taylor's mother," Carly explained.

"It's the first time he's lived away from home," Susan said, almost apologetically. "He's not used to being alone."

Finn rapidly recalibrated. "Taylor is the boarder."

As if on cue, the lanky young astrophysicist came down the stairs. "Was that the pizza guy?" He saw Susan and did a double take. "Mom, what are you doing here?"

"She brought you dinner." Carly could see Susan's point of view. Having her only son leave home for the first time must be hard. But bringing dinner uninvited and unannounced to a son who wanted independence seemed a tad intrusive.

Susan gave Carly a quizzical smile. "You're ordering pizza? Just as well I came by. There's enough pot roast for everyone."

"My aunt Irene died last week, suddenly and unexpectedly," Carly explained. "It's been kind of hectic." Patience, calm, understanding. That's how her aunt would have responded to this situation.

"I'm so sorry," Susan said. "Taylor didn't say anything." She looked at her son, who hunched his bony shoulders into a shrug.

"You'll stay and eat with us, of course, Susan?" Finn said.

"Well, I don't like to impose…" The older

woman patted her hair. "But it is a long drive and I haven't had dinner."

Surprise, surprise. Carly threw a sympathetic glance at Taylor. "Is that okay?"

Taylor nodded, tight-lipped.

"I have mashed potatoes and green beans, too," Susan said, indicating the thermal bag slung over her shoulder. "This is a lovely home," she went on as they all trooped into the kitchen. "So big. Just made for a family." She glanced between Carly and Finn. "Do you two have children?"

"Not yet," Finn said with a mischievous wink at Carly.

She frowned at him. "We're not a couple."

Susan looked from one to the other.

"Please, sit down," Carly said. "I'll just pop my home-made bread in the oven."

She prodded the flaccid loaf. It didn't seem to have risen much but she put it in the oven anyway. At least she hadn't ordered the pizza yet, so there was no need to cancel.

Susan sat at the table right in front of the scribbled-on room rental ads in the local paper that Taylor had left out. "This is your writing, Taylor. Are you looking for new accommodation already?" She turned to Carly. "Is there a problem now that your aunt has passed?"

"Carly is selling the house," Taylor said.

"Is that so." Susan's soft lips pressed together. "Taylor, honey, you come home with me tonight. You don't need the distraction of Realtors and buyers traipsing through the house while you're trying to work. You'll have to move again anyway, better to do it now before you get settled. The commute isn't bad. Why, I got here in just under an hour. Or, you could transfer to a college in Seattle and the drive would take half the time."

"I can't transfer, Mom." Taylor's Adam's apple bobbed up and down. "I've got funding, a supervisory committee, a tutorial job. The telescope is booked."

Taylor going home would make life easier for Carly. He wasn't her problem, and letting him stay was only postponing the inevitable. But while Carly also felt for Susan, on her own for the first time in what must be decades, she couldn't let Taylor down.

"There's no problem." Carly scooped away the newspaper and crumpled it. "I'm going to honor my aunt's commitments. Taylor is welcome to stay for the summer term. If the house sells sooner than that, I'll arrange for closing to take place at the end of August."

Taylor's and Finn's astonished gazes homed in on her, two sets of eyebrows raised. Susan made a soft sound of disappointment.

"It'll be fine." Carly stared them all down. She hoped this would seem like a good idea in the morning. And then, because they were still looking stunned, she decided a change of scenery would help move the evening along. "On second thought, let's eat in the dining room. Finn, can you give me a hand?"

FINN SET OUT Irene's best china around the dining table while Carly and Susan duked it out in the kitchen for control of warming up the pot roast in the microwave. In his opinion, a less formal meal would be more likely to defuse the tension between Taylor and his mom, but Carly seemed bent on proving to Susan that Taylor hadn't stumbled into a crack house, or worse, a place where people ate fast food from the box with their hands.

"You're a mother hen, just like Irene," he murmured to her as she brought in the casserole dish clutched between two oven mitts and set it on a hot mat.

"That woman isn't going to have a single thing to hold against me or this house," Carly whispered. "She insisted Taylor show her his room. She treats him as if he's five years old instead of a PhD student."

"He'll figure out how to deal with her on his own." Finn knew firsthand how much it sucked to have a mother interfere in his life, even when she believed she had his best interests at heart. "He has to make his own mistakes."

"Wanting independence isn't a mistake." Carly pulled off the oven mitts. "Taylor needs to stand up for himself but it doesn't hurt for him to know someone has his back."

Finn cracked a tiny smile. She was so earnest, so sincere, so passionate in her desire to do good. And that was why he liked her so much. Unless her efforts were turned toward him, that is. "Okay, but don't say I didn't warn you. The house might be harder to sell if you've got a tenant."

"I'll take that chance. It could be a couple of months before I find a buyer. And then there's escrow. I can stretch that out three, even four months." She moved the salt and pepper from the sideboard to the table. "Why did you tell Susan we don't have children yet? Is that some kind of joke? Because after what we talked about in the tower, I don't get it."

He'd only said it because he'd been annoyed that she'd broken away from him so abruptly and shut down any discussion of their kiss. Playing the friends card seemed premature, and a tad presumptuous. Exploring their attraction didn't necessarily mean commitment. Just because they'd kissed wasn't any reason for her to panic.

"I spoke lightheartedly," he said. "Don't give it another thought."

"So you don't want us to have children together?" she asked. "Just to be clear."

"Children are not on my radar," he vowed.

She blew out an exaggerated breath. "Whew. That's a relief."

Finn went on setting the table. Maybe she was right and they should keep their relationship platonic. He was in an unstable period of his life right now. She was busy cementing her own status with a prestige job. All that being said, they did have unfinished business. "I'd like to know though, is it because you're still mad at me for that summer? I had too much on my plate back then."

"It's not that." She brought down crystal water glasses from the sideboard. "I'm simply not in the market for a relationship."

Talk about being in denial... Up in the tower, Finn had felt her body heat rise and the way she moved restlessly in his arms. But he wasn't going to push her where she didn't want to go. "Fine."

"So we're good?" Carly asked.

"We're always good," he growled. "No matter what."

The doorbell rang.

Carly picked up the oven mitts and laid them neatly next to the casserole. "Now who?"

Finn followed her out to the foyer. He did a double take when he saw Annie standing there with her dimpled knock-knees below her miniskirt, pulling nervously at her hair.

"Sorry to bother you." Her gaze darted from Carly to Finn. She stuck the end of her ponytail in her mouth and then dragged it out again, spitting hair. "Finn, can I talk to you for a minute?"

"We were just about to have dinner." Finn glanced at Carly. "Can we hold off eating for five minutes?"

"Sure," Carly said. "The bread isn't done yet anyway."

"What is it?" Finn asked Annie. She was shifting her weight from one flat, pointed shoe to the other. Whatever it was must be important for her to work up her courage to come and see him.

"You know how you were going to let me sing the other day?" Annie said. "I thought if you heard me, you could tell Dingo and the other guys I'm okay. If you think I am, that is. If it's not too much trouble. But you're busy, I can see that. Thanks anyway." She started to turn away.

"Wait. I'd be happy to listen to you." Finn looked at Carly. If ever a person needed help, Annie did.

Carly picked up on his silent communication.

"You're welcome to stay for dinner," she said to Annie. "We have plenty of food."

"Really?" Annie looked to Finn for confirmation.

"Why not?" he said. "The more the merrier."

"Oh, thank you. Thank you both so much." Annie stepped inside and smiled. "Is that pot roast I smell? I love pot roast. It's my favorite. And baking bread? Awesome!"

"Thanks," Finn whispered to Carly as they led Annie into the dining room.

"Now who's the mother hen?" Carly murmured.

Taylor and Susan came downstairs. Introductions were made. After an awkward shuffle, Carly directed Taylor and Susan to sit next to each other with Annie opposite. That left her and Finn at either end of the table, spots usually reserved for the mom and dad. He flashed her an ironic smile and she rolled her eyes.

"The bread." Carly jumped up again. "Go ahead and start. I'll be right back."

Susan took the lid off the casserole and passed it across to Annie. Finn started on the vegetables and for a few minutes they were occupied in passing food around.

"It's nice when friends drop in for dinner," Susan said, smiling at Annie.

"Oh, I'm not…" Annie cast an anxious glance at Finn.

"It is, isn't it?" Finn said. "This pot roast is delicious, Susan."

"Yes, what did you put in the gravy?" Annie asked.

"I can write out the recipe, if you like," Susan said, beaming. She turned to her son. "Better than pizza, isn't it, Taylor?"

"Your pot roast is the best, Mom," he said dutifully.

"I like your and Taylor's sweaters," Annie said to Susan. "Did you knit them?"

Now that Annie was certain of her welcome, she became chatty. She seemed to take it for granted that Taylor and Susan were longtime friends of Finn's and Carly's. Susan and Taylor accepted Annie without question. Finn was cool with all that. A home-cooked meal was a treat for him, too. Irene's portrait, still propped on the mantelpiece, smiled benignly at them. She would have approved of the hospitality and she would have adored that such a diverse group had come together over a meal.

Carly came quietly back into the room empty-handed and slid into her chair. "Didn't work," she said in reply to his questioning glance.

"Bring it in," Susan said. "Let's see it. Takes a lot to make bread inedible."

It took some convincing before Carly would produce the bread but eventually she agreed and shamefacedly carried in a bread board with her sourdough loaf. A golden brown oval, it was flat at the ends and rose to barely an inch in the middle.

"I bet it tastes good," Finn said.

"Either it's overproofed or there's a problem with the starter," Susan diagnosed.

"Starter, I think," Carly said, cutting the dough.

Susan sniffed a slice and took a tiny bite. "It's got a good flavor. Try again."

Carly asked how to tell when the starter was ready to use and Susan responded with a dissertation on bread making.

Finn chatted to Annie about music while Taylor listened, casting curious glances across the table at the waitress. Susan noticed and when there was a lull, began talking about her son's research into pulsars. It was clear from the way Taylor kept gently correcting her that she had no idea what he actually did.

But she was proud of him, Finn could see that. Interfering mothers always were proud. And the prouder they were, the more they pushed their offspring to do things the right way, their way. Finn knew all about that. Taylor was quietly chafing under his mother's attention but was too polite to say anything rude.

"Taylor, do you play basketball?" Finn said, to rescue him. It was a reasonable question given the guy's height but the nerd factor left room for doubt.

"I did in high school." Brightening, Taylor pushed his glasses up his nose. "I heard a rumor that a pro basketball team is coming back to Seattle."

"That would be cool," Finn said. The next twenty minutes were a passionate discussion of professional sports teams in the Seattle area.

After dinner, Taylor excused himself to prepare for a tutorial tomorrow. Carly and Susan cleared the table and went to clean the kitchen.

"Ready to show me what you've got?" Finn said to Annie.

With a flashing smile, she nodded, ponytail bobbing.

He crossed the room and sat on the piano bench, warming up his fingers with a few quick scales. "What do you like to sing?"

"Rock, blues, R&B, soul, pop, jazz—anything, really. I love Amy Winehouse and Adele." She stroked the shiny edge of the concert grand then ran the hem of her cardigan over it in case her fingertips had left prints. "Have you got music?"

Now that they'd arrived at this moment he almost wished he could send her away so she wouldn't embarrass herself. With her pudgy cheeks, round brown eyes and dimple in her chin she looked far too young and too innocent to sing Amy Winehouse's raw and gritty music with any credibility. But he'd promised.

"You start singing, I'll improvise." He set his phone to record. Then he began playing minor chords in a bluesy arrangement. If she had any talent at all, even if it wasn't suitable for Dingo's band, he would do what he could to encourage and help her. "When you're ready."

Annie closed her eyes and took two deep breaths, focusing inward. Finn kept his head down so as not to make her any more nervous than she already was. His hands marked time with a quiet, repetitive R&B rhythm. He'd almost lulled himself into a meditative state when the raw power of her voice channeling Amy Winehouse woke him with a start.

His mouth dropped open in sheer surprise before he recovered and started playing properly. His hands found the beat and then the melody and meshed them together, keeping the volume low so as not to overpower the singing. No chance of that he realized as Annie's voice swelled into the chorus. He risked a glance at her. Her eyes were open now but were fixed on some distant vision only she could see. She no longer looked or sounded like a child. Anguish and emotion she could surely never have experienced in her life were somehow conveyed through the tremor of her vocal cords. Swaying with the music, she snapped her fingers and moved her shoulders and hips in a sexy, sensual movement that kept time with the soulful beat.

Dimly Finn became aware of Carly and Susan in the hallway, listening. Then of Taylor, quietly coming down the stairs and standing behind them.

Annie finished abruptly, almost before the last bar was done. "What do you think?"

Still stunned, he shut off the recording.

"That bad?" Annie asked, fearfully awaiting his verdict.

"That good!" He grinned. "You've got one helluva voice."

"Really?" She smiled tentatively as if afraid to believe it.

"I've never in my life heard anything like that from a complete amateur." He rose from the piano to give her a high five. "If Dingo doesn't use you in his band he's a fool and there are plenty who will."

He looked over to Carly and the others. "Am I right?"

They broke into applause and cheers.

Annie burst into tears.

CHAPTER TEN

IT WAS NEARLY 11:00 p.m. before Carly sat down by herself on the couch with her laptop. All in all, it had been an emotional and exhausting evening. Finn had recorded Annie singing three songs and promised to speak to Dingo the next day, before driving the elated girl home. As Carly mixed up another batch of sourdough she heard Susan again plead with Taylor to come home. Taylor had refused, nicely but firmly.

Although Carly was tired she was far too wired to sleep. Finally she had a moment to herself and could investigate more about what happened to Irene. She Googled *brain aneurysm*, selected a respected medical site, and started to read. The more she read, the more depressed she became. She didn't hear Finn come in until he appeared in the living room.

"What's so fascinating?" he asked.

"You mean, terrifying." She passed a hand over her face then leaned back. "Did you know that a person can have a brain aneurysm for months or years and not know it? They're like a ticking time bomb and at any moment the aneurysm can burst. Boom and they're dead."

Finn sat beside her on the couch. "So there's no warning?"

"Most of the time there are no symptoms until it ruptures," Carly said. "I feel awful that I didn't know, didn't do something."

"Don't." Finn shifted closer and put his arm around her. "Irene had a good life. She wouldn't want you to feel bad. She'd want you to look to the future."

"I know. She always had such a positive outlook on life." Carly leaned against him, soaking in his warmth.

He played with her fingers, rubbing his thumb across her nails. "If you knew you were going to die tomorrow, what would you do tonight?"

"I wouldn't go hiking, that's for sure." Her broken chuckle made a tear fall to her cheek. She brushed it away. "Sorry I've been such a downer lately. Normally I coo over pictures of kittens and put wildflowers in jam jars and stuff like that."

"Don't be sorry," he said gruffly. "You're grieving."

"I know and it'll never pass completely," she said, remembering her mother's death. "You learn to live with it. There'll be darker times, like now, and other days when you cope. And some days the sun will shine."

Her fingers were interwoven with his, their thumbs stroking. Together with him, she felt stronger than alone.

If there was no tomorrow, what would she choose as her last act? Would she worry about how long a relationship lasted? No, that would be meaningless. Would she waste her time worrying about all the potentially bad things that could happen? Again, pointless. Or would she celebrate the joy in life? Try to find a crumb of happiness to end her days?

She looked into Finn's eyes. Glimmering in their dark irises she saw light. Warmth. And yes, hope. If she were dying, who better to spend her last night with than Finn? He was one of a handful of people whom she'd cared about most of her life and even though long separated, had never forgotten. His calm, steady strength put things into perspective for her.

Her end was far from imminent but she still had unanswered questions—about him, about herself, about them.

"I would do this." She kissed him, at first lightly then, seeing the heat flare in his eyes and the sound of startled pleasure, she pressed her lips against his again, slowly, sensuously.

Savoring the firmness of his mouth, the warm gust of his breath.

His arms came around her, pulling her close. She sank into him and then she couldn't stop kissing him. Angling her mouth for more, she savored the slide of his tongue against hers, the heat of his skin beneath her fingertips. His hands moved over her and she slid down on the couch so he could lie on top of her. Heat spread through her at the intimate touch even through their clothes. She kissed him like a drowning woman gulps for oxygen, as if she could never get enough, as if the world was coming to an end and she would inhale him along with her last breath. As if he was life itself.

WHEN FINN KISSED Carly all his doubts receded and the clamor in his brain stilled. Whatever else was going on in his life, this was pure and right. Everything he'd said about hope and belief in the future distilled into the desire to wash away her heartache with gentle kisses and soft strokes. But when she pulled him down onto her, lust took over.

They fumbled with each other's clothes, furiously working at buttons and zippers, awkwardly shifting to push down pants and hike up skirt, laughing with eagerness and nerves. How many times had he sat at the piano for his lesson and stolen glances at Carly curled up on the window seat with a book, wishing he could be doing exactly what he was doing now? His mother's warnings had held him back. *She's too good for you. She'll play with you and then break your heart. Concentrate on your music. That's the only thing that matters. The only thing that will last. Your only chance to rise above your station in life. Then you can have any woman you want.*

He squeezed his eyes shut, willing his mother's voice out of his brain before the moment was ruined. Right or wrong, he wanted Carly. He'd always wanted her. And now he was with her and she was willing and eager. He wasn't going to turn her down, not when he'd waited years. Oh, the sweet taste of her nipple puckering beneath his tongue. The fullness of her plump breast, the firmness of her belly, the heartbreaking tenderness of her navel.

When they were fully naked, stretched out, her moving beneath him, he groaned with wanting. Her lithe body, the sensation of skin against skin, of her breasts pressed against his chest and his cock finding its way between her legs like a divining rod searching for the lodestone, made him crazy to be inside her.

Through the blood-hot lust haze he remembered to use protection. Leaning off the couch he grabbed his pants, found his wallet and fumbled for a condom. When he finally entered her he looked into her eyes and was humbled by the trust and happiness he saw there. They both stilled and he touched her cheek, and then her lips, abrading the soft skin with his fingertips. She was real, not a dream or a fantasy.

He began to move, slowly at first, then faster as her hips pushed up hard to meet his thrusts. And all the time their eyes were locked in fierce intimacy. Only when she came did her head fall back with a little cry and her eyelids closed, ecstasy softening her features, rolling through her and melting her limbs beneath him. That made him even harder if that was possible. He pumped into her, his body rigid. Her legs came around his hips and pulled him closer, squeezing. The orgasm rolled through him, picked him up and flung him high and then sent him floating back to earth. To the couch and Carly, warm and damp with sweat. He buried his nose in the earthy scent of her skin.

He pressed his lips to her neck and started to shift his weight, worried he was too heavy.

"Stay here at the house," she said, holding him tightly with arms and legs. "I don't just mean tonight."

"You're looking for a sex slave," he teased.

Eyes shut, she smiled. "That's it."

"I'll get my things from the hotel tomorrow."

He eased back down, more relaxed and content than he could recall being in a long, long time. They fit together perfectly, legs entwined, his hand cupping her breast protectively, their breath mingling. He drifted in and out of a sleepy bliss. Whatever else was going on, whatever else would happen or wouldn't happen, he would always have this memory of Carly gazing up at him with desire in her eyes and love in her touch. They'd made love together and they couldn't unmake it.

CARLY CAME AWAKE with a pervading feeling of well-being throughout her body, mind and soul. Finn lay curled around her on the couch, breathing evenly, his eyes closed. Lightly, she stroked his hair back from his forehead and smiled as she watched him sleep.

Making love with him had been even better than she'd always dreamed it would be. Possibly they shouldn't have given in and done the deed but if the world did end tomorrow at least she could die happy. In a moment she would take him up to her room and they would do it all over again, more slowly. Take time to really get to know each other's bodies. She wanted to find out what made him purr and what revved his engine.

Her smile faded as reality found a way in

through a crack in her happiness. What was the point in getting involved? In another two days she would be back in New York. He would be in Los Angeles. A long-distance relationship worked for some but she liked routine and certainty and the idea of coming home to the man she loved at the end of a long day.

Anyway, who knew how long this early phase bliss would last, especially when there were already no-go zones in their relationship. Finn wasn't willing to let her in, not if he wouldn't talk about the five-hundred-pound elephant that had been keeping him from performing.

"Finn?" They were both cooling down and she wanted to be under the covers.

"Hmm?" He started kissing her face.

"Let's go to bed."

They gathered their clothes and crept up the stairs. Taylor's light was out, thankfully. What she and Finn did was none of anyone's business but theirs. Besides, it was temporary. The less anyone knew, the fewer explanations would be necessary when it ended.

She pulled him into the shower and they washed each other. Then he smoothed lotion over her whole body. Finally, back in her room, he made love to her again, slowly. In a seated position on her single bed, with her straddling him, they explored each other, touching, kissing, stroking, licking. Letting the tension build and build, holding off until they were both panting with need. She found another condom somewhere in her bag and made a ritual out of sheathing him. By the time she finally lowered herself over him with a long moan, he was growling with impatience. But he slowed them down again and made her wait while he stroked and kissed and built the tension all over again.

Tension so fierce she wanted to scream. Her nails dug into his back. Before she could change the pace herself, he did, thrusting into her in long, hard strokes that sent her into the stratosphere. She came within seconds. Before the waves of sensation had peaked, he came, too. They clung together, rocking gently, which set her off a second and then a third time.

Finally, exhausted, they slept, curled together in her single bed. Her last thought before she drifted off was that while her mind might be telling her this was temporary, Finn was already burrowing his way into her heart.

FINN WOKE WITH a crick in his neck from sleeping with his head half off the pillow. He stretched the tight muscles carefully so as not to wake Carly. Then he propped his head on his elbow and gazed at her. So beautiful. So sexy.

Last night when he'd held her in his arms,

twelve years and a continent separating them had evaporated as if it was nothing. Forging a relationship going forward wouldn't be easy but he'd waited for her too long to let her go again. Was it possible to turn their budding romance into something lasting?

He rolled out of bed and headed for the shower. As the water sluiced over his head, he was grateful that Carly had stopped pushing him away. They had a lot of lost time to make up for and he would enjoy every minute.

She was still sleeping when he checked in on her again, lying on her side with her tousled blond hair over her face and the sheet tucked up beneath her arms. He bent to kiss her cheek. She stirred and rolled onto her back, her eyes still closed. The sheet slipped, exposing a rounded breast and one smooth rosy nipple. Unable to help himself, he brushed his lips lightly across the tip to feel the incredible softness. Beneath his gaze it budded and his groin tightened.

She opened her eyes and seeing him, smiled. "Come back to bed."

"Tempting." He loved lazy morning sex and Carly was soft and sleepy and willing. And he was so very hard. "Can I take a rain check? I believe you said the plumber is coming this morning?"

"Oh, right. The downstairs bathroom." She

sat up, glancing at the clock. "I need to go to the grocery store. Then I'm going to pack up Irene's room. Putting off the task won't make it go away."

"Do you want help?"

"I'll be fine, but thanks." She reached for her dressing gown and slipped it on. "I thought you'd head straight to Dingo's house so he could listen to Annie's recording."

"He's at work. I'll see him this afternoon," Finn said. "Annie's voice has a lot of potential but it's untrained. Dingo's going to hear that. I hope she doesn't get her hopes up too high."

"You could train her," Carly said, picking through her suitcase for clean clothes.

He huffed out a laugh. "I'm not a music teacher."

"You had voice lessons for years, along with the piano lessons," Carly argued. "You know what she needs to learn."

"The thing is…" The real reason was surprisingly hard to come out with. "I won't be here long enough—"

"Right, of course." She smiled, a little too brightly. "Which is a nice segue into talking about last night."

"I didn't mean—"

"It was wonderful, and you were wonderful," she rushed on. "But we both know it's temporary."

"Carly," he said firmly, stemming the flow. "It only has to be temporary if we want it to be. I don't want you to go out of my life again."

"Which brings us back around to maintaining a friendship."

"That's a given," he said, hiding his disappointment. He wanted more.

"Pinky promise?" She crooked her baby finger.

"Pinky promise." He linked fingers and squeezed. Then he turned her hand over and kissed the palm. "We both have a lot on our plate right now. We don't have to make life-altering decisions after one night of mind-blowing sex. Let's take this one day at a time."

She gave him a lopsided smile. "Mind-blowing, huh?"

He knocked his head. "Hollow. I'm short about five pounds of gray matter."

The doorbell rang.

Finn leaned in to kiss her and then rolled off the bed. "That'll be the plumber."

CARLY SAT DOWN at the kitchen table to make a grocery list. She and Finn had agreed to be friends—that was the good news. The bad news was, cementing their friendship didn't stop her from being infatuated. Back when he was simply the object of her fantasies, her feelings were easier to keep under control. Now that they'd made love she was hyperaware of him. Like now, for instance. How could she think about milk and eggs when the sound of his deep, rumbling voice down the hall talking with the plumber made her hot all over again?

She finished her list and before leaving the house she tidied the living room to eliminate any signs of their lovemaking. As she plumped and straightened the cushions, the previous night came back to her. The uplifting rush of looking into Finn's eyes as he moved inside her. The moonlight on his naked chest, the scent and texture of his skin, the sound of his breath in her ear. Remembering, her skin tingled. She felt giddy, almost light-headed, awash with warmth and pleasure.

Then out of the blue, she was flooded with guilt and shame. The only reason she and Finn were together was because Irene had died. It wasn't a big leap to think that her aunt's death was also the reason they'd made love. It was a well-established phenomenon that after a brush with death people turned to sex as an instinctual life-affirming gesture.

She dropped to the couch and buried her face in her hands. This morning Finn had seemed to want to move beyond friendship. But what if making love hadn't been fate or kismet or soul mates calling to each other but instead a simple reaction to death? She hated that their feelings could be boiled down so dispassionately. Not love, or even the beginnings of love. Probably not even infatuation. Just biology. Maybe a little chemistry. Okay, a lot of chemistry. After all, she'd been attracted to him as a teenager. That was then. She was grown up now and too pragmatic to get moony-eyed over a guy who was still trying to figure out his life. He might think he was fine, but she knew he wasn't one hundred percent happy.

What they'd done last night couldn't happen again. No matter that Finn was the one bright spot in this whole awful episode and he'd been wonderful to her. Or that the thought of cutting short their romance made her feel as if she would suffer another huge loss. A missed opportunity to finally explore what they'd started so long ago.

The plumber went past on his way to get something from his truck. She glanced at her watch and realized she'd been clutching a pillow to her stomach while her mind whirled in useless circles for the better part of ten minutes.

Had she actually believed she was in control of her life? She was a mess, unable to sort out her thoughts or her emotions. Finn didn't need her problems even if she wanted an ongoing relationship with him. Which her rational mind was doing its best to warn her was a mistake.

Brushing aside her tears, she grabbed her grocery list and headed out. At the store, she raced her cart around the aisles, tossing in fresh fruit and vegetables and whatever. There were so many things she needed to do. So little time. Finish packing Irene's effects. Call a real estate agent for an appraisal of the property. Call an estate auctioneer—no, first ask Irene's friends if they wanted anything. No, first set aside the bequeathed items for Uncle Larry, Brenda and the others. And Irene's portrait and the seascape for herself.

She needed more time, that was all there was to it. As she turned down the cereal aisle she brought up her boss's number on her phone and got Leanne.

"Hi, Leanne, it's Carly." She spoke quickly, tossing items in her cart. "I'd like to talk with Herb if he's available but first, about my business cards. I've consulted an expert. I'm going with serif."

She must have sounded definite because Leanne didn't argue this time. Carly breathed a sigh of relief that the ridiculousness was at an end. Leanne put Herb on the line.

"Hi, Herb." Carly took a deep breath and plunged in. "I'm calling to ask a favor. My aunt left me her house and all her personal effects. I need to put the house on the market and get everything organized so that when I return to New York I can concentrate fully on my job. If it's okay with you, I'd like to borrow future vacation time to stay another week. I guarantee I'll be back for the meeting on the eighth."

"Well…" Herb said slowly. "What's the status on the Wallis Group?"

"I sent them a prospectus and all the info on our firm," she told him. "I've made contact with their HR person. At the moment the ball is in their court. I'm monitoring my emails and if anything comes up I'll be on it. If I don't hear anything in a week I'll follow up."

"Sounds like that's under control," Herb said. "Let me know if there are developments that you can't handle from the west coast. And talk to Leanne about assigning any other urgent cases to another consultant. Otherwise, we'll see you on the eighth."

"Thanks, Herb," Carly said, relieved. "I really appreciate this." She hung up and stood there blinking. A huge weight had just been lifted from her shoulders.

Back at the house, Rufus greeted her with wagging tail and followed her as she made the rest of her calls and put the groceries away. Then she grabbed a stack of cartons and started for the stairs, the dog bounding ahead. Now that she had a deadline reprieve she had to get on with things.

Entering her aunt's room was weird, as if she was intruding on personal space. Rufus prowled, sniffing everything, and finally settled beside the bed, his muzzle resting on one of Irene's sandals. Irene was present everywhere, from the dangly bead earrings on the dresser to the paisley pashmina shawl draped over the wing chair in the corner, to the biography of Leonard Bernstein on the bedside table.

Oh, and there was the bluebird brooch sitting in a little porcelain dish on the dresser. The enameled bluebird with its wings spread, throat lifted and beak open as if he was singing his heart out. Carly smiled. Irene used to lend it to her students to wear for good luck before a recital or an exam at the conservatory. Countless young people had been encouraged by the talisman and gone on to make Irene proud.

Carly put down the brooch and picked up her aunt's shawl. A whiff of delicate floral perfume instantly transported her back to her childhood. She and Irene used to sit on the porch in the warm dusk and talk quietly. As the shadows grew long and the heat of the day faded, Irene would wrap herself and Carly in the shawl and they would sit until the stars came out.

Carly gently folded the shawl and set it aside.

Then she started to empty the low bookshelf. There were a lot of New Age self-help books about the health benefits of meditation, more biographies of famous musicians, the odd thriller and plenty of literary and women's fiction.

She picked up a plain black leather-bound volume. Curious, she opened it and saw handwriting. Irene's journal. A quick skim suggested a mixture of random thoughts, daily events and recorded dreams. Carly closed it quickly. She wouldn't dream of reading Irene's journal if her aunt was alive. Was it an invasion of privacy now that she'd passed? It felt too soon, her own grief too raw. Hard enough to pack up Irene's things without hearing her voice leap off the page. And yet…part of her longed for that connection to her aunt. And just maybe there would be something about Finn in there, some clue as to what made him tick that he wasn't telling her, that she couldn't guess for herself. Although that, too, seemed an invasion.

"Carly?" Finn said from the doorway. In his skinny black jeans and gray T-shirt he looked scruffy and sexy, very much the rock star at home.

She started guiltily. "Hey."

"Irene's friends are here to see if they can do anything." He stepped back.

The woman with the long gray braid and the grandmotherly-looking blonde from the funeral filled the doorway. "I'm Roberta and this is Jeanette. Can we do anything to help, like pack Irene's clothes to go to a charity?"

"I remember you both," Carly said, suddenly very glad these women had arrived to help her deal with the memories. "Thank you, that would be wonderful. If…if there's any item you would like to have, please take it."

Roberta and Jeanette exchanged a glance and shook their heads. "No, but thanks, anyway."

Leaving the women tackling the closet, Carly picked up the shawl and journal and went into the hall to speak to Finn, Rufus at her heels. "Is the plumber still here?"

"Yeah, and the job looks worse than he'd initially thought," Finn said. "He's ripping out the pipes in the laundry room."

"I thought the bathroom was the problem."

"Like I said, it's bigger than he thought." She must have looked worried because Finn placed a palm on her cheek. "It'll be over soon."

"I've got another week off work. I need to fly home next Sunday. " Her gaze met his. Neither said a word. It was all very well to pledge friendship, but when the future was too nebulous to pin down, saying goodbye would be gut-wrenching.

"I've got to go to Dingo's," he finally said awkwardly. "I'm playing the band Annie's recording."

She kissed him lightly on the mouth. "Good luck."

CHAPTER ELEVEN

FINN PAUSED IN the middle of Dingo's driveway to listen to the band playing the instrumental bridge of an old Queen rock anthem. Leroy had the drum solo down pat and Billy rocked the bass. Dingo, well, he could compete with the best on lead guitar. The instrumental section crescendoed and segued into the bars leading up to the next verse. He could already imagine Annie belting out the words in her gutsy, soulful voice.

He started forward again, eager to let the guys hear her recording. A strong male voice came in smoothly on the backbeat and he stopped short. Tom must have come through with a lead singer. This guy was good. No way was Dingo going to go with Annie now even if he loved her tape.

Finn slipped inside the studio and perched on a stool as they finished the song. The newcomer looked the part of an old-time rocker, too, with tight jeans and sleeveless ripped shirt as he strutted about tossing his mane of blond hair. He was no amateur, either. His voice was trained, his presentation polished, and his timing was impeccable. He finished with a flourish of the handheld mic.

Finn clapped enthusiastically and exchanged grins with Leroy and Billy. "Awesome."

"Take five, guys." Dingo leaned his guitar against an amp.

Leroy eased off the drum stool and stretched. Billy headed for the bar fridge for beer.

"This is Leith," Dingo said, introducing the lead singer to Finn. "He's from Seattle and has been performing solo and in various bands for years. Leith, this is Finn Farrell, the guy responsible for you being here."

Finn extended a hand to Leith. "Nice to meet you. You've got a great sound."

"Thanks. I've heard a lot about you." Leith gave a firm shake and bumped fists. "I appreciate you putting the word out to Tom. I signed with him two months ago. Never thought I'd get a gig this good so quickly. Mind you, they haven't given me the nod yet."

"We'll make a decision soon," Dingo said. "Meanwhile, beer's in the fridge." Leith headed over to where Leroy and Billy were opening bottles and Dingo turned to Finn. "Are you staying for rehearsal?"

"Nah, I've only got a few minutes," Finn said. "There's work to do up at the house."

Dingo gave him an appraising half smile. "You're really going the extra mile for Carly. Do I detect a little love interest?"

"You've got a vivid imagination, man," Finn said.

"And you play your cards close to your chest," Dingo rejoined. "But then, you always did."

"I didn't come to jaw about my love life," Finn began.

"What's up?" Dingo glanced over his shoulder and lowered his voice. "If you've changed your mind about joining the band, even temporarily, that's cool."

"Is there a problem with Leith?" Finn asked, matching Dingo's quiet tone.

"He's great—as far as he goes," Dingo said. "But he only sings. We're still short a keyboardist."

"I haven't changed my mind but I did find a singer for you," Finn said. "She doesn't play an instrument, either, but she has a voice that has to be heard to be believed. Untrained but so much power. If Leith doesn't work out she'd be a good alternative."

Finn pressed a USB stick into Dingo's palm. He'd fiddled with the sound mix a little on his laptop music production program but hadn't needed to do anything to enhance Annie's voice.

Dingo held the flash drive with callused fingertips. "Who is she? What experience has she got?"

"If you like what you hear then we'll talk," Finn said. "No obligation. If not lead, then maybe you could use her as a backup singer."

"This better not be Annie," Dingo said, plugging the stick into a USB port on a laptop hooked up to his sound system.

"Just listen." Finn trusted his instincts when it came to music but these guys had a vision of their band and that was their prerogative. It all came down to what they thought of her voice.

The guys' chatter faded to murmurs at the opening piano chords. Dingo glanced at Finn, no doubt wondering if that was him playing. Then Annie started to sing. The effect was even more powerful without the visual of her schoolgirl look and her mousy hair in a straggly ponytail. The guys exchanged surprised looks. No one even brought a beer bottle to their lips until the song ended. Even then, the stunned silence lasted another few seconds.

"Wow!" Dingo said. "Who is she?"

"Does it matter?" Finn said. "You guys don't need her…" He nodded to Leith. "But maybe you could recommend another band that's looking for a singer?"

"Hold on a sec. We might be able to use her

on backup vocals," Dingo said, clearly trying to hedge his bets. "What do you guys think?" he said to the band, including Leith in his question.

"Amazing."

"Awesome."

"If she looks as good as she sounds, sign her up."

"Is she available?" Dingo asked. "Can you get her down here?"

"She's got a day job. I'll have to check when she's free," Finn said, stalling. No matter how good her voice, Annie would need to work on her look if the band was going to accept her. Rightly or wrongly, they had a prejudice against her. With her talent she would find another band but she seemed to want to work with this one.

"Let us know, okay?" Dingo said.

"I'll be in touch soon." Finn lifted a hand. "Catch you all later."

CARLY WAS FRYING ground beef and onions for tacos when Finn arrived home. Rufus was swirling around the kitchen, nosing the floor for fallen tidbits. His feathery red tail wagged furiously when he saw Finn come through the door. If Carly had a tail she would have been wagging it, too. As it was, she couldn't help smiling in response to Finn's infectious grin. The black waves flopping over his forehead made her want to run her fingers through his hair and mess it up even more.

"Hey."

"Hey, yourself." She stirred the meat, acting casual and feeling anything but. Would he kiss her? Should she put this spoon down and go kiss him? Or were they both going to pretend that they hadn't made doomed love—until it happened again?

"How was it clearing out Irene's room?" he asked.

Okay, so they weren't rushing into each other's arms. Well, she had no right to be disappointed. She was the one who'd said she wanted to be friends. "Not as bad as I'd feared. It helped having Roberta and Jeanette there. We emptied the closet and the dresser and they took all the clothing to a charity."

"You didn't want to keep anything of hers?"

"I kept her shawl and her journal," Carly said. "Journals, plural. She's got at least a dozen. Oh, and her bluebird brooch. Do you remember that?"

"Of course," Finn said. "She gave it to me to wear the night of the concert. I was so agitated I forgot to put it on."

"That explains everything then," Carly said with a dry smile. Could he take a teasing or was the subject too touchy? He gave her a withering look but he was smiling, too.

He came closer and touched the small of her back as he peered into the fry pan. "Smells good. Tacos?"

"Yep." She nudged her hip into his. "Did the band love Annie's tape?"

"Big time," Finn said. "Only snag is, my agent already sent them a vocalist. Leith was there today, rehearsing with them. He's good, and he's professional. Dingo and the guys aren't going to let him go for Annie, no matter how much they liked her voice."

"Oh, what a shame," Carly said. "I mean, it's great that they've got the band member they need but too bad for Annie."

"They're considering her for backup vocals so all isn't lost yet."

"If she was my client, I'd advise her to accept," Carly said. "The experience will lead to other avenues."

"Exactly." Finn sat. "Just one teeny problem. I haven't told Dingo and the guys they were listening to Annie. They don't see a girl barely out of high school as having potential."

"That's so shortsighted," Carly said. "The minute she opens her mouth you have to believe she's a rock chick."

"Would you do me a favor and style her for the audition?" Finn asked.

"Sure, that would be fun." Carly's mind leaped ahead to what she could do with hair, clothes and makeup. "How far is she willing to go to change her appearance?"

"I bet she'd die her hair orange and wear a clown suit if it gave her a shot at singing with the band," Finn said.

"Let's hope it won't come to that. Do you like chilies?"

"The hotter the better." He nuzzled her neck and then planted a kiss below her ear. "You smell delicious."

She shook a liberal amount of chili flakes into the meat mixture and then turned down the heat under the pan.

His mouth fit so nicely to hers that it felt only natural to open to him. His kiss was unhurried and thorough, his tongue seeking and exploring while his hands reacquainted themselves with her back, her butt, then slid back up to cup her breasts. His thumbs pressed on her nipples and she pushed her hips closer to his.

Finn took her by the hips and swung her around until she was backed against the table. With a hop and a lift, she was on it. He grasped her knees and spread her legs then stepped between them. One by one, he undid the buttons of her cotton shirt. Now that they'd gone down this road every touch, every word, felt more serious, as if they'd embarked on a real romance.

She was out of her depth in unfamiliar waters. In hindsight, her previous love affairs had been superficial. Movies, dinners, concerts, sex, a lot of shallow talk and not much feeling. Was the heightened intensity she experienced with Finn a leftover of unrequited puppy love or a consequence of her emotional turmoil over Irene's death?

Or could they truly be soul mates? Taking one day at a time as Finn had suggested was easier said than done, at least for her. She liked to know where she was going and what was coming next. Lately, nothing seemed certain. Not her job, not the house, not even life itself.

He eased back and touched a finger to her chin. "Something's wrong."

"Thinking too much. Sorry." She smiled ruefully. "It's been kind of a heavy day. I'm up and down, all over the place."

"Another time then." Slowly he re-buttoned her blouse.

Every button closed felt like he was putting her away from him. She wanted to tell him to go back to touching her, but didn't know how. "What did the plumber say?"

"The pipes in the downstairs bathroom and

laundry need replacing. They're so old they're corroded in spots," Finn told her. "While he was ripping the walls apart he noticed some dodgy-looking wiring and suggested we call in an electrician."

"It's snowballing," Carly said.

"It's all fixable," Finn assured her. "Do you want me to take care of the tradesmen?"

"Yes, please," Carly said. "The Realtor is coming tomorrow to appraise the property. I'll have to do a big cleanup tonight."

Finn kissed her lightly on the lips, her closed eyelids and her forehead. "Let me know what I can do to help."

Hold me. Love me. Never let me go. She eased away, smiling, fighting her need to cling to him. "Thanks, but I've got it covered."

THE NEXT MORNING Carly bent to retrieve a piece of lint from the otherwise spotless kitchen floor. The downstairs bathroom and the laundry room were a mess because the plumber was working in there but the rest of the house was clean and tidy. She'd stayed up till midnight, working to prepare it for the Realtor's assessment.

Finn had gone to bed early—in a room two doors down from hers. When she'd climbed the stairs at midnight, she'd seen the light under his door and hesitated. She was confused about what had happened in the kitchen. Had he thought she was pushing him away? Or did he simply need time alone? Had he come to the conclusion that sex with her was a mistake?

But oh, he could make her feel things without even touching her. He'd played the piano most of the evening, giving the house a pervading atmosphere of peace. Putting down the mop, she'd sat on the landing and just listened. Under the spell of the soothing music, she'd forgotten about her troubles for a time.

This morning they'd met in the kitchen and hadn't had a chance to talk. She'd been busy with last-minute cleaning and he was taking books and miscellaneous stuff to the thrift store. Whatever they wouldn't accept he would deliver to the dump.

The doorbell rang and she went to answer it.

"Hi," she greeted the man on the step. "Carly Maxwell."

"Sam Wallace, Fairhaven Realty. Nice to meet you." White-haired with the deep tan and slick appearance of a salesman, he extended a hand glinting with a gold-and-onyx pinky ring. But his smile seemed genuine and there was no doubting his sincerity when he said, "I'm real sorry about your aunt. Irene taught my daughter how to play the piano. That was a few years ago now but we remember her with fondness."

"Thank you," Carly said. "Please come in."

Sam stepped inside, looking around. "This is a beautiful house and a great location. Most of the period features are intact, I see."

"Including the original plumbing and wiring," Carly said, leading him into the living room. "I'm having that fixed before it goes on the market."

"Good plan," Sam said. "Move-in ready is more marketable than a fixer-upper."

"Is it better to include the furniture with the house or sell it separately?" Carly asked.

"Either way. You can negotiate that with the buyer. But the less clutter, the better." Sam stood before the bay window. "Fine view."

"I should also mention," Carly said. "I've got a tenant who will be here till the end of August."

"We can work around that." Sam crossed to the dining area, his observant gaze surveying from floor to high molded ceiling. "Fireplace functional?"

"I believe so."

The Realtor turned to the French doors looking onto Irene's dormant vegetable and herb garden. "You'd be wise to turn the yard into low maintenance. Most people, both partners are working and don't have time to garden."

"My aunt was on her own and she always found the time," Carly said.

Sam shrugged. "It's up to you, of course."

A frown tightened Carly's forehead. The thought of looking out on concrete and gravel was beyond depressing. No proper veggie patch. No lying in the cool green grass on a summer day and pointing out cloud shapes to a little girl, the way her aunt had done with her in long ago years. And what would that mean for any pets? A person could make time for anything if they wanted to. It was all a matter of priorities.

Gosh, who did that sound like? Carly felt a shiver run across the back of her neck and she glanced over her shoulder, half expecting to see Irene standing there, gently imparting one of her life lessons. There was no one, of course. Carly didn't believe in ghosts. Nor did she subscribe to New Age philosophy the way Irene had. But just for a moment, she'd felt her aunt's spirit as real and solid and loving as if she were still alive.

Carly rubbed her arms and caught up with Sam, who had wandered in the direction of the kitchen. She spent the next twenty minutes showing him the rest of the house, answering his questions and asking her own.

As he left he handed her his business card. "I'll call you when I've drawn up a valuation."

"Ball park?" she said.

He rocked a splayed hand. "Three and a half to four hundred. If the wiring and plumbing are up to code."

A quick mental calculation suggested that would give her enough for a down payment on a decent apartment in Manhattan. With her increased salary she would be set to have the life she'd been working toward. Professional, upmarket, successful. "Wonderful. Thanks again."

She closed the door slowly. It was starting to sink in what selling would mean. Strangers would live in Irene's house. There would be no more music. Possibly no more vegetables or homemade bread. No more of the wonderful life Irene had made for herself and for the people she loved.

But Irene would have been the first one to say, don't hang on to material possessions, don't cling to the past. Move on. Live for the moment. Above all, be true to yourself and live your own authentic life.

Carly glanced at the font on Sam's business card. Sure enough, it was serif. Times New Roman or something like it. She placed it on the hall table and headed out to the backyard. There was something she needed to do for Irene. She didn't have time but she could find it. Heck, she would make it. It was all a matter of priorities.

WHEN FINN GOT home he found Taylor in the kitchen, poring over a cookbook even though it wasn't even noon. "Have you seen Carly?"

"She's in the backyard," Taylor said. "Planting a vegetable garden."

"Right," Finn said in disbelief. Because she didn't have enough to do. She'd seemed pretty stressed ever since they'd made love although he wasn't sure if that was the cause. Last night she'd scrubbed the house from top to bottom, refusing his help, and then hadn't knocked on his door before bed even though he'd left his light on. Things weren't as free and easy between them as he'd thought. If he were the paranoid type he might even think she was avoiding him.

She was wearing Irene's backyard boots and slashing inefficiently with a hoe at the weeds in the vegetable garden. A smudge of dirt ran across her cheek and the faint freckles on her nose stood out in the bright sunlight, making him think of the young girl he used to know. Her blouse gaped at the top where a button had come undone, revealing the swell of her breast, reminding him she was now very much a woman.

"What are you doing?" he asked, although it was obvious. The question really was not what, but why.

"Planting a garden," she said. "This year could be the last." She relayed the advice the Realtor had given her. "I can't bear the thought of paving the yard over. Maybe if a potential buyer sees a garden growing they'll decide to keep it."

Finn picked up the battered notebook lying on the grass and flipped through the pages. Irene had drawn diagrams showing where she'd sown different seeds, all dated with notes on when the vegetables had flowered, and later ripened. Planting a garden she would never harvest had to be the definition of an optimist. Or insanity.

"I thought you were in a hurry to return to New York," he said. "What about your job? What if you plant a bunch of plants and then you're not here to look after them? What about the house for that matter? And Taylor? Have you thought this through?"

"Taylor is trustworthy enough to be left in charge while I'm in Manhattan," Carly said. "Sam, the Realtor, can show the house to potential buyers. It's all good." She leaned on the hoe and wiped her damp forehead with the back of a gloved hand. "As for the plants, I have no idea what will happen to them. All I know is, I need to do this."

"I suppose Taylor might tend the garden," Finn said. "I never thought he'd be cooking, either and yet there he is, researching the subject as if he's writing a thesis."

Carly went back to hoeing. Bits of dirt and

grass flew in the air. Rufus leaped after them trying to snatch the tufts, yelping with every leap. Finn watched her inept hoe work for a minute or two and then stepped into the garden bed. "Here, let me show you how to do that."

Reluctantly, she handed over the hoe. "The miniature trowel and fork I use for balcony gardening didn't exactly prepare me for this."

He brought the hoe down sharply, gave a twist of the blade and lifted it, turning over a chunk of earth. Then he chopped at the clod to loosen the roots. Finally, he leaned over and tugged lightly to remove the clump of clover and nut grass.

"How do you know how to do this?" she asked.

"My mom was a gardener," he said. "She grew the best tomatoes I've ever tasted." Maybe she still did. He wouldn't know.

"Has she gotten back to you yet?" Carly said.

"Nope." Finn attacked a clump of dandelions. "This rift has gone on for so long, maybe too long for us to come back from it."

"Or there's a simple explanation for why she hasn't contacted you," Carly said. "You should try again."

He leaned on the hoe. "I'll give her till tomorrow. Maybe she's been busy."

"I bet she's dying to see you." Carly touched his arm. "You're a very special person, Finn Farrell. Your mom knows that better than anyone."

Except that his mother looked upon him as a failure, and when he saw himself through her eyes, it was hard not to think that way, too. Sure, he was making a living songwriting and he enjoyed it, but it wasn't what he'd once dreamed of.

Shaking his head to rid himself of those self-destructive thoughts, he handed the hoe back to Carly. "You try."

Imitating his actions, she brought down the hoe, twisted and lifted. It took her a time or two, but she got the hang of it. How long this gardening fit would last, he had no idea, but if it took Carly's mind off her aunt's death and helped her move toward closure then why not?

He found a shovel leaning against the garden shed and set to work following the path she'd hoed, digging down a good foot and turning over the soil. He had to admit, it felt good to be doing something that was about the future, not the past, even if they wouldn't be here to see the fruits of their labors.

Pausing, he glanced over at Carly, working determinedly to break up the turf. A wave of affection flowed over him. They had something bigger than friendship, deeper than lust. If they could put down roots together, this was where they would be, in this dark, rich soil in Irene's backyard.

CHAPTER TWELVE

"ROCK CHICKS NEED big statement hair." Carly walked around Annie, who sat on a chair in the middle of the kitchen. She lifted a wispy strand of dishwater brown. "Do you want to go black, red, blond or a richer brown?"

"Black," Annie said. "My idol is Amy Winehouse for her voice and style."

"Her voice was amazing," Carly agreed. "Black hair it is. Maybe some extensions to add volume. Are you prepared to backcomb?"

Annie put a hand over her heart. "Whatever it takes."

Through the kitchen window Finn could be seen in the garden, driving in stakes for the tomato seedlings Frankie had brought over. Taylor was at the stove, sautéing onions and garlic for spaghetti Bolognese. A pile of other vegetables waited to be chopped. The kitchen gave off a good vibe. With the bread rising, Taylor cooking and everyone busy with projects, the house felt warm and lived in.

Taylor lowered the heat on the onions and

turned his attention to the zucchini. "Do either of you know how many millimeters the zucchini should be on every side? The recipe doesn't say."

"Just dice them small," Carly advised. "It's not rocket science."

"It would be easier if it was," Taylor muttered, lining up the strips of squash and bringing down his knife precisely.

"You could grate them," Annie said. "That's how I get the kids to eat their vegetables."

"Do you have children?" Taylor asked, eyebrows raised in surprise.

"Ew, no," Annie said. "I don't even have a boyfriend." Beneath the indignation, Carly heard what sounded like a hint. "When I said kids, I was talking about my three little sisters."

"I'm an only child," Taylor said wistfully. "It must be nice to be part of a big family."

"Kids are expensive to raise and they take a lot of work," Annie said, sounding old beyond her years. "You're lucky you get to go to college."

Carly checked her loaf of sourdough rising under a cloth next to the stove. She could leave it for another hour or so. "Annie, we need to go to the store to pick up a few things for your makeover."

"Okay." The girl drifted over to stand next to Taylor and peer at the cookbook. "It doesn't say so but I always add a pinch of sugar to the tomato sauce."

"I've read about that. It's because tomatoes are acidic." His cheeks had turned pink at Annie's proximity. "I thought about adding baking soda to lower the pH."

Carly observed the pair with a smile. If Taylor wasn't such a geek he might realize that Annie was in awe of him. If Annie didn't have self-esteem issues she might realize Taylor was fascinated by her worldliness.

"I'd go with sugar if I were you." Annie pulled on her ponytail and smiled up at him. "See you later."

Taylor flushed a deep red.

Carly drove them to the drugstore first and Annie selected a hair color called Midnight Sea, a deep blue-black that would look dramatic under lights.

"This is a big change, considering I might not get past the audition," Annie said doubtfully.

"Think of it as an investment in your future. Then once you look the part, you'll need some attitude," Carly said.

Annie pretended to search the shelves. "What I need is a big ol' box of sass."

"Seriously, fake it till you make it really does work," Carly said. "I applied for a position above what I was qualified for. I got the job and sure, I'm on a learning curve but I'm coping."

"I'm not a professional," Annie said. "I don't have a degree. Heck, I barely finished high school."

"You've got street smarts," Carly said. "You're stronger than you think. You deal with disgruntled customers, the lunch rush, coworkers, and at home you help take care of your little sisters."

Annie sighed. "My sisters are great and I love them, but they make a mess of our room."

"You share with them?" Carly said, trying to picture four girls in one bedroom. "How old are they?"

"Twelve, ten and seven." Annie examined a tube of mascara. "Last week they got into my makeup while I was at work and ruined everything."

"Why don't you move out on your own?" Carly asked.

"Can't afford it," Annie said matter-of-factly. She put the mascara back on the shelf. "I can't afford to buy a lot of stuff for this audition, either."

"You can pay me back after your first gig." Carly dropped the mascara into her shopping basket. "Let's check out the next aisle."

They tested lipstick and foundation on their wrists, laughed over sparkly blue eye shadow

and tossed it in the basket along with a growing assortment of cosmetics. It was fun, Carly
thought, like having a younger sister to shop
with. Annie didn't realize how lucky she was.

They left the drugstore with bulging shopping
bags and walked around the block to the thrift
store. Carly headed past shelves of secondhand
books and dishes to the racks of clothing.

"We'll go with a retro look to complement
the classic rock Finn says the band plays." Carly
flipped through the racks and picked out a black
leather sheath with a plunging neckline and a
high hemline. "You would look so hot in this."

Annie held it up against herself. "It'll be tight
on me."

"In other words, perfect," Carly said.

Together they found a few more outfits—
leather hot pants, slinky tops, short skirts and
a new pair of fishnet stockings. Annie carried
them off to the tiny changing room in the corner of the store.

Carly drifted over to the shoe section hoping to find a pair of thigh-high boots for Annie.
An older woman with curly dark hair wearing a
navy blazer over white shirt and dark blue jeans
was sifting through a pile of shoes for the match
to a brown loafer.

"Excuse me," Carly said, edging past her to
get to the boots.

The woman moved out of the way and as she did so, glanced up. "Carly?"

She did a double take. "Mrs. Farrell?"

With a little laugh, Nora Farrell pressed a hand to her chest. "I didn't know you were still in town. How are you?"

"I'm okay," Carly said. "How have you been?"

"Fine. I'm so sorry Bob and I couldn't make it to the funeral. We…had another commitment that day."

Or had Nora not gone because she thought Finn would be there? It was so sad and so wrong that Finn and his mom held a grudge all these years. Families were supposed to forgive each other.

"Finn missed the service, too, but came to the reception," Carly said. "He's been helping me fix up the house for sale."

"He's still here?" Nora said.

"I feel badly that I'm hogging his time. I'm sure you would like to see more of him," Carly added, feeling the other woman out.

"Finn does what he wants. He always has." There was both sorrow and resentment in her tone. She found the brown loafer and dropped it to the floor to slip a foot inside. "He came by the house but I wasn't there and he hasn't contacted us again."

"He sent you a text the other day. He was kind of bummed that you didn't reply."

"I didn't get it." Nora fished her phone from her purse and scrolled through her messages. "No, nothing. He probably doesn't have my new number." Her mouth twisted. "I've only had this phone for two years."

"Um…it's short notice, but would you and your husband like to come to dinner tonight?" Carly said impulsively. Meeting on neutral territory might help thaw the frost between mother and son.

"Oh, I don't know." Nora took a half step back and glanced around as if looking for an escape route. "I'm sure you've got too much to do without having dinner guests."

"It's no trouble," Carly said. "My boarder is cooking. It's nothing fancy but judging by the food piled up in the kitchen we'll have enough to feed an army."

"Well, in that case, yes, I would love to," Nora said. "But you should check with Finn first."

"I'll call him right now." She got her phone out, a bit nervous about putting him on the spot.

Nora discreetly moved to the other side of the shoe display, but she was still in earshot. She glanced back with a look so vulnerable that Carly's heart ached for her. Finn needed to see how much his mother missed him.

"He's not answering," she said when his phone went to voice mail. "But I'm positive it'll be fine. Come by at six o'clock. You remember where Irene's house is, don't you?"

Nora smiled drily. "I must have made that trip a million times over the years."

"Yo!" Annie swaggered toward them in figure-hugging black leather. Grinning, she struck a pose, hand on jutted hip. "So, what do ya think?"

Carly laughed out loud. "Perfect." She turned to Nora. "This is Annie, Finn's protégé. She's going to be the next big thing in rock music. Annie, this is Finn's mother."

"I'm sure she'll be a great success," Nora said politely.

Annie deflated, hunching and pulling on her ponytail. "I'm not a professional singer yet. Carly, are you sure this is the right look for me?"

"Wait till we do your hair before you question it." Carly gave her a meaningful look and Annie slowly straightened up. Carly turned back to Nora. "Annie's just starting out. She's got a tremendous voice."

"Well, I hope she lives up to her potential," Nora said.

O-kay. There'd been a distinct note of frost in Nora's tone. Carly was starting to have misgivings about the dinner invitation. Nora might yearn for her son but she was a tad judgmental. "She will, with the right encouragement and support."

"Bob and I will see you tonight." Carrying the pair of loafers, Nora wended her way to the cashier.

"Let's go home and do your hair." Carly looped an arm through Annie's. "Can you stay for dinner, too?" She hoped Finn and his parents would talk but the more people around to act as buffer, the smoother the evening would go. Break the ice with food, then the Farrells could take it from there. If they chose to.

"Really? Thanks!" Annie did a little skip.

"It's only spaghetti," Carly cautioned. "Taylor's not an experienced cook."

"I don't care," Annie said. "Tonight is sausage night at home and if I'm not there then the girls will get my share. They're growing and need the protein."

A lump formed in Carly's throat.

"When my mom's on shift, my stepdad cooks," Annie went on. "He thinks he's some kinda chef and dumps in ingredients without measuring anything. Half the time it's indelible."

"Do you mean inedible?" Carly said, repressing a smile. Annie was too cute.

The girl tossed her hair. "Yeah, that's what I said." Then she shrugged. "But we eat it because we got nothing else. At least I get a square meal at Rhonda's on the days I work."

"How many days a week is that?"

"Three usually," Annie said. "And if someone's sick I get called in."

"Would you like another part-time job?" Carly asked, making her second impulsive offer of the day. "I need someone to help me sort out my aunt's things and get the house ready for sale. I can't pay much but you could have room and board on top of wages."

Annie's eyes lit. "I'd have to go home for a couple hours every day and check on my sisters, make sure they're doing their homework."

"That's fine," Carly agreed.

"Cool." Annie grinned. "I'd like that."

"You invited my parents for dinner?" Finn's hands collapsed on the keys in the middle of a delicate musical phrase with a discordant clang. "A little warning would have been nice."

"I called but your phone went to voice mail," Carly said. "Then you were out when I got home. I've been upstairs doing Annie's makeover all afternoon and I didn't hear you come in till you started playing."

He tried the passage again but his fingers wouldn't cooperate. "Did my mother say why she didn't reply to my text?"

"She didn't receive it. She has a new number." Carly came closer to the piano. "What's wrong? I thought you wanted to reconcile."

"I do. And I don't." The fight had been so acrimonious he hated to stir that up again.

"You should have seen Nora's face when she spoke about you," Carly said. "She's hurting but she's ready to forgive and forget, I'm sure of it."

Finn snorted. "Forgive? That would imply I have something to apologize for. She knew I didn't want to go to Juilliard and she kept pushing me."

"I don't mean you should apologize for pursuing your own musical interests," Carly said. "But for your part in letting the estrangement continue for so long."

Finn's fingers moved of their own accord into a dark moody piece. Nora's lack of support for his own music hurt just as much now as it had when he was eighteen. He could feel the anger rising in him, anger he'd tamped down for years.

Carly drummed her fingers on the polished surface of the piano, putting his nerves even more on edge. "The longer this goes on, the harder it will be to overcome. You don't want to wait until she's on her deathbed and be trying to make up for lost time at the eleventh hour."

"So I should just put the past behind me and act like nothing happened?"

"Would that be so terrible?" Carly asked.

The thought of letting go of the resentment he'd been carrying around left him feeling strangely empty. In a weird way, that whole episode had defined him for so long he hardly knew who he used to be. Or who he might have become if it hadn't happened. What if he'd wasted the past twelve years of his life?

"How long are you going to blame her for you not being able to perform?" Carly persisted.

Finn glanced up sharply. "I don't do that."

"Maybe not consciously," Carly said. "But deep down, I wonder."

Was there something in what Carly said? If Nora hadn't put so much pressure on him he wouldn't have been too upset to play the night of the concert.

"All I want is for her to accept my music," he said. "If she did that I'd meet her halfway."

The doorbell rang.

"I'll get it." Carly crossed the living room and went out to the foyer to greet his parents. "Come in. It's nice to see you both. Can I take your coats?"

"I'd forgotten how beautiful your aunt's home was," his mom said, slipping off her wrap. "Bob, look at that crown molding. And the leadlight transom, oh my."

Finn got up from the piano but his feet felt

stuck to the Persian carpet. His hands curled and uncurled at his side. His mom was talking too fast, a sure sign she was nervous. He cast a glance at Irene's portrait over the mantelpiece. *If you're listening, beam down a little fairy dust to help me through this evening.*

They might all need it. Taylor, clearly freaked about cooking for a large group, clattered pots and pans in the kitchen as if playing cymbals in the "1812 Overture." While Nora, Bob and Carly were still standing in the foyer, Annie descended the staircase. Her jet-black hair was teased and set into a beehive and she wore heavy makeup and a miniskirt with a tight top. Seeing his parents, she froze like a deer in headlights and then slipped unnoticed around the corner in the direction of the kitchen.

"Nora watches those home renovation shows," Bob confided as Carly led them into the living room where Finn waited. "One day I came home and she'd ripped up the carpet looking for hardwood flooring."

"All I found was plywood," Nora said with a trilling laugh. "But this house, this is the real deal."

Finn came forward and shook his father's hand. "Hi, Dad." He paused. "Hello, Mother," he added stiffly.

"Finn." Nora gave him a peck on the cheek.

An awkward silence fell. Even Carly didn't seem to know what to do. Fortunately, just then Taylor came in bearing a steaming platter of spaghetti topped with a rich red meat sauce followed by Annie with a bowl of salad. There was a moment of confusion before everyone found a place at the table. Once again Carly and Finn were at the ends. Taylor and Annie sat on one side and Bob and Nora on the other with Nora somehow ending up next to Carly, the farthest point from Finn.

Carly opened the wine and poured for everyone except Taylor, who politely declined, and Annie, who was underage. "Please help yourself to the food and pass things along."

"I don't eat red meat," Nora said, apologetically, handing the platter of spaghetti to Bob.

"Oh, I'm sorry, I didn't know," Carly said, taken aback.

"When did you become a vegetarian?" Finn asked.

"I gave it up years ago." Nora's pursed lips stifled a sigh as if to say, *if you cared you would know that about me.*

This was even harder than he'd thought it would be. He hadn't expected they would instantly reconcile but he hadn't anticipated this stiff reticence either, especially after the heated arguments of the past.

"Have some bread." Carly passed the basket to Nora. "I made it myself."

"Would you like salad, Mrs. Farrell?" Annie handed across the bowl.

"Thank you," Nora said. "Didn't you have brown hair this afternoon?"

"Yes," Annie said, twirling spaghetti on her fork. "I'm having a makeover for a music gig."

"I think you look awesome," Taylor said. When Annie smiled shyly at him, he blushed from his bobbing Adam's apple to the roots of his blond hair.

"So, Mom…" Twelve years apart and Finn couldn't think of a thing to say to his mother. "Are you still working at the liquor store?"

"I'm an administrative assistant at the primary school now." She buttered a slice of bread. "What are you doing?"

"Writing songs," he said. "Playing backup on studio recordings."

"Not performing?" Her voice was carefully neutral, but he heard undertones of disapproval.

"No." He concentrated on winding noodles around his fork. Only Nora could make him feel ashamed and angry at the same time, like a child caught doing something wrong.

Another awkward silence.

"What do you do, Taylor?" Bob asked. Taylor

launched into an enthusiastic description of his research into pulsars.

At the other end of the table Carly seemed worried by Nora's meager dinner. "Did you have enough to eat? If you'd told me your food requirements we could have prepared something else as well."

"I don't like to cause a fuss." Nora reached for another slice of the sourdough. "I hope Finn isn't imposing on you too much."

"Not at all," Carly said. "I don't know what I'd do without his help in fixing up the house."

"You don't have work to do in LA, Finn?" Nora said.

Again, it wasn't so much what she said that got his back up as the faint note of implied criticism. "I'm my own boss."

Nora's mouth opened to speak. Bob touched her hand in a silent warning.

"Finn's very successful," Carly said. "One of his songs was in the top ten."

"Rock music?" Nora said as if she'd tasted a worm in the salad.

"Not exactly, although there are similar elements," Carly said, floundering for definition. "It's hybrid, right, Finn?"

"Right." He shouldn't have to explain it to his parents. They should know.

Just as he should have known his mother was

now vegetarian and had gotten a new phone number. And that his dad had gone gray and wore glasses.

"Are you married, Carly?" Nora asked, changing the subject.

Carly choked on a sip of wine. "I'm focusing on my career at the moment."

"Finn's not the settling down kind, either," Nora said.

"Maybe there are reasons Finn hasn't settled down," Carly said with a pleasant smile. "Maybe he's never met the right woman."

Nora shrugged. "He's had plenty of girlfriends."

"How would you even know that about me?" Finn demanded.

"Joe tells us things." She turned back to Carly. "You, I imagine, will end up with someone on Wall Street."

In other words, not her son who didn't have anything to offer a woman with Carly's background? Finn grimaced. He didn't want to react to everything his mother said but he couldn't stop himself. This was exactly the kind of tense situation he hadn't wanted to drag Carly into.

"Let me take your plate," Annie said to him, jumping up to gather the empty dishes.

"I'll give you a hand." Taylor gathered the

platter and salad bowl and the pair beat a hasty retreat to the kitchen.

A beat passed then Nora said, "Finn, are you ever going to go back to playing classical music?"

Okay, that was it. He rose abruptly. "I'll put the kettle on for coffee."

When he got to the kitchen Annie and Taylor were storing the leftover food in the fridge. "You guys can take off. I'll clean up."

"Well, okay," Taylor said. "I have tutorial assignments to grade."

"I should get going, too," Annie said. "I've got an early shift at the café tomorrow. Thanks for dinner."

Finn filled the kettle and measured out coffee. Too agitated to go back in the dining room, he started stacking dishes in the dishwasher.

His mother entered carrying wineglasses. She set them down hard on the counter. "Can I have a word with you?"

"Don't you think you've said enough?" The tension inside flared to anger. "The life I've made might not be the one you wanted for me but it's what I want. Why can't you accept me as I am?"

"You could have had a stellar career," Nora said, unrepentant. "I wanted you to have opportunities, not get stuck in Fairhaven. I couldn't let you throw away your future on playing rock music in a garage band."

"I didn't get stuck here, though, did I? I made a career for myself on my own terms. Whether you agree or not, I've done okay."

"You're not doing what you're best at," Nora insisted. "You're not performing."

"Do you think I don't know that?" Finn said. "You pushed me to follow your vision and I lost what I loved the most."

"When you ran out of town I was left to pick up the pieces," she flung back. "Apologizing to all our friends who supported you, explaining that you'd been under a lot of pressure because you wanted the scholarship so badly—"

"That's a lie," he snapped. "You shouldn't have said that."

"I had to save face." Her cheeks turned red. "For years I'd been telling everyone you were going to be a big success, a concert pianist, and make it on the world stage. You could have been someone."

"I am someone," he said. "The name Finn Farrell means something in the music world, even if it's not the part of that world you thought I'd be in." He flipped a hand, tired of the circular argument. "Ah, forget it. You'll never believe in me."

"I will when I see you perform again," Nora

said. "Until then you're hiding your light under a bushel."

Hiding. Like a coward. Was that what she thought of him? "Okay, then. Next Sunday at Rhonda's," he declared rashly. "I'll play at the open mike."

Carly had just entered the room and stopped dead. "Finn, are you sure?"

"Why not?" He spoke offhandedly though his heart was racing.

"What time?" Nora said.

"One o'clock." *Be there or forever hold your tongue.*

"Nora?" Bob came into the room with their coats draped over his arm. "Everything okay? We should go."

"Yes." Nora found a brittle smile. "Carly, thank you for dinner." She gave Finn an awkward embrace. "It was nice to see you, son."

He returned her hug, but was too churned up inside to say anything.

Finn let Carly show them out. He couldn't believe he'd just committed to playing in public. When was he going to stop letting himself be manipulated by Nora?

And yet, part of him wanted to play at Rhonda's. To take that step forward. To prove to himself and to everyone that he could do it.

If his mother showed up, then it would mean she'd taken a step forward, too.

Carly was right. He still had a lot of anger. His choice was to let it eat away at him forever… or find a way to break free of his self-imposed limitations.

CHAPTER THIRTEEN

WHEN CARLY RETURNED from driving Annie home she followed the crashing chords of Beethoven's Fifth Symphony into the living room. The lamp in the corner shed a glow that illuminated the grand piano and Finn relentlessly pounding the keys. Her heart went out to him after that acrimonious exchange with his mother.

Carly slid onto the bench next to him, seeking his warmth after being chilled by the spring evening. And to give comfort if Finn needed it. She waited until he finished playing and then asked, "Are you okay?"

"Yeah, fine," he said, starting another piece, quieter but no less dark and moody.

"I'm sorry that didn't work out better."

"Not your fault." Finn ran a chord progression deep into the bass clef.

"Annie's moving in," Carly said. "She's going to talk it over with her mom. She helps look after her sisters but their house is tiny. There would be definite benefits to their family to have one less person living there."

"It's only temporary," Finn said. "Then she's right back where she started."

"Change happens one step at a time." Carly smoothed a fingertip along the polished wood below the keys. "Maybe the band will take her on and she can quit the café and move out on her own—"

"And they all lived happily ever after," he said sardonically.

"Don't be cynical, Finn, it's not like you. Good things happen all the time, especially if you help them along." Carly studied his profile and the droop to his mouth. "Are you sure you're all right?"

"Positive." He sounded dispirited though, and his fingers on the keys were heavy, as if playing was an effort.

"It's great that you're going to play open mike," Carly said. "And that your mom is coming to hear you."

His hands stilled abruptly. "If I can't do it, it'll just confirm to her that she was right all along."

"You can do it," Carly insisted. "Start with me, an audience of one." She rose and sat in a chair facing the piano, knees and feet together, hands folded on her lap expectantly. "I'm ready."

Finn gave her a long, inscrutable glance. Then he ran his hands over the piano in a series of ascending notes, over and over until Carly thought he'd forgotten she was there. Finally, he began to play a melody and then to sing.

He played her a love song. His voice was soft and seductive, a young man extolling the beauty of a girl. The words and his soulful dark eyes melted Carly's heart. Then the tone changed, became so yearning that she ached. With his rough-smooth voice soaring, he filled the room with such love and pain, heartache and longing that the hairs on her arms stood on end. It took her until the second verse and a phrase about a lighted bedroom window that she realized he was singing about her.

The final notes died away.

"That was beautiful," she whispered, almost speechless because of the huge lump in her throat. "Thank you." So he had felt something for her back then. She'd never been sure.

"You were my inspiration, in case you didn't guess. It was the first song I ever wrote, when I was sixteen." He smiled a lopsided smile. "I've refined it since."

"Oh, Finn." Carly rose and put her arms around him, pressing her cheek to his. She thought of all the years they'd lost and held him tighter. "You will smash it at the open mike."

"Maybe." He pulled her onto his lap and kissed her. His mouth was hot and seeking, his tongue boldly exploring. Carly responded eagerly, her pulse skipping erratically as his hands moved over her, sliding beneath her top. He started to lift the hem, his gaze questioning. In reply, she pulled it over her head and flung it aside. Digging her fingers into his hair she drew his face to her breast, moaning when he loosened her bra and sucked a nipple into his mouth. Afraid she would tip him off the piano bench, she leaned backward and her elbows crashed onto the keys.

"Upstairs?" she suggested but he was already standing and lifting her, letting her butt come down on the ivories with a crash as he slipped her panties off.

"Right here will do fine." His eyes burned as he unbuckled his belt. Before shucking his pants he found a condom and ripped it open.

Carly spread her legs, planting her feet either side of him on the bench, and undid his shirt buttons. Only the table lamp glowed but the curtains were open to the deep twilight sky. A car went past slowly and turned in a few doors down. She should draw the curtains but she was too keyed up and truthfully, the exposure added another layer of excitement to the rough and ready sex. He was pushing into her, eyes locked, one hand braced on the piano top, the other holding her right breast, squeezing her nipple. His breath came fast and hot and their bodies slammed together, the sound mingling with the ongoing crashing of piano keys.

Taylor was upstairs. Would he come down to investigate or would he assume Finn was experimenting with atonal music? She thrust her hips against Finn's, squeezing her legs, creating as much friction as possible. A vase atop the piano vibrated, wobbled and fell to the floor in a soft thud on the carpet. Sheet music slithered off the rack. Finn slammed his mouth onto hers as he pushed into her hard and harder and the tension gripping her core spiraled upward to a crescendo as his hands crashed down on a major chord. She clung to his shoulders, shaking with the force of her climax. He trembled beneath her fingers as he found his own release.

"Not sure Irene had this in mind when she left you her piano," she said weakly.

Finn laughed under his breath and kissed her eyes, nose and lips. "As long as I keep it tuned she won't mind."

CARLY WOKE IN the pitch-black night, squashed into her single bed with Finn. Lifting her head she glanced at the bedside clock. Three o'clock. Wide awake, her mind active, she knew she wouldn't get back to sleep. Careful not to disturb Finn, she slipped out of bed.

She wrapped Irene's shawl around herself and

padded down the hall to her aunt's room. With the bed stripped and the closet empty there was a lost feeling to the room. She curled up in the reading chair and reached for Irene's most recent journal, skimming over mundane passages. When Finn's name jumped out at her she slowed to read carefully. Irene had noted when a particular song made the charts. Carly marveled. She hadn't realized that one was his, too.

Pages later, in October of the previous year, Irene mentioned having a headache that had lasted two days. Migraine medication had helped but hadn't completely eradicated it. She thought maybe it was a hangover from her birthday party on the weekend. Reading, Carly felt sick to her stomach. The headache got worse. Irene went to the doctor. Doctor sent her for tests. Carly flipped faster, scanning the pages. Blood tests okay. Headache persisting. Irene went for a brain MRI. In an entry dated December fifteenth, she wrote in stark letters pressed hard into the paper, *I have a brain aneurysm.*

Carly's hand went to her mouth. Her aunt had known about the aneurysm for six months before her death. That there was no hope quickly became apparent.

The specialist says it's positioned right next to a major nerve and so he can't put something in to alleviate the pressure. Basically, there is no treatment. I will be walking along the street one day and it will burst. I will have a major stroke or die. I would prefer death.

Carly closed the book around her finger. *Oh, Irene.*

Her aunt had known at Christmas, which she'd spent with Carly and her father in New York. They'd seen a comedy at the theater, walked in the snow in Central Park and toasted the New Year with French champagne. Irene hadn't said a word even though she'd known it could be the last time she would see her niece and her brother-in-law.

Carly began to read again.

My visit to New York was wonderful, everything I hoped. I'm so glad I got to see Carly and Randolph. Glad, too, that I didn't spoil our time together by speaking of my condition. I don't want them to be upset or worry. Today I meditated for two hours. It helps with the headaches. I'm coming to terms with this, to a level of acceptance I wouldn't have thought possible after I was first diagnosed. I've had a good life. I can truly say that if I passed tomorrow I would die happy and fulfilled. Oh, there's more I'd love to do, places I would visit, loved ones I want to spend more time with. But no matter if I lived to be a hundred, there will never be enough time. That's just the way it is.

Again Carly had to stop reading and breathe through the ache in her chest. It had been one thing to know some of the facts and to speculate about the rest, but to read Irene's experience in her own words, in her handwriting, brought her situation home in a very personal, intimate way.

She wiped her eyes and kept reading. Oh, here was her name, linked to Finn's.

I hope I can persuade Carly and Finn to come on the cruise with me. They haven't met in many years. Frankie says I'm a meddling old matchmaker and should butt out. But I fantasize about them living together in this house and raising a family.

An acute stab of longing made Carly pause again. She could imagine her and Finn together in this house only too well. Kids, dog, garden, the whole nine yards. At the same time it felt like a dream, something out of reach.

Neither Carly nor Finn can spare the time for a cruise. Carly's email was all about her new job. I'm glad she's excited but I'm afraid she's turned her back on what she's really good at— helping people—and won't be happy in the long run. I worry about Finn, too. So much talent gone to waste. In that, (and that alone), Nora is right. She's too controlling and doesn't even realize she's driven him away. Finn will never get unstuck until he makes peace with her. Oh well, what do I know? One thing I'm positive about is that Carly and Finn would be good for each other. Maybe I can find another way to bring them together this summer.

Carly closed the journal. In a horrible way Irene had brought them together.

She turned off the lamp, closed her eyes and tried to meditate, hoping some of Irene's peace would rub off on her. Wrapped in her aunt's shawl, she would give anything right now to feel her aunt's spirit envelope her with warmth and love.

She couldn't bring Irene back but there was one thing she could do for Finn—help him get back onstage where he belonged.

"FROM THE TOP, one more time." Looking expectantly at Annie, Finn played the opening chords of a Janis Joplin song. He wanted her warmed up before they headed down to Dingo's studio. "Why don't you incorporate some of those dance moves you worked on."

"I'm not sure I can dance and sing at the same time." Annie wore a tight, short skirt and a form-fitting tank top, bangles and high heels. She looked the part except for the way she slouched and pulled nervously on her hair.

He bit his tongue so as not to remind her again to stand up straight and proud. Carly had coached her on that, too. "Use your body language to express the emotion of the song."

"I'm fat," she said flatly. "I look stupid bouncing around."

"Fat?" Finn repeated, dumbfounded. "No way. You're…curvy." He would have said more but he didn't want to creep her out or give her the wrong idea about his interest in her. He took his hands off the keys and sat back. "I know what you're feeling. You don't like everyone looking at you. It's hard at first but you do get used to it. Then you get to like it."

Then you crave it.

He'd forgotten that. But seeing the audition through Annie's eyes, seeing her on the cusp of becoming a singer, it all came back. The validation, the reward for all the hours of hard work, and most of all, the rapport that came from connecting with the audience, even if it was only other students and their families. At times he ached to feel that again. He could only imagine how much bigger that connection would be if he was performing his own songs.

"Don't think about yourself or how nervous you are. Think about the people you're singing to," he said, passing on Irene's wisdom. "You're a conduit for the music. Concentrate on sharing that with the audience. Shut your eyes if it helps."

"I'll try." Annie closed her eyes and began

to hum. Finn played the opening bars several times before she joined in. With her eyes still closed she swayed to the beat, her movements natural and unrehearsed. Her voice soared, full and rich. She didn't see the electrician carrying a spool of electrical cable stop in the hall to listen. Or Taylor, hurrying out with a briefcase, pause, spellbound.

As the last notes sounded Annie opened her eyes and blinked, looking as if she wondered where she was. Noticing the electrician and Taylor, she blushed, then turned to Finn. "Was that better?"

"Sing like that at the audition and you're a shoe-in." Finn shut the piano lid and rose. "Let's go." He grabbed his car keys off the hall table and sat on the chair to pull his boots on.

Taylor walked Annie down the steps. "I don't know much about music but I believe I'm seeing the birth of a new star. I wouldn't be surprised if you went supernova."

"Are stars born or made?" Annie asked, teasing him.

Taylor began to explain in all seriousness how stars had come into existence.

Finn chuckled. Then looked up as Carly hurried down the stairs. She was wearing a blue jacket that brought out the color of her eyes. Her ripped jeans were no doubt designer but her feet were bare inside her ten-dollar sneakers. "Oh, good, you haven't left yet. Where's Annie?"

"Outside." He snaked an arm out to draw her in and buried his face in her neck. He needed to talk to her, tell her how wonderful she was and how much he wanted to be with her. Instead, all he could say was, "You smell great."

Laughing, she wriggled out of his arms. "I've got to give something to Annie." And she hurried out to where Annie and Taylor stood talking on the sidewalk.

Finn followed. Usually he was the one putting space between himself and a new sexual partner, wanting to take things slowly. With Carly, however, he felt an odd urgency to cement what they'd had, take it to another level of intimacy. Did he mean love? Surely it was too soon to be thinking along those lines. But sleeping together was starting to feel important, not at all like a temporary arrangement where they could say goodbye and walk away easily.

Despite his intention not to drag her into his problems with his mom, she was neck deep in the muck. Her words echoed in his mind. *How long are you going to make your mom an excuse for not performing?* Was that what he'd done, really?

He met Carly as she was coming back up the

stairs. "Do you want to come to the audition, give Annie moral support?"

"I wish I could but I'm going to the crematorium to pick up Irene's ashes," Carly said.

"Shoot. I said I'd go with you."

"It's fine," Carly said. "But later you could come with me to spread her ashes. There's a full moon this evening. I'd like to think of her floating out to sea with the tide on a golden path to light her way."

"Very fitting. Afterward, you and I will go out to eat. We'll have a nice wine and relax." He smoothed his thumb over the faint crease between Carly's eyebrows. It was time she had a night off from dealing with everyone else's problems.

"Taylor and Annie..." she began.

"Can take care of themselves." He cocked one eyebrow. "Who knows? They might like to be alone, too."

Carly grinned. "Wouldn't it be cool if they got together?"

"They're very different people," Finn said.

"Opposites attract," Carly reminded him. "Look at us."

He only smiled. Yeah, look at them. With no clue where they were going.

"Fingers crossed for Annie's audition," Carly

added. "I lent her Irene's bluebird brooch for the audition."

"You're a lot like your aunt, you know that?" Finn kissed her. "Generous and kind."

"That's one of the nicest things anyone's ever said about me." She gave him a quick hug then ran up the steps and into the house.

Finn headed for the Mustang. Annie was adjusting the blue enameled brooch on her leather dress. "Carly lent me this for good luck. It belonged to her aunt."

"Irene used to let students wear it during recitals to give them confidence," Finn said. "And you know what, it worked. Everyone who wore the bird did really well."

As they drove across town Finn coached Annie with last-minute tips on her breathing and voice projection. He parked outside Dingo's house and swiveled to face her. "A touch of nerves isn't necessarily bad. It gives you the adrenaline you need to perform. If today doesn't work out, something else will. Remember that you love singing and go out there and enjoy yourself."

"Whatever happens, thank you for everything," Annie said. "I want you to know how much I appreciate it. I wish…" She ducked her head.

"What?"

"I wish you could be my voice coach. I didn't realize there was so much for me to learn."

Finn tapped the steering wheel, avoiding the longing in her kohl-rimmed brown eyes. Annie needed a teacher and he enjoyed working with her. "I'm only in town long enough to help Carly get her aunt's house ready for sale. While I'm here, I'll teach you what I can. How about that?"

"That would be great." Her face lit. Then she bit her lip. "But um, how much do you charge?"

"Forget it! I'm not a professional teacher. It'll be fun for me, too."

They got out of the car and walked down the driveway, Annie unsteady on her high heels. The band was playing a rock/pop blend and they could hear the music through the closed door.

Outside, Finn paused. "I haven't told them who you are yet. With that makeup, haircut and those clothes you look completely different. Hopefully you'll get through the audition before they recognize you. If they say something, just keep singing. No matter what, the show must go on."

"Carly says I need attitude." Annie threw her shoulders back and took a few paces in an exaggerated swagger. "How's this?"

"Nothing wrong with pumping yourself up," Finn said. "Eventually you will discover who you are and feel comfortable enough to be your authentic self. For now, it's showtime."

Finn introduced her as Tia, the singer from the recording. Annie smiled and nodded and didn't speak. The guys were polite. Dingo complimented her voice. Annie fidgeted.

"Let's get down to it," Finn said, not wanting Annie to get any more nervous than she already was. "She's going to start with an Amy Winehouse number. I'll play keyboard. You guys join when you're ready."

Annie went up to the standing microphone. Finn played the opening bar and nodded at Annie. She came in right on cue. The first few lines were a bit wobbly but he caught her eye and touched his solar plexus to remind her to breathe from her diaphragm. Her voice got stronger.

Leroy came in on drums with a reggae beat. The percussion acted like a vote of confidence to Annie. Her voice swelled and she started using hand gestures and moving her hips. If Finn shut his eyes he could almost swear he heard the original artist. It was uncanny. Now the guitars were playing and the fuller sound made Annie project her voice more. She looked at him and smiled. Relief flickered through him. She was having a good time.

Finn didn't pause when the song finished but segued straight into the Doors tune the band was rehearsing. This would show how versatile she was. Annie grabbed the mic off the stand and belted out the song, stalking across the tiny open space. Dingo shot him a surprised grin.

The guys were digging it, no question. And rightly so, she was that good. The second song ended with a flourish of drums. Annie grinned and looked over at Finn for his reaction. He gave her a discreet two thumbs up.

There was a moment of silence. Then Dingo and the guys all started talking at once. They wanted to know where she was from, who she'd played with before, how come they'd never heard of her.

Before she could answer their questions Tyler ran into the studio, yelling, "Annie, Annie."

"Hey, little munchkin." Annie crouched and held out her arms to the boy.

Tyler stopped dead, thrown into doubt by her altered appearance. Finn could almost see the little wheels turning in the toddler's head. She sounded like his babysitter but she had black hair and stuff on her face.

"Tyler, it's me, Annie. I've got a costume on, like Halloween."

The boy ran into her open arms and was enveloped in a hug.

"Annie?" Dingo shook his head. "I never

would have recognized you. How the heck did Tyler know?"

"He knows my singing voice. When I'm baby-sitting, we play with the karaoke machine." She ruffled the boy's curls. "He loves rock music. Don't you, tiger?"

"Me sing, too." The toddler broke free of her embrace and danced around, playing air guitar.

"Give us a minute," Dingo said to Annie and went over to the other band members. The trio stood in a huddle, casting occasional doubtful glances at Annie.

She led Tyler outside onto the grass at the side of the house.

Finn joined the band members. They might have accepted her before they knew who she was but they were obviously finding it hard to over-come the prejudice of taking a teenage babysitter into their hard rock band. "What do you think?"

"She's good but…" Dingo trailed away with a shrug. "She's Annie. Sorry."

Finn swore under his breath. He bet they would take her if he came as part of the package. Well, why not, he'd already said he'd do open mike. If he could manage that, he could handle the RockAround concert. He hoped.

"I'll make you a deal," Finn said. "I'll play keyboard and sing at the RockAround gig—"

He held up a hand to quell the immediate chorus of approval. "On one condition."

"I have a hunch what it might be. But go on, let's hear it," Dingo said, crossing his arms over his chest.

"Make that two conditions." Finn swallowed. He was either taking another step forward—or setting himself up for a fall. "I get to showcase one of my original songs."

"No problem," Dingo said. "Right guys?" Nods all around.

"And," Finn went on. "You bring Annie in to sing backup." Rumblings but nothing too loud. Finn pressed harder. "Plus, she and I sing a duet."

"Duet?" Leroy snorted. "That's not hard rock."

"We'll find something suitable," Finn said. "You should expand your repertoire if you want to make the big time. There's a wider market for a versatile band than there is for golden oldies."

"We'll talk it over and let you know," Dingo said.

"Cool." Finn walked out into the sunshine and told Annie what was happening.

She threw her arms around him and hugged him. "I can't believe it. That's amazing."

"Don't get your hopes up too high," he cautioned. "They might not go for it."

Truth be told, he was excited himself. And at the same time, scared to death. He was counting on Carly being willing to help him prepare.

CHAPTER FOURTEEN

IT WAS A perfect evening for spreading Irene's ashes. The sun was low on the horizon but despite the late hour it was still warm enough for shorts and a sleeveless T-shirt. Carly waded into the water carrying the heavy blue-and-silver urn. Wavelets lapped at her thighs and a light breeze lifted her hair. Finn strode through the water to her right, his rolled-up jeans soaked to above his knees. Rufus bounded between them, barking joyously.

Finn seemed lighter, happier tonight and his upbeat mood was contagious. Even the seriousness of the occasion couldn't quell the feeling of buoyancy that permeated the air. Irene had known she was going to die prematurely but had kept living life on her terms. She hadn't let fear rule her. Carly wanted this last send-off to be perfect, befitting the beautiful, strong person Irene had been.

"Here looks good," Carly said, stopping. Any deeper and she might lose her footing and drop the urn.

Finn closed the gap between them. "How do you want to do this?"

She'd been considering that very subject all day. This was her last physical contact with Irene and she didn't want to just dump the contents of the urn in the ocean. It had to be meaningful. "I'm going to take a handful, think of a time she and I spent together and then fling the ashes. Then another handful, and another, till it's all gone. You can do the same if you want."

"It will take a while but it'll be nice to reminisce," Finn said. "We have to tell each other our anecdotes."

"Of course." Carly screwed off the lid and peered inside. The urn was two thirds full of a gray, gritty material mixed with lighter ash.

She plunged her fingers into it and closed them around a handful, remembering the comedy show she and Irene had seen last December in New York. She described the evening to Finn. "The show was good, but Irene and I laughed more during the taxi ride home than we did at the theater."

"Here goes." Carly pulled out a handful of ashes. Visualizing Irene's laughing face, she threw the ashes across the water. Then offered the urn to Finn. "Your turn."

He reached inside and his smile grew.

"What are you thinking of?" Carly said.

"Irene doing her Barbra Streisand imitation," Finn said. "She was note perfect and her gestures and mannerisms spot on." He opened his mouth and sang, mimicking Irene mimicking Streisand in a voice that sounded eerily like both Irene and the great singer.

He flung the ashes just as a gust of wind came out of nowhere. Irene's remains blew back in their faces. Carly shrieked and ducked, a hand up to keep the ashes out of her eyes. Then she stumbled on the soft ocean floor and fell back in the water, clutching the urn to her chest.

Finn reached for her arm and missed. He tried to grab the urn but was too late to save it from tipping. Carly went under, stinging salt water rushing up her nose. The urn was wrenched from her by a wave. She floundered in the chilly ocean, trying to regain her footing.

Finn gripped her upper arm and hauled her upright. When he'd made sure she was firmly planted on two feet, he duck dived in search of the urn. Carly spotted the lid floating five yards away and Rufus, like a good retriever, paddled over to bring it back.

"Good boy," Carly said as she took the lid from him.

Finn surfaced holding the urn, saltwater and ashes spilling from the mouth. He flicked wet hair out of his face and Carly groaned. The ceremony she'd envisaged was a shambles. "This isn't how I wanted her last send-off."

"Irene liked spontaneity." Finn felt around in the urn. "There's still some ash in there. You could get a few handfuls out."

"No, the mood is ruined. Let's just pour the rest of her out. We'll do it together." She put her hands on the lip and bottom of the urn. Meeting his gaze, she said, "One, two, three...go."

They tipped the urn over. The contents streamed into the ocean. The heavier pieces sank through the clear water, the lighter particles hung suspended in the upper layers of the water or floated on the surface. Soon they were standing in the middle of Irene's swirling remains.

Carly looked down, horrified. "Oh wow. If I don't laugh, I'll cry."

"Irene would have laughed." Finn swished a hand through the water and picked up gray flecks. "I just hope I'm not going to be picking her out of my boxers for the next week."

An appalled giggle spurted from Carly. "I'm going to wash that woman right out of my hair," she sang off-key.

"We're not exactly sending her on her way." Finn nodded at the incoming tide carrying the flotsam. "She's heading straight for the beach."

"I didn't even think about the direction of the

tide," Carly said. "I imagined her floating out to sea and traveling the world on ocean currents."

"Maybe this is better. She'll stay here, in one of her favorite places." Finn started wading out to where the water was deeper. "Let's rinse off with a swim farther out."

Carly glanced toward the shore. There was no one around. She pulled off her top and slipped out of her shorts, then removed her bra and panties.

Finn stripped naked, too. He took their clothing and the urn to the beach and then swam back out to join her.

The setting sun turned the bay to molten gold and burnished their gleaming skin. Laughing for the sheer joy of being alive, they splashed, ducked and chased each other and dove over waves. Rufus barked and circled, trying to get in the game.

Tiring, Carly turned over and floated on her back to gaze up at the fathomless sky, turned a deep indigo by twilight. Soon they would go in. But not yet. Out of the corner of her eye she glimpsed Finn not far away, also on his back. She sculled toward him and held his hand. She told him that her aunt had known about her aneurysm and how brave she'd been. Quietly they reminisced about good times they'd had with Irene, then gradually fell silent. Cool water lapped at Carly's sides but the air held warmth. Her mind emptied. Serenity flowed over and through her. In this moment she felt at peace.

THE NEXT MORNING, Carly opened her eyes to see Finn propped up in her bed, scrolling through his phone messages. His sleep-ruffled hair was dark against the snowy pillow and his strong features relaxed into a grin as he read something he liked.

How good would it be to wake up with him every morning for the rest of her life? To breakfast together and share their plans for the coming day. To come home to him at night and unload or celebrate or just curl up on the couch and watch television together. To be part of his life from here on out…

Her mouth twisted. Nice fantasy but not going to happen. She was going back to New York on Sunday and he'd be going back to LA. If she got the Wallis Group account she would be very busy for the foreseeable future.

"Morning," she said lazily and ran her fingertips along his stubbled jaw.

He set his phone aside and gave her a lingering kiss. "Dingo agreed to take Annie as backup singer if I join the band."

"Fantastic," she said. "Congratulations."

He turned on his side, propping his head on his hand. "Now I have to step up. I need to overcome my anxiety. It's not just my fate riding on this but Annie's, Dingo's and the whole band. I haven't even proven myself at open mike and I've signed up for RockAround."

"I'll help," Carly said, sitting up eagerly. "Let's go to Seattle and check out the venue. No one will be around during the day. You can get a feel for the room, walk out onto the stage. It'll make Rhonda's stage look like child's play. If there's a piano you could play it."

"Or I'll run screaming from it with a panic attack," Finn said. "Do you have tips on dealing with that?"

"Yes, but…" She searched his gaze, suddenly doubtful. "I'm not sure I'm your best source of advice about this since we're in a relationship."

"Are we in a relationship?" His fingertip traced a delicate line from her jaw down her neck to the curve of her collarbone. "I thought you more or less said we were friends with benefits."

"The point is, we're intimate." Carly captured his finger before he went any lower. "I've only worked as a counselor. It's not the same thing as a therapist. You could find someone locally who is more qualified and more objective."

"You know me better than a stranger," Finn said. "I trust you and I don't have a lot of time.

With you I don't have to explain my backstory or wait for an appointment."

"True," she conceded. "But if something goes wrong, don't blame me."

"What could go wrong?" Finn slid a hand down her belly, beneath the sheets.

All sorts of things could go wrong. He was proud and sensitive. He'd finally accepted that he needed help—that alone was a breakthrough—but she was hardly objective. As if to prove the point, her brain now turned to mush as his clever fingers brought her pleasure. She edged closer, feeling him rise against her. Her last coherent thought before she surrendered to the moment was, if she couldn't help him overcome his anxiety would he still trust her? Or would he shun her for having seen him at his most vulnerable?

FINN DRUMMED THE steering wheel as he drove south to Seattle. A low level of tension had been building inside him since they left Fairhaven. What if he couldn't get over the anxiety? If he fell apart he would not only embarrass himself, he'd screw things up for everyone else. What had he been thinking when he'd rashly said he'd play at open mike? And RockAround…was he insane? No, he couldn't do this. There was too much at stake.

The whole way, Carly had been chattering excitedly about how thrilled she was that he was taking steps to overcome his problem and how he would make a comeback and start performing his own music from now on.

"I don't know about a career performing," he said. "I'm not even sure I should be doing Rock-Around. I've been thinking about that Molto Music job. You were right, it would give me security with a solid income."

"It doesn't have to be either, or," Carly objected. "You could apply at Molto and do the RockAround gig, then see how it goes. No matter what, it's worthwhile addressing your issues. Wouldn't it be better to choose your career based on what you want rather than having to accept what you can manage? Irene didn't let her condition stop her from doing anything she wanted to do."

"It's not that simple," he said. "Even if I overcome the anxiety there are no guarantees in this business. The music industry chews up talented performers and spits them out every day of the week."

"Finn, you're throwing up roadblocks." Carly put her hand on his knee and squeezed. "Anxiety is a common problem. There's no shame in it. It takes a strong man to admit you need help."

"I don't know," he said. "I'm getting cold feet."

"Do you know how many psychiatrists it takes

to change a lightbulb?" She waited a beat. "Only one, but the lightbulb has to want to change."

He groaned. "Hey, bad jokes are my thing."

"Do you want to change, Finn?"

He was on a seesaw—one minute wanting to, the next minute, running scared. He'd been doing okay in LA, in his comfort zone. But he was tired of fear holding him back. Tired of making excuses for why he wouldn't perform. Tired of letting people down. He didn't think he could face Annie if he had to tell her she wouldn't get her big break because he was scared.

Finally, he nodded. "Yeah, I'm ready."

"Good," Carly said. "And remember, it doesn't matter what anyone else thinks. What's important is that you want this for yourself."

She was wrong there. What she thought mattered to him. But he said nothing and took the exit for Seattle, following the GPS prompts to the RockAround nightclub downtown. They found a place to park and walked a block to the venue. The main concert area was a vast room of black walls and red pillars, deserted on this weekday afternoon. Chairs were upturned on tables set up on two levels facing the stage.

An electrician was working on a panel next to the stage. Behind the bar, a thirtysomething guy with a bushy red beard was replacing beer kegs.

Finn walked up to the bartender. "I'm with the

warm-up band playing next Saturday. Mind if I check out the stage so I can get an idea of how we're going to set up?"

"Sure, go ahead." The bartender gestured with a wave.

Carly glanced around the room. "How many people does this place hold?"

"Fifteen hundred in here," the bartender said. "There's another room with a jukebox that seats five hundred."

"Do you usually fill up on the weekend?" she asked.

"Standing room only," he said.

Finn wandered over to the stage and up the stairs onto it. Now Carly was chatting to the electrician. He walked around the stage, trying to picture the hall filled with people. A slight queasiness took up residence in the pit of his stomach.

"So what should I be doing?" he asked when Carly rejoined him.

"You need to feel comfortable around the source of your phobia," she said. "By confronting your fears you begin to see them as simple problems to be solved and not something overwhelming. Like now, you're up there and nothing bad is happening."

"My fear is facing an audience. There's no audience," he pointed out.

"First we conquer the empty concert hall, then we work on the audience," she said. "What I want to do is take you through that concert. Cast your mind back to the moments before you walked out. What was going on backstage?"

"I was fighting with my parents," he said. "I wanted to play one of my own compositions, but Nora insisted I practice the repertoire I would be doing at the Juilliard audition. I didn't even want to go to Juilliard. She was emotionally blackmailing me into it, said I owed it to her. It got pretty heated. Finally I agreed to play the audition repertoire on the condition that even if I got a scholarship to Juilliard, I wasn't going to accept. I'm sure she thought she would change my mind later."

"Go behind the curtain," Carly said. "Then walk out as if you're going to perform."

Finn crossed the stage and ducked behind the heavy velvet curtains. It was dark, with a stale dusty smell that brought the evening of the concert forcefully back to life. His heart began to race. Things he'd forgotten leaped to the forefront of his mind. He'd yelled terrible things to his mother, obscenities he couldn't believe had passed his lips in her presence. Sweat broke out on his forehead, beneath his arms. The whole audience must have heard what a jerk he was.

"Finn?" Carly called. "Are you coming out?"

He emerged from between the curtains. The stage lights came on in a blinding flash. He froze, his chest so tight he couldn't breathe.

"Talk to me," Carly said in a low, calming voice. "What are you feeling?"

He looked down at his shaking hands. If there'd been a piano onstage he couldn't have played a note if his life depended on it.

"Ashamed," he whispered. "I was awful, stupid, and said terrible things. You were in the front row. Could you hear me yelling at my mother backstage?"

"The orchestra was tuning up," Carly said. "No one heard anything."

"I don't know why she bothered pushing me so hard," he said. "I wasn't good enough to get into Juilliard. She threw away years of her life on a slacker. I didn't have the character or the drive to put in the hard work to make it to the top. I wanted to fool around, and hang out with Dingo and the guys."

"Are those your words, or hers?" Carly asked, still in that calm voice.

He rubbed his temples. Fragmented memories came and then slipped away. "I... I don't know."

"She was angry because you wanted to play your own music," Carly went on.

"Well, yeah. Because that's not what I had been trained for."

"Your tastes changed," Carly said. "Why shouldn't you pursue your own interests?"

"Because she'd sacrificed so much for me. She worked two jobs to pay for my lessons. My brother didn't get to go on a school trip to Japan because that money was spent on me." His hands hung slackly at his sides as the black stain of shame spread to encompass his whole life. "The whole time I was a fraud. I wasn't good enough to get into Juilliard."

"Why do you say that?" Carly asked.

"I wasn't prepared for the audition," he said. "I'd wasted time writing my own music instead of practicing. I wasn't note perfect. She knew that but still insisted I perform."

"How did that make you feel," Carly said. "About yourself, about your mom."

"I was going to be humiliated and I knew it." He raked his hands through his hair and pulled at springy locks. "I was furious with her. But I had no right to be angry. It was my own fault."

"Maybe, maybe not. Does any of that mean you weren't capable of learning and performing well enough to make the grade for Juilliard?" Carly said. "Don't just say yes because that's the message your subconscious has been sending you for the past twelve years. Stop, and really think about it. And remember, there's no right or wrong answer. You've proven that you can make a living writing songs. There's no pressure to perform. Personally, I couldn't care less if you never play an instrument again. But objectively speaking, is your talent and your skill enough?"

"I was a good student. I had talent. For a long time I was dedicated."

"Irene thought you were a prodigy," Carly said.

"Talent isn't enough." Finn stared at the scuffed legs of the chairs piled on top of a table. Wisps of memories blew away before he could grasp them. Then he stilled. He saw himself waiting in the wings, peeking out at the audience. Seeing the rows of faces receding into the darkness. His knees turning to jelly, the sweating hands, the band tightening around his chest. Then Nora calling him back for last-minute instructions. Him refusing to go on. Then the fight. And all this time he'd been remembering the sequence of events backwards.

He looked at Carly. "I was panicking even before the fight with my mom. The stage fright caused the fight, not the other way around."

"Really?" Carly said, looking puzzled. "This wasn't the first time you'd been in front of an audience. There were recitals."

"It was my first time in a big auditorium," he said. "I had no problem playing at Irene's house and in small venues but as soon as I got on that stage I freaked out." His eyes fell shut as he remembered something else that made him flush with shame. "The last thing Nora said to me was, *The show must go on. A professional performs no matter what.* I went out there and fell apart. That's when I knew I wasn't ever going to make it as a performer, classical or otherwise."

"Finn, you were barely eighteen years old. You weren't a professional." Carly climbed the steps onto the stage and sat beside him, putting a steadying hand on his arm. "You were young and under enormous pressure to not only perform but to excel. Nora was your mother, your tutor, your financial support, your disciplinarian and your biggest cheerleader. She'd opened the doors to the world of music for you but she was also calling the shots. If you didn't do what she wanted she made you feel guilty. It's no wonder you had an anxiety attack."

Finn sank to the floor and hung his legs over the edge of the stage. Gradually things began to sink in as he slowly wrapped his head around all the contradictions. "Have I been sabotaging myself all this time to get back at my mother?"

"Whether you're punishing yourself or Nora by not performing, I don't know," Carly said. "But you've crushed your own ambitions for the past twelve years. The question you have to ask yourself, is, do you continue to make yourself and her pay? Or do you let it go?"

Finn stared at Carly. The real question was, even if he wanted to let it go, would he be able to?

CHAPTER FIFTEEN

FINN GOT OUT his straight razor, lathered up suds and soaped his jaw. Time to get rid of the scruff and put a fresh face on to meet the future. He drew the razor in a slow sweep down his cheek, hearing the rasp of blade against flesh. Outside in the hall, Annie's footsteps went past. Even though it was Saturday, Taylor had gone to the university to work in his lab and Carly was checking on her latest batch of sourdough. With four people living in the house it really felt like a home.

Looking back over the past week he realized he'd undergone subtle changes. Spreading Irene's ashes, even with the unorthodox turn that ritual had taken, had been surprisingly okay. Love didn't die, memories lived on. Meeting his mother had lanced an old, infected wound. It still hurt but the healing had begun with her agreeing to hear him perform his own music. Finally, at the RockAround, he'd gained insight into the wrong beliefs that had been holding him back.

He felt as if he was starting over. The question

remained whether he could overcome his phobia in time for the big gig, but with Carly on his team, miracles were possible.

As well as the open mike tomorrow, Dingo's band was booked at the bar the following Saturday. It would be a test of both him and Annie. He'd blocked out some time over the coming week to work with her, but in the meantime, he had plans of his own.

He rinsed the last of the foam off his razor and washed his face. Thinking of what lay ahead for him today, his heart started to race. Staring into the mirror, he deliberately slowed his breathing. *You've got this.*

But so many people were counting on him— *Stop. Breathe.* The world would go on with or without him.

People would be watching, waiting for him to fail.

He was doing this because he wanted to share the music he loved.

Hold that thought. Turning away from the mirror, he toweled off.

"'BYE. LATE FOR WORK." Annie grabbed her purse and a piece of toast before rushing out the door.

"See you later." Carly folded the sourdough into the shape of a loaf and laid it into the mold. Now that she was feeding the starter regularly the bread was rising just fine. She put the dough near the stove to keep warm, washed her hands and went out to check on the garden.

Rufus rushed ahead of her and picked up his ball, tail wagging hopefully. She threw it for him and walked along the vegetable patch, checking for new growth, pulling a weed here and there. As well as tomatoes, she'd planted beans, radishes, arugula and zucchini, all vegetables Finn had assured her were easy to grow.

It was hard to believe she was leaving tomorrow. She didn't want to think about that yet. The RockAround concert was on May 27th, the Friday of the Memorial Day weekend. Only three weeks away. She would come out for the concert and stay for the weekend. By then the radishes and arugula should be ready to pick.

The plumber and electrician were nearly finished their repairs. Peter King would act as her proxy to pay the tradesmen upon completion. Once that was done, she would put the house on the market. She'd decided to offer the house for sale furnished except for the contents of the master bedroom. She couldn't bear the thought of anyone sleeping in her aunt's bed in this house so she'd donated it along with the dresser and nightstands.

A three-month escrow would give Taylor plenty of time to complete his summer research and find another place to live in the fall. By then Annie would either have a permanent place with the band or she would have to go back home. Carly hoped it would be the former, but if Finn didn't stay with the band, Dingo might not keep Annie...

Stop. She couldn't worry about everyone. Finn had been mysterious about his plans for today, telling her he had things to do downtown. Maybe he was checking out the craft fair that was setting up in the historic district for the weekend. Maybe he was going to Rhonda's to sit on the stage and go through the same exercise they'd done at the RockAround. Whatever he was up to, he hadn't asked her to come along and it made her feel slightly hurt. Which was stupid because she had things to do herself. But they only had two days left and she wanted to spend every minute possible with him.

Time was passing much too quickly.

Finn wandered onto the outdoor stage at the Village Green in the historic district of Fairhaven carrying a guitar he'd borrowed from Dingo. There was more foot traffic on Main Street, but with the craft fair on free space was at a premium. And, to be honest, at the Village Green, a small oasis in the heart of downtown, there would be fewer people. Across the street were outdoor cafés but he was hidden from their view by a row of trees.

His palms were damp as he sat on the steps and tuned Dingo's old acoustic. Taking long, slow breaths he tried to calm himself. He could do this. An older couple were walking their spaniel at the far end of the green. He ignored them. He was just a guy, playing his guitar. Hopefully any listeners would attribute the beads of sweat on his brow to the sun beating down. And if he kept his eyes shut no one would see the glaze of panic in them.

He played without singing for five or so minutes because he didn't trust his voice not to shake. Then he hummed along to the tune, a song he'd composed a few years ago when he'd been feeling homesick for Fairhaven. When he felt comfortable with that he started to sing, eyes still closed, feeling the warmth of the sun's rays on his face. The lyrics referenced local landmarks and the tune was upbeat, capturing the atmosphere of the quaint, friendly community.

The sweet scent of lilacs planted around the green mingled with salt air from the ocean a couple of blocks away. The call of wheeling gulls formed a raucous backup that made him smile and he lifted his voice louder.

A clink to his left made him open his eyes. A woman pushing a stroller smiled at him. With a start he realized she'd thrown coins into the open guitar case on the stage. He hadn't planned to busk for money, he'd just wanted to experience performing in public in an unthreatening venue. But it felt good knowing that this young mother liked his song. He smiled and nodded his thanks. This wasn't so hard.

CARLY SIGNED THE necessary documents at the realty office and passed them back to Sam. "I'll be in touch by phone but if there's anything you need to know immediately you can contact Peter King. He has power of attorney for financial transactions related to the house."

Sam rose and shook her hand. "Pleasure doing business with you, Carly. It's an excellent property in a sought-after area. You should have no trouble selling."

"I don't want to close till the end of summer," she reminded him. "I have tenants. And a garden."

The Realtor chuckled. "You're a lot like your aunt, you know that?"

Outside, the street had been blocked off for the craft fair. Stalls shaded by colorful umbrellas were laden with handmade wooden furniture and toys, homespun woolen garments, pottery, hemp products, handcrafted cheese, wine, hydroponic herbs and punnets of early strawberries.

Carly walked through the stalls, drinking it all in. She wished she could stay for the summer and relive everything she loved about the town and the area. But that was impossible. Once the house was sold she wasn't likely to come back here.

"Carly!" Frankie caught up with her. "How have you been?"

"Busy," Carly said, hugging her. "I don't recall this fair from the old days. Is it new?"

"It's been an annual event for a couple of years." Frankie paused in front of a display of painted glass ornaments. "These would make nice Christmas gifts."

"Gorgeous." Carly touched wooden wind chimes and listened to the hollow melody. "I've been meaning to tell you, I'm putting the house up for sale. Taylor and Annie will stay till the end of summer."

"What about you?" Frankie asked.

"I'm heading back to New York tomorrow night."

"So soon? Seems like you just got here."

"I have to get back to work." Carly moved on to a stall selling homemade jams and chutney. They looked delicious but her suitcase was already overflowing. Suddenly the market, while interesting, seemed pointless and she felt her mood spiraling down. "Do you want to grab a coffee?"

"Sure," Frankie said. "Rhonda's?"

They'd just come level with the coffee shop. Carly glanced through the windows at the tables crowded with market goers, tourists and Seattleites up for the weekend. "Is there someplace quieter?"

"This way." Frankie headed down a side street and they walked to the next block where there were several outdoor cafés. A busker was playing on the Village Green and a dozen or so people sat on the grass or stood in a semicircle, listening. Carly snatched a sprig of lilac as she passed a flowering bush and held it to her nose.

"That guy sounds pretty good," Frankie said.

Carly tilted her head and her eyes widened. "That's Finn. Come on."

Throwing down the lilac, she walked up the shallow steps onto the Green and started across the lawn. Finn was singing with his eyes closed. His voice wasn't as strong as it could be and once he stopped midverse and just hummed. Then he recovered to sing the final verse and finished with a flourish of twanging strings. The audience clapped politely.

Carly waved but he didn't see her. He was smiling and nodding to the audience as people tossed money into his guitar case. Strumming, he said a few words before launching into his next song. Even out in the open with no acoustics he really did have an amazing voice. A couple who'd been walking toward a coffee shop stopped and turned to go onto the Green instead.

"Are you going to go over and say hi?" Frankie asked.

"No, let's not disturb him," Carly said, not wanting to add extra pressure.

Already he didn't need her. The thought gave her a pang deep down inside. Well, good for him. He had no idea how wonderful he was. When he started to fly he would be so far above her she'd never catch him.

FINN STACKED THE last quarter. The kitchen table was dotted with piles of coins neatly arranged in rows from largest denomination to smallest. He almost felt prouder of these earnings than of his royalties for the Screaming Reindeer song. The money thrown into the guitar case had been longer in coming and harder won.

The front door opened and he recognized Carly's footsteps in the hall. "In here," he called.

She was wearing city clothes, a navy pencil skirt, white blouse and stiletto ankle boots. His cheerfulness faltered at the reminder that tomorrow she would be going back to New York. But he was damned if he was going to waste the precious time they had left feeling down.

"Thirty-three dollars and sixty-five cents, one lollipop and a coupon for a free margarita at Pedro's." He grinned. "Not bad for my first day as a performer. It will almost pay the fine I got for busking without a permit."

Carly hugged him. "You were awesome. I was so proud of you. And it was a smart way to ease into performing in public with minimal pressure."

He leaned back, surprised. "You were there? I didn't see you." Not that he would have, with his eyes either shut or staring fixedly at the guitar strings.

"Frankie and I were going for coffee and didn't want to interrupt you." She got a bottle of white wine from the fridge. "I think this deserves a celebratory toast."

Finn raised the coupon. "How about tacos and margaritas instead?"

"You're on."

Finn took her hand as they walked down the hill to town in the warm spring evening. The present mood was a far cry from the day they'd roamed these streets looking for Rufus. He was still on a high from successful busking. Carly was in a goofy mood, making up outrageous future careers for the kids they passed.

"That little girl," she said of a five-year-old in pigtails walking with her mom and a shaggy-headed boy. "She's going to be a world authority on shredded cheese. Her brother will get work as a Rasputin impersonator."

"You're pulling my leg," Finn said laughing. "There's no such thing."

"You would be amazed the weird jobs out there," Carly said. "Mind you, Rasputin is a niche market. Tough to break into."

"What about that kid?" Finn nodded to a cherubic boy being towed in a cart behind his dad riding a bicycle.

Carly tapped her cheek, pretending to ponder the matter. "He'll have a job fishing bicycles out of the canals in Amsterdam."

"You know these things because?" Finn asked, smiling.

"I'm a recruitment consultant," she said. "I'm trained to identify people's special abilities and place them in their perfect job."

"Okay, then, what makes you believe I'd be a good match with Molto?" Finn asked.

"The wicked glint in your eye when you're counting up your money. I'm kidding, of course. It's your songwriting ability." She glanced sideways at him. "Are you really thinking of calling them?"

"I put in my application last week."

"Good for you."

They came to the edge of the historic district and the market set up on the main street. The conversation turned to the contents of the stalls. Finn's thoughts, however, were on the future. He wanted Carly in his life, not temporarily but permanently and on a daily basis.

The application to Molto felt like a cop-out. He didn't really want it but he'd figured the only way he could get Carly to even think about moving west to be with him was by proving he was stable and reliable. He couldn't say that though because he knew all too well what it felt like to be pressured by someone you loved. Assuming she loved him.

She might be more willing to give up her job in New York if they lived in Fairhaven. It was the scene of some of his worst memories but there were good memories, too. Summer days with Carly on Irene's porch, jamming with Dingo, the woods, the beach, riding for miles on his bike with his friends. He'd grown up here, traveling the years from a boy to a teenager to a young man. The town was home in a way that LA would never be. And it was a great place to raise a family.

"Look at this rocking chair." Carly came to a halt in front of a display of hand-crafted maple wood furniture.

The chair had rounded, clean lines, a broad leather seat, and a tall back with a design of a sun and moon carved into it. She sat and rocked gently. "It's super comfortable."

"Kinda out of the box for a city girl like you." He was eyeing the king-size headboard carved from the same fine-grained, rose-hued wood. It wouldn't go in his ultramodern Hollywood rancher but he liked it a lot. Casually he pocketed the woodworker's business card. "It would be perfect for Irene's house."

Dreamily, Carly smoothed a hand over the maple wood arm. "In the kitchen, next to the stove." She rose and pushed him into the chair. "Isn't that the most comfortable thing you've ever sat in?"

"Not bad," he said, rocking. "Although it's not in the same league as my old duct-taped recliner."

"You keep ruining my image of the hotshot LA creative. Are you sure you don't live in a biker den or a frat house?"

"Shh, I'm creating right now." He closed his eyes and pictured himself in the rocker, strumming a guitar and watching the sunset over the bay. "I'd rather have it on the porch."

She placed a hand warmly on his shoulder. "We could get two chairs. One for me, one for you."

He placed his hand atop hers. Side by side,

rocking through life. With his eyes still closed, he smiled. These few weeks with Carly had been the best.

When he opened his eyes Carly was watching him, a wistful smile on her face. Rocking chairs, huh. Carly was after a fancy office in downtown Manhattan.

He pushed that depressing thought aside. All too soon they would both have to return to reality. Let tonight be about romance.

Surging to his feet, he whirled her into his arms and danced her away in an impromptu polka, dodging pedestrians and dogs on leashes. Laughing, she let herself be twirled, leaning into his supporting arm and letting her head fall back. At the end of the block, he picked her up by the waist and spun her around, letting her slide down his body.

"What was that about?" Her face was flushed and her eyes sparkling.

"Just feeling good," he said.

"Silly." She put her hand in his and they walked up the steps of the Mexican restaurant.

Pedro's was Saturday night busy so they had their margaritas in the bar while they waited for a table, surrounded by colorful pottery and posters of Cabo and Baja.

"Are you excited about open mike tomorrow?" Carly dipped a tortilla chip in salsa.

"Equal parts excited and scared." He spun the bowl-shaped margarita glass around to get more salt. Good for the throat.

"A few nerves aren't necessarily a bad thing." Carly wiped her fingers on a napkin and got out her phone. "I thought I'd tell a few people about the open mike. Are you okay with that?"

"Go ahead," he said, still on a high. "The only thing worse than playing to an audience is playing to an empty room."

"There, I've sent a mass text to everyone I know in town and posted on social media." She reached for another chip. "At the Village Green were you anxious at all?"

"Sure, a little, but it went better than I expected. My confidence wasn't all it could be but I felt as if I really connected to the audience. Reminded me of what I've been missing."

It had also made him realize what the future might hold. If all went well at open mike and then at the bar and at RockAround, who knew where he could proceed from there? With the band or on his own. He had no illusions the road ahead would be easy but suddenly his world had opened up. He wouldn't need Molto.

"That's great," she said. "So, you feel ready to play tomorrow? You really want to do this?"

Was she seeking reassurance that he wouldn't bail? Fair enough. That concert twelve years ago was tough to live down. "I really want to play. I promise I won't run out of the café again, no matter what happens."

The waitress showed them to a table and not long after, plates of enchiladas and tacos arrived. Finn joked and teased Carly, who complained that he'd given her a side ache from laughing. But like a somber note anchoring the light-hearted melody was the thought that the minutes were ticking away till the time he would lose her.

Impulsively he reached for her hand across the table, felt her smooth skin beneath the calluses on his finger pads. "Don't go back to New York. Don't sell the house. Let's finish what we started."

Carly only seemed to hear the last sentence. "Not that again!" Laughing, she rubbed her ankle up his calf. "I'm going to make you eat those words." She leaned forward, showing her cleavage above her V-neck blouse. "When we get home, you're going to give me an all-over body massage until I get a happy ending, if you know what I mean. Finish what you started."

He kept smiling, hiding his disappointment that she'd completely misread him. A happy ending to him meant home, family, lasting love. Whereas he'd been speaking seriously of the future of their relationship, she had reduced their connection to a sexual fling.

Well, they had been joking around all night. He knew he meant more to her than just a roll in the hay. But a seed of uncertainty had been planted. She'd said from the beginning that she didn't want anything complicated. If he started over as a performer he could be struggling for a while. Would Carly take him seriously as a relationship prospect, or would he always be the bad boy from the wrong side of the tracks? Even a job at Molto might not be respectable enough for a woman who operated in the high echelons of the business world.

"Finn?" she said.

Pushing aside his dark thoughts he smiled lasciviously and rubbed small circles in her palm, letting her know he was thinking about doing the same thing on a completely different part of her anatomy. "I'm all about happy endings."

Sexual chemistry and humor, these were things they were good at. Safe things. He would never make Carly choose between him and her dream job. But like the bite of chili on his tongue, the fear that this was all there was between them stung his heart.

CHAPTER SIXTEEN

SUNDAY MORNING CARLY rose before the birds, unable to sleep. Finn had gone out early for a run with Rufus to shed any last nerves. Word was spreading that he was going to be at open mike today. Someone had reposted her tweet onto the Fairhaven Facebook page and added that Finn was the songwriter behind the Screaming Reindeer hit. When she zipped down to the grocery store for milk for breakfast she'd overheard the woman in front of her at the cash register talking about him. Apparently she'd known him in high school and remembered his and Dingo's garage band.

As she left the supermarket she called Nora to remind her. "Don't change your mind, please. Finn would be so disappointed if you didn't come."

"Will he come is the question," Nora said.

"Of course he will. Yesterday he was busking on the Green. He had the crowd eating out of his hand."

Nora made a noise that might have meant anything, approval or the opposite. "Bob and I will be there. What time?"

"He wants to be the first act, to get it over with," Carly said. "So about 12:30 p.m. Annie's going to reserve us a table. I'll pick you and Bob up at 12:20 pm."

Carly started the car and headed back up the hill. She passed Finn jogging, Rufus at his heels, and rolled down the window. "Hey, hot stuff. Going my way?"

He grinned and waved. She roared past, glancing in the rearview mirror. His smile had faded and a furrow had creased the space between his eyebrows. A moment of doubt swept over her. Was she making too much of him playing today? A little pressure could be a good thing. But too much and he might fold.

Nah, he was just hurting on his homeward uphill stretch of the run. Finn was just as excited about today as she was, even if he didn't show it as overtly. He'd said so last night. She believed him. After all they'd been through together and all the soul-baring, late-night discussions, he wouldn't lie to her.

Yesterday had been perfect, starting from the thrill of seeing him perform on the Village Green, to him dancing her down the street, to the sexy banter at Pedro's to the swoon-worthy "happy ending."

She was putting away the milk when he came through the back door all sweaty and sexy in his body-hugging T-shirt and shorts. "Good run?"

"Good to get back into it," he grunted. "I was getting out of shape."

"Your shape looks fine to me." She slid a hand over his tight butt.

He glanced at the clock. "Got to shower and get dressed."

"I told your mom we'd pick up her and your dad on our way to Rhonda's," Carly said. Finn's face went blank. Uh-oh. Had she gone too far by bringing his parents when he and Nora weren't entirely comfortable together? "Is that a problem? I thought it would be okay since you were the one who invited her."

He plucked his damp T-shirt away from his chest. "Thing is, I'm going to Dingo's first. We're going to tape my song live and I'm going to help him set up the recording equipment."

"Oh, okay, sure." Her breath released in a relieved sigh. For a moment there… "If you were having second thoughts, you'd tell me about them, wouldn't you?"

"I'm not having second thoughts." He opened the fridge, took out the juice carton and poured himself a glass. "This is an essential step toward performing at RockAround. I'm committed to that."

He'd been committed to the concert back in high school, too. She watched his throat move as he swallowed a couple of long gulps of juice. Oh for goodness' sake, why was she worrying? This was nothing like the same thing. Back then he'd been pressured into performing music he didn't want to play for a music school he didn't want to go to. Today's open mike was him playing his own song, his way.

"Well, good." She blotted his temples with a tissue. "You're all sweaty. I can practically smell the testosterone oozing out of your pores."

He grabbed her playfully around the waist. She squealed and squirmed as he backed her against the counter, pressing into her hips. She slid her hands up under his T-shirt over hot bare skin slick with perspiration. After last night she thought she would have been satiated for a week. Instead she was wet and she could feel how hard he was.

Finn's gaze shifted and he stilled abruptly. He was looking past her to her packed suitcases sitting in the hall at the base of the stairs. He took a deep breath and released her. The fun had drained out of the moment. "What time is your flight?"

"I'm going straight from the open mike to the airport." He'd known for weeks she was leaving but she'd deliberately avoided mentioning her departure in the past few days, not wanting to ruin the good times. She'd planned to wait to talk about the future until after the open mike, when he was relaxed. They would find a quiet place, away from the café. She didn't know what they would decide, only that she couldn't leave without addressing where they went from here. Had she left it too late? "We should talk."

"I need to shower."

"Finn, is everything okay?" she asked, touching his arm as he passed her. She had a feeling that if he hadn't seen her suitcases she would have been sitting on the table right now with him pushing into her, oblivious to the time.

"Fine." He lifted a hand as he walked away and let it fall—like an ax on a chopping block. "Everything's fine."

If everything was fine, why did his voice sound so strained?

"I'll see you at the café," she called after him as he ran up the stairs. Then the bathroom door closed and she heard the shower. Carly stood uncertainly in the foyer. "Break a leg."

CARLY FELT A twinge of unease when she saw the sandwich board that stood outside Rhonda's café advertising the open mike afternoon. Underneath someone had attached a handwritten notice in bold letters proclaiming the appearance today of Fairhaven songwriter, Finn Farrell.

Yesterday Finn had seemed absolutely fine with playing in front of an audience, but today with the pressure mounting, she wasn't as sure of him. Putting on a smile, she opened the heavy glass door and ushered Nora and Bob in ahead of her.

Annie saw her and hurried out from behind the counter, all smiles. She led them to an empty table near the stage and whipped off the reserved sign. "We don't usually reserve tables but my boss said I could for today. I kind of hyped Finn to them, talking about RockAround and how he's rejoined his old band and is starting his comeback in his hometown."

"Great publicity." Carly hoped Finn hadn't gotten wind of that.

"See the guy in the green shirt by the pillar?" Annie said. "He's the arts reporter with the *Bellingham Times*. Dingo called him." She took their lunch orders and added, "I've got to get back to work. Sunday is always busy but today the café is filling faster than usual."

Annie was right. The room was nearly at capacity already and open mike hadn't even started. There was a definite buzz growing over Finn's appearance. There would be many locals who had admired the child prodigy's talent and had liked him as a youth. But no doubt there were also plenty of people who remembered his infamous epic fail. Maybe they were coming to see if history would repeat itself.

"Excuse me, can we use this chair?" a man asked, his hand already on the seat she was saving for Finn.

"Sorry, no, my boyfriend will be here any minute." Carly glanced at Nora to see what the older woman made of that statement but Nora's expression was impassive. Carly shrugged. She and Finn were sleeping together. They cared about each other. They'd promised not to lose contact again. Calling him her boyfriend wasn't out of line but she couldn't help worrying that she was jinxing herself. She and Finn hadn't had that conversation yet.

Nora checked her watch. "When is he coming?"

"He should be here by now." Carly checked the time on her phone. "He must have gotten held up."

"He'll be here," Bob said, but he didn't sound overly confident.

Nora's chicken Caesar salad, Bill's soup and Carly's toasted panini arrived and for the next fifteen minutes they concentrated on eating. Finn still hadn't arrived when they'd finished.

"Where is he?" Nora said, glancing around.

"It's only quarter to one. Plenty of time." Carly frowned. "It's strange that Dingo's late, too. I hope they didn't have an accident."

"In a mile and a half?" Nora shook her head, lips compressed. "This is just like Finn."

"He'll be here," Bob said staunchly.

"I'll text him." Carly wiped her hands on a napkin and sent a message. Everything ok? She listened for the whistle of incoming. A full minute passed. Two minutes. "He must be driving and can't answer."

"Driving out of town," Nora said grimly.

"Now, dear." Bob put a hand on his wife's shoulder.

Carly noticed that other people in the café were looking at the stage and checking the clock on the wall over the coffee machine, or glancing at their watches or phones. To Carly's anxious ears the murmur of conversation sounded querulous.

Annie came to collect empty dishes. "Where are Finn and Dingo?"

"I don't know," Carly said. "I don't have Dingo's number. Do you?"

"My phone is in my purse in the back room but I can get it—Never mind," Annie said, straightening. "Dingo's here."

The tall Aussie with the long ponytail strode across the front of the café and stepped onto the stage. The room erupted into enthusiastic applause. The panini suddenly felt like a rock in Carly's stomach. Where was Finn?

Dingo held up a hand to the audience to quell the clapping. "Thanks for your patience, guys. Sorry for the delay. We'll get started in a minute."

He made his way to Carly's table. Crouching at her side, he kept his voice low. "Where's Finn? I've been waiting for him at my place. He didn't show."

"What?" Carly squeaked. "He should have been there half an hour ago."

Just then, the door opened again and in walked Finn. Every eye in the room turned his way. His gaze scanned the room, found Carly and then he looked away. Her heart sank at his pale face and strained expression. Mechanically he walked up to the stage. He tapped the microphone and it emitted a static shriek.

"Thanks for coming, everyone." He dragged a shaking hand through his wild black locks. "Sorry to disappoint if anyone came to see me but I won't be performing today. I—I can't." He sucked in a breath that was amplified by the microphone. His voice broke. "Please stay, though. There'll be lots of great music."

With that he walked off the stage and headed for the exit. Carly pushed back her chair and ran after him. He was waiting for her around the corner in the parking lot. At least this time he wasn't running away. Hands shoved in the pockets of his skinny jeans, wide shoulders hunched beneath his brown leather bomber jacket, he looked the picture of misery.

"Talk to me," Carly said, stopping a few feet away.

"I'm not ready." Finn gazed at her bleakly. "The Village Green yesterday was okay because it just happened. There was no one there when I began to play. The crowd grew in ones and twos. Even then there were no more than a couple of dozen people listening at any one time."

"Never mind." She came closer and rubbed his arm. "Step by step, you'll get there. Maybe the bar gig will be better."

"No, I'm going back to LA today, now." He gestured to the Mustang parked behind them. "I'll take Rufus. It's not fair to leave him with Taylor and Annie. Who knows if one of them would be able to keep him when they move out."

"You're giving up." Anger burst into flame in her chest.

He looked away. "I never wanted this anyway."

"That's so not true," she cried. "Where is the guy I was with yesterday? The one who believed in himself? Oh, he's gone." She flung a hand out.

"Left the building. Because leaving is what you do. Letting people down is what you do."

"Carly," Finn said in an agonized voice. "That's not fair."

"Isn't it?" It was bad enough that he'd bailed on open mike and wasn't giving himself a chance to overcome his problem. He was leaving her, too. She'd spent years feeling lost and bereft and now he was doing it to her again.

She walked over to Rufus, who had his head out of the car window, and put her arms around his neck, stroking his soft red coat. He licked her hand and she buried her face in his fur. "Goodbye, sweetheart," she whispered, her eyes blurring. "Going with Finn is for the best. You wouldn't like it in New York."

"Carly." Finn touched her arm. "Let's not part like this."

"Don't." She shook his hand off and turned away quickly to avoid seeing the pain in his eyes. She couldn't go through this again. He might want to be friends, stay in touch, but when the going got rough, he took the easy way out. As for romance, what a joke. "We're done."

FINN GOT IN the Mustang and fixed his gaze fiercely on the road ahead. He should feel relieved that the ordeal was over. So what if he'd bailed on open mike? Those people in the café had already forgotten him and were listening to whoever was next on the playlist.

Except for Carly. And Nora. Dingo, Annie, Taylor, the guys in the band. All his old friends. The woman at the hardware store he'd rashly told and who'd promised to come and watch him.

The entire awful morning replayed in his brain.

On his way to Dingo's house he'd passed through town and seen the sandwich board with his name on it and the lunch crowd visible through the plate glass windows. That's when the anxiety had started, the racing pulse, the ever-tightening band around his chest.

Panicking, he'd kept going past Dingo's street to Chuckanut Drive. He'd thrown a few rocks in the water at Teddy Bear beach, trying to psych himself up and failing. But he couldn't leave without facing the people he was letting down. Nor could he leave without saying goodbye to Carly. Remembering the look in her eyes as she'd reamed him out made him groan aloud. *We're done*. He couldn't bring himself to even think about her.

Now he sped up the freeway entrance and onto the I-5 South. He turned the radio to full volume to block his thoughts, hit cruise control and just drove. It was better this way. He was a songwriter, not a performer. It was a mistake to think he could change. Failing was what he did. It was who he was.

And why should he put himself out there? He'd only been doing it for Carly's sake. But she wasn't going to stick around. Her life was back in New York. Her high-falutin' job was waiting for her. No matter what he did, he would always be the boy from the wrong side of town. Sure, that might appeal to a teenage girl but not to a grown woman.

Better to leave now before he ruined the Rock-Around gig for Dingo and the guys. And Annie now, too. His fist pounded the steering wheel at the thought of her disappointment adding to the pile. He could picture them all talking about him at the café, wondering what was truly wrong with him.

Any small gain in reconciliation with his mother would be lost. No doubt she'd expected this. Her words from long ago continued to ring in his ears. *A professional doesn't buckle under pressure. The show must go on.*

Well, the show was going to have to go on without him.

At Tacoma he headed for the coast. His troubles would only continue once he got to Los Angeles so he might as well take the longest route possible and think about where he was going in life. He tried but his mind was empty and desolate, like the fog-shrouded Oregon coastline. Mile after mile of narrow winding road sandwiched between looming dark forests and the thundering gray ocean.

He drove until 2:00 a.m., stopping only for gas and to drive through a burger place. Finally he crashed at a motel halfway down the Oregon coast for a few hours' sleep. At dawn, he made the mistake of looking at his phone and saw dozens of text messages and voice mails. Half of the messages were from Carly. He turned the phone off, not ready to talk to her, or anyone. If they hated him, he hated himself more.

He bought a couple of breakfast sandwiches and walked down to the beach to sit on a rickety wooden jetty. Rufus wolfed down his sandwich and then sniffed around the piles of kelp mounded on the sand. Finn sat on the damp pier, legs dangling, and watched the waves rolling in from the horizon to break on the rocky point in a spume of white spray.

What was he doing with his life? What had happened to that kid who had dreamed of becoming a musician? After fleeing Fairhaven as an eighteen-year-old he'd taken a job in a record store, barely able to afford to eat and pay rent in that fleabag of a first apartment. He'd hung around bars and music venues, gotten to know people. Finally scored a gig playing backup.

Gradually he'd added songwriting to his repertoire and his reputation as a pianist and writer
had grown.

It was a safe route, one that paid the bills but
didn't put him under emotional duress. What
was wrong with that? He'd fulfilled part of his
mother's wish for him and found a way out of
poverty and into independence. He didn't need
to perform to survive, and even thrive. He had
a perfectly adequate life doing what he did. It
wasn't fair for other people—Carly, his mother,
Irene—to expect more from him. Why couldn't
they accept him as he was? If he was happy then
what did it matter to anyone else?

If he was happy.

We're done.

Suddenly restless, he whistled for Rufus. The
dog loped back, his long red feathers wet and
coated with sand. Finn scolded him affection-
ately and wiped him down with an old towel he
kept in the trunk.

At the town's single gas station he tanked up
the Mustang and got back on the road. Sunrise
lent a pearly glow to the smooth stone monoliths
scattered along the beach. Around midday he'd
had enough of the slow coastal road and headed
east through the redwood forests to the freeway.
Now he just wanted to be home and sleep in his

own bed. At rest stops he stretched his legs and fueled up on coffee as he walked Rufus.

Another ten hours and he turned into his driveway in Laurel Canyon. He washed down a sleeping pill with a slug of scotch and went to bed.

CARLY GOT TO the office early Monday morning ready to tackle the backlog of work that had built in her absence. Files were stacked in piles on her desk and her in-tray was overflowing. Her email, which she hadn't opened in days, bristled with urgent flags. Excellent. There was so much to do that she wouldn't have time to think.

It felt good to be back wearing a suit and heels and having her hair and makeup done. This was who she was, professional and competent. She would throw herself into work, far away from messy emotional entanglements with unsatisfactory men.

After skimming her emails for the most urgent, she found a message from her contact at Wallis Group. He said things were progressing and he hoped to have an answer for her by early in the week. In other words, anytime now. Quickly she looked down the list of emails but there was nothing else from him yet.

She went back to the top and opened a résumé from a CEO of a tech company in Colorado who was looking to relocate to Silicon Valley. Impressive credentials. Impeccable work history. Yada yada. In less than thirty seconds her eyes glazed over and her thoughts drifted to yesterday.

Finn had bailed on the open mike. She still couldn't believe it. *Sorry.* Was that all he could say to everyone who'd believed in him and supported him? Everyone who'd put themselves on the line for him?

She'd even put her heart on the line.

He'd appeared to be making headway and then wham, he'd backslid. Well, she'd known all along it wouldn't be easy. When he'd admitted to the audience at Rhonda's that he couldn't perform, she'd felt his pain as if it were her own. But he shouldn't give up.

He must still be feeling bad if he wouldn't answer her calls and texts. She wished he would get in touch with her so she could find out where his head was at and talk some hope into him.

Herb stopped by her door. "Carly, good to have you back. Everything under control out west?"

"Everything's fine," she said, smiling. "It's great to be back."

Her smile faded as Herb moved away. Was it good to be back though? Ever since she'd touched down at JFK she'd felt out of sorts, as if she'd left a limb back in Fairhaven. Or maybe her heart.

She went back to skimming her inbox, deleting junk and answering emails that could be dealt with quickly.

Leanne knocked on her door and came in bearing a small white box on her open palms like a ring bearer at a wedding. "Ta da! Your new business cards. Check them out, make sure your name is spelled right."

Carly lifted the lid and removed one. Carly Maxwell, Executive Recruitment Consultant.

A tumult of mixed emotions swept through her. This was what she'd been working toward the past five years. All her plans and dreams were coming to fruition. Executive recruitment consultant, partner, senior partner. Who knows, maybe one day she would be CEO?

So why wasn't she over the moon?

"They're perfect, thanks," she said to Leanne. Her computer chirped and she was relieved at the distraction. "Excuse me, this could be an email I've been waiting for."

"I'll go see how your furniture order is coming along," Leanne said and hurried off, her heels clacking on the tiled floor.

Carly clicked into her inbox. When she saw the Wallis letterhead her pulse sped up. Quickly she opened and scanned the contents. Yes! She'd gotten the account. They were moving their entire recruiting needs to Hamlin and Brand and she would be their main contact.

Then right on the heels of elation came the anticlimax. She would be locked into this kind of work for the foreseeable future. Locked into? This was what she'd wanted. Wasn't it?

She reached for her phone and brought up Finn's number to send a text. Got the Wallis account. That sounded so impersonal but she didn't know what else to say to him. Why hadn't he responded to any of her texts? Yes, she'd said they were done but he'd sworn to be her friend. Her heart squeezed painfully. She wanted his friendship but she wanted his love, too.

Without adding anything more to her message she hit send.

Finn was halfway through a bottle of scotch at two in the afternoon when he got Carly's latest message. He raised his glass to her success and sloshed alcohol onto the grass beside his sun lounger. Rufus padded over to see what the excitement was about.

"She got the big account." Finn scratched behind the Irish setter's silky red ears. "I'm not surprised. She's a smart cookie, and ambitious. Bet she's doing a happy dance."

He took another swig of the bottle and gazed

through the pine trees rising out of the steep-sided ravine. A dark pall fell over the sunny day. His head was fuzzy and his heart heavy when he thought of how badly he'd blown things with her.

He tapped out a message. Congrats. Knew u could do it.

He thought about saying more but what? Their paths had come together briefly for Irene's funeral and now they had diverged again. Best to accept his limitations and the limitations of their relationship. His mother was right, he wasn't the settling down kind.

Except that he ached to hold Carly again, to sit on that damn veranda with her and watch the sunset while they rocked away in their hand-carved chairs. He longed to see her eyes light up when the sourdough rose and hear her groan when he made a lame joke.

His phone rang, dragging him out of his recollections. "Hey, Tom."

"Where have you been?" his agent demanded. "I've been trying to get hold of you for the past two days."

"Been on the road," Finn said. "Back home now. What's up?"

"Your latest tune is up for an award on Friday," Tom said. "Can you make it to the ceremony?"

"What day is today?" he mumbled.

"Are you drunk?" Tom asked, incredulous.

"I'm working on it."

"Well, sober up because we have things to discuss," Tom said briskly. "Molto contacted me to arrange an interview. Did you apply for a songwriting job there?"

"I sent them my résumé," Finn said. "Put you down as my contact. Thought you could negotiate me a better contract."

"Finn, are you thinking clearly? Your career is on the upswing. Do you really want to throw that away and go work for a large corporation?"

No, but he'd considered it might be handy to have a steady paycheck. Did that matter now that he and Carly weren't together? He dragged a hand over his face. They never would be a couple now that he'd shown his true colors. He didn't know what he wanted anymore.

"Make a time for me to see Molto," he said. "I'll decide later if I go or not."

Tom muttered something incoherent that Finn ignored. Rufus dropped his ball at Finn's side and waited, panting hopefully. Halfheartedly Finn picked up the ball and tossed it to the other side of the lawn. The dog raced after it, tail flying like a flag.

"Dingo contacted me," Tom went on. "I understand you said you would join his band? Is that still happening? It would be great if you started performing. We need to think about your brand. Is it being part of a band, or a solo artist? How do we best promote your YouTube music videos on the back of the RockAround concert?"

"About RockAround…" Finn put his fingers to his temple. "Can you find the guys another lead singer and keyboardist?"

There was a long pause. "So you're bailing," Tom said flatly.

"I'm bailing," Finn admitted.

"Kind of short notice, isn't it?" There was a cold edge to his voice.

Finn threw the ball again for Rufus. "Can't be helped. And no, I don't want to talk about it."

There was a long silence. Finally Tom said, "I'll pick you up at seven on Friday." He seemed about to hang up when he added, "Finn?"

"Yeah?"

"I have the number of someone who could help you," Tom said. "He's at a big research medical center and specializes in cutting-edge therapy. He works with a lot of returned vets with PTSD and has had amazing results."

Finn thought about a fridge magnet he'd seen once. *Everything you want is on the other side of fear.* That made it sound as if overcoming anxiety was simple. It wasn't. Fear was a raging forest fire, an unclimbable mountain. Fear was a vast glacier pitted with bottomless chasms. If he tried to get to the other side of fear he would either be consumed or broken.

"Nah, I'm good," he said at last. "See you Friday."

CHAPTER SEVENTEEN

CARLY CLIMBED UP to her third-floor brownstone apartment on Friday night carrying a bottle of champagne and a selection of gourmet appetizers from the deli. In a half hour or so her friends Althea and Erica would come over for a drink before they all went out on the town to celebrate her getting the Wallis account.

She put the bubbly in the fridge next to the jar of sourdough starter she'd brought from Irene's house. She'd left some starter back in Fairhaven in case Taylor or Annie got ambitious. Now that she'd begun using it, she was committed to keeping it going.

After arranging the snacks on a baking tray she tidied up. Compared to the spaciousness of Irene's house, her studio apartment felt cramped, almost claustrophobic. Never mind, it wouldn't be long before she could afford a bigger place.

Hard on the heels of that thought came a wave of the depression that had dogged her since leaving Fairhaven. For a brief, heady period, she'd really thought she and Finn had forged something lasting. The west coast versus east coast thing was a problem but with enough will, they could solve it. With her salary she would be able to fly reasonably frequently between New York and Los Angeles. And he could stay with her for long periods. A songwriter could work anywhere, right?

Career-wise, he'd been so close to breaking out of his self-imposed slump. He'd been trying, he really had. And then he'd just…given up. Where was the young Finn, the guy who had practiced classical piano for hours on end, day after day, and still found time to explore different music and develop his own style? Where was the outcast son who had nevertheless made a name for himself as a songwriter? The guy who'd counted his busking coins as if they were riches, the man who had for one shining moment, believed in himself as a performer?

Where was the guy who'd kissed her in the tower? The man who'd made love to her, not as if the world was ending, but as if it had just begun?

When he'd given up on himself, he'd given up on them, too.

Her phone rang. Wiping her hands on a tea towel, she picked up. "Hello?"

"Carly, it's Sam, from Fairhaven Realty. We

had an open house on Wednesday. I've got great news."

"Yes?" Carly's pulse kicked up a notch but she didn't know if it was excitement or dread. She opened a cupboard and brought down small plates and champagne flutes.

"A couple from Seattle have made an offer," Sam went on. "They've underbid your asking price by twenty thousand but if you're looking for a quick sale it might be worth considering."

"Did you tell them I need an extended settlement period?" Carly said.

"They're fine with that, as long as they can move in before the school year starts. They've got a couple of kids in primary school."

"Any other bites?" Carly asked.

"Some interest but nothing solid. It's a big house, lots of maintenance," Sam said. "It's not for everyone."

"I can put in a counteroffer, right?" Carly asked.

"Midway would be reasonable," Sam said. "They like the house and would probably be willing to come up a little."

"But it would still be below my asking price and it's only the first offer." Carly hesitated. "I need to think this over."

"By all means, but if you're considering it,

don't take too long. They've got their eye on several houses in the area."

"I'll get back to you by the end of business tomorrow."

Carly hung up and went to the fridge for the champagne. The glass she poured wasn't in celebration. Everything seemed to be happening at warp speed. Her expanded job, Finn back in LA, the house on the brink of being sold. The weeks in Fairhaven had felt like an idyll, sandwiched between "before" and "after" segments of real life. There was a musical term for an interlude—*intermezzo*. That's what their romance had been, an intermezzo.

Her fingers sought out Finn's number. She'd told herself she wasn't going to be the first to call. Instead, she would give him space to figure things out—and let herself cool down. But he'd been such a part of Irene's life and the house that it seemed only right she talk over her decision with him.

The phone rang and rang. She tried to tell herself he could be at a studio working but her fuse had shortened where he was concerned. If he let it go to voice mail…

"Yo?" he answered at last.

"Finn, hey." She felt awkward and angry. "Did I get you at a bad time?"

"No, it's fine." His voice sounded gravelly,

wary. "Congratulations again. I should have called but I was…tied up."

Tied up. That could mean anything from a studio session to solitary day drinking.

"Doesn't matter," she said, even though it did. "Sam just called. Someone put an offer on the house."

"Great," Finn said. "I guess."

"It's what we did all that work for," she said. "The buyers are willing to have a long settlement so that's good for Taylor and Annie. It's under my asking price but not so far below as to be out of the question."

"I don't sense you jumping for joy," Finn said, sounding more alert. "What's the problem?"

"Not a problem exactly." Carly couldn't put a finger on her resistance. "If I hold out I might be able to get a higher price. On the other hand, they're the only people who have shown interest. If I let them go, I might be passing up my only chance to sell to someone willing to meet my conditions."

"Ah, the old bird in the hand dilemma," Finn said. "What's your gut feeling?"

"My gut feeling doesn't make logical sense." She walked to the window overlooking the street, gridlocked in the early evening. Horns honked. Someone shouted. The noise didn't bother her. She liked the bustle of the city. So where did this

uneasy feeling come from that had been claw-
ing at her ever since she signed the agreement
with Sam's realty agency?

"I think," she said slowly, "I want to keep the
house."

"I thought you couldn't afford to," Finn said.
"I thought you wanted to buy an apartment in
New York with the proceeds."

"Yes, yes." Why was it suddenly annoying
that he was parroting her words back to her? "I
didn't say it makes sense."

"What you're experiencing is a case of Fear
Of Missing Out," he said. "Otherwise known as
wanting to have your cake and eat it, too."

"You're right, it's a dumb idea. I was going to
crunch the numbers on the option of keeping it
as a rental property but I'd only be delaying the
inevitable. It's not as though I'd ever live there."

"How is being back at your dream job?" Finn
asked, changing the subject. "Everything you
hoped it would be?"

"It's fine. I told you I got that big account I'd
been angling for. It'll be a lot of work but could
lead to even bigger things."

And yet, all day she'd been dogged by that
feeling of anticlimax. An "is this all there is?"
feeling. Which was crazy.

"That's great," Finn said. "You'll be helping
a lot of people."

"Yeah." People that she mostly would never see. How could she not have realized that her job entailed a lot of paper pushing and little personal contact with her clients?

"And the business cards?" Finn went on. "Did they turn out?"

"Serif was definitely the way to go. You were right." The longer they chatted, the harder it was to remember why she was mad at him. "How's Rufus? Do you have a fenced yard? Can you get his brand of dog food there?"

"He's settling in fine. I took him for a walk up in the hills this morning. He loved chasing the ground squirrels." Finn was silent a moment and then cleared his throat. "He...he misses you."

"I miss him, too." Carly's eyes welled. She gulped champagne.

She was supposed to be celebrating, not having a pity party. She'd gotten everything she wanted. Except for Finn. And the house and Rufus. Well, a person couldn't have everything, could they?"

"I have news, too," he said. "I've got an interview with Molto."

"That's great," Carly said. "If you get the job, would you be based in Los Angeles?"

"Yeah, good huh?" Despite his words, he sounded down, the opposite of the guy who'd sat at the table grinning and counting spare change.

"It's time I got real. I'm thirty years old. Dreams don't come true just because you want them to."

"No, they don't," she said, a bit too sharply. "You have to make them happen."

"I thought you'd be pleased about Molto," he said. "You showed me the ad."

She sighed. "I am, I guess. If you are."

"My Screaming Reindeer song is nominated for another award," he went on, ignoring her lack of enthusiasm.

"You should be getting that nomination."

"It's not a big deal, just some radio station award," Finn said dismissively. "Not like I missed out on a Grammy."

"The publicity will be great for you," Carly said, trying to be upbeat. "Congratulations."

"I know you're disappointed in me...."

"I'm disappointed for you." Her fingers tightened on her phone.

There was a long silence.

She pressed the damp napkin to her eyes. This was no way to stay in contact. Any sympathy she offered would look like pity, which he would hate, and any constructive criticism would look like well, criticism. "I'm your friend no matter what. Do you understand?"

More silence.

"Sure." His voice became detached, almost offhand. "Big deal or not, I have to go put on a monkey suit. Tom's picking me up soon. Congrats again."

Carly hung up. She let out a long breath and then went to the bathroom to splash cold water on her face. As Finn had said, it was time to get real. The romance was most definitely over.

FINN GOT TO his feet and whistled and clapped as the Screaming Reindeer were called onstage to accept the award for most requested song of the year.

"Congratulations." Tom pulled him into a hug and slapped his back.

Finn subsided into his seat. The blonde in the shimmery silver dress on his right—Amber or Amy, something like that—smiled. She'd been coming on to him all evening even though he'd done nothing to encourage her.

Finn was happy for the band but in his deep, dark, heart of hearts he was envious. And bitter. Black and bitter as the life he led. Carly was right. It should have been him accepting this award. Of course there was no saying his rendition would have won an award but he would never know because he'd never given himself the opportunity.

This was his life, the one he'd chosen. It was fine. He was making a living, his songwriting was gaining recognition and he had Tom looking out for his interests. What was he worried about?

The rest of the evening he drank steadily to blot out all the things he didn't want to think about. The RockAround gig, Carly, his mother—

Oh, man. Another thought hit him. Irene's house going into the hands of strangers. He and Carly would never again sit on the porch and watch the sunset. Never climb up to the tower for a clandestine kiss. Never harvest the vegetables they'd planted. Never fill the house with rug rats of their own.

"Are you all right?" Tom said, a hand on his shoulder. "You just groaned."

"Yeah, fine," Finn said wearily. "I should get going." He dragged his tux jacket off the back of the chair. "You stay," he said when Tom also rose. "You've got another client up for an award."

"I can take you home," Amber or Amy said, looping an arm through his. He thought she was trying to keep him upright until her hand strayed to his butt.

"Thanks, no." Clumsily, he disengaged himself. "I'll get a cab." Before anyone could stop him, he wove through the tables toward the exit.

HE WOKE UP lying on his back on the ground. His head hurt too much to open his eyes but he could tell by the red glow behind his eyelids that his surroundings were bright. Something warm and wet was wiping across his face. He felt around gingerly, hoping he wasn't on a public sidewalk. He felt grass. A park? Could be just as bad.

What was that wetness? Cracking an eyelid he saw a long pink tongue descend toward his nose. Rufus, trying to rouse him.

"G'way, dog." He batted at the Irish setter and dragged himself onto his elbows. He was in his backyard in his underwear. His tux jacket and pants, socks and shirt were spread around the pool area. His hair felt damp and his boxers were damp, too. An empty scotch bottle lay on the tiles next to a lounge chair.

Apparently he'd thought it a good idea to go for a midnight swim alone and blind drunk. So this was what rock bottom felt like. He was lucky he hadn't drowned.

"C'm here, Rufus. Sorry, boy." He slung an arm around the dog's neck and buried his face in his fur. "Disgusting." Rufus whined. "Not you," Finn said. "Me. I'm disgusting."

Rufus made a long, low growling sound that sounded almost like talking.

"I should do something about it?" Finn asked wearily. "Yes, I should but..."

He searched for an excuse and found none. There were no *buts* to cover how low he'd sunk. He had no legitimate reason to complain about a single thing and yet he was miserable. He couldn't even pretend to have dreams anymore and that was wrong.

As he lay there on the grass, gazing up at the relentlessly blue sky, his brain cleared and he could view his life dispassionately. His career, whichever direction it took, was secondary to his happiness. The accolades and applause were all very well, but in the end it didn't matter as much as the people in his life. The most important of whom was Carly. He'd had a chance to be with her and he'd blown it. He'd blown it with his family and his friends and his community. All because he'd lost his self-respect and his integrity as a man and as a musician.

Somewhere over the years, an essential part of himself had gotten lost. He had to get it back. He had to get Carly back. And Irene's house. He had to find his way home to his family and Fairhaven.

He was done hiding and being a coward. It was time to tackle that mountain. There was only one way to the other side. He couldn't go around, he couldn't go over. He had to go through the fear.

Finn crawled over to his jacket and fumbled in the pocket for his phone. "Tom? Have you still got the name of that guy at the research center?"

CARLY WENT OVER her list of pros and cons for selling the house. It boiled down to a battle between head and heart. Selling was smart financially speaking because she could put down a deposit on a nice apartment in New York. Keeping the house, on the other hand, would mean she would retain her connection to Fairhaven, her aunt and Finn. Bonus points that Taylor and Annie could rent indefinitely.

Not that she expected to see Finn again any time soon now that he'd backed out of the Rock-Around gig. In any case, she'd decided regretfully she couldn't afford the time away from work to go to the concert even though she would have liked to be there for Annie. The girl's latest flurry of text messages had been bursting with excitement, but also worry because the band still hadn't found a keyboardist.

Carly tapped her pen on the paper and returned to the problem at hand. Head or heart? If she were her client she would advise herself to follow her head. No one ever got into trouble by choosing the smart course of action. They might not be happy but they would be safe. At the same time, it was impossible to discount the precious memories and sentimental value of Irene's home.

Her phone rang. It was Sam. Shoot, he wanted her decision.

"You have another offer," the Realtor said. "It's over your asking price by fifty thousand dollars."

"Wow." Something had to be wrong with this picture. "I suppose they want a quick settlement."

"No, one hundred and twenty days is fine."

"What's the catch?" Carly asked.

"No catch." Sam paused. "Well, maybe one. The buyer is Finn Farrell. He made the offer over the phone but he says he'll be in tomorrow to put in a formal offer."

"Finn," she repeated in disbelief. He'd just talked her into selling. So he could nab the house for himself? Why? After his disastrous no-show at Rhonda's there was no way he'd want to go back to Fairhaven to live. Did he think it a good investment? What exactly was he thinking? Why had he made the offer without saying a word to her?

"What should I tell him?" Sam said. "Will you accept? I don't think you'll do better."

"I... I need to talk to him myself," Carly said. "I'll get back to you."

She hung up and immediately called Finn. "What are you doing?"

"I take it Sam contacted you?" he asked. "Financing is assured, there's no problem there."

"I'm not worried about that." Carly noticed he

sounded a lot sharper than the other day. "I want to know why you want to buy it."

"Does it matter?" Finn said. "Isn't the point that the house won't be going into the hands of strangers? That's what's been bothering you the most, isn't it?"

"Yes, but I don't want…" She pinched between her eyes, suddenly struck by a horrible vision of him living there with another woman. "You're not responsible for what I want."

"Just say yes and there'll be one less thing for you to worry about." When she didn't reply Finn changed the subject. "I'm going away for a week or ten days. Before I leave, I'll send you an e-ticket to the RockAround gig. Will you come?"

"Are you going?" Carly asked.

"I'm in the band," Finn said. "So, yeah, I'll be there."

Carly blinked. "I didn't know you'd changed your mind about performing. Annie didn't mention it."

"I only decided this morning. I'm flying up to Fairhaven this afternoon to talk to Dingo about it."

"Finn, it's wonderful that you're going to try again but…" Would he let her and everyone else down a third time? To fly across the country, get her hopes up again, only for him to back out at the last minute. She didn't think she could take the disappointment again.

"Trust me," he said persuasively. Not just sharper but irrepressible. "You've always believed in me. Believe in me one more time. Because now I finally believe in myself. It's going to be okay."

"The concert is only two weeks away," she protested. "How are you going to get ready in such a short time?"

"I've found an intensive therapy—or rather, Tom found it—that apparently works miracles," he said. "Give me one more chance. In fact, marry me, Carly. I love you. We'll live on South Hill and fill that big old house with babies, just like Irene wanted us to."

"Now I know you're crazy." She laughed even though she wanted to curse and her heart did backflips at talk of love and marriage. Typical Finn, making her amused and flustered all at the same time. What was she supposed to say to such an off-the-cuff proposal? She wouldn't dignify it with an answer of any kind. "No one proposes over the phone."

"I'd rather do it in person but that isn't possible right now. I'll ask you again at the concert."

"I'm not going to the concert," she said. "I have too much work to do."

"It's a holiday long weekend."

"I need to get on top of things."

"Please, Carly," Finn said, his voice becoming husky. He paused a beat. "The lightbulb wants to change."

Carly almost said yes, but she forced herself to keep silent instead. She wished him good luck and then called Sam back to tell him she needed time to think about Finn's offer. If she lost the other offer, so be it, but she wasn't saying yes to Finn until she was confident his words were genuine. She would give him a couple of days and then talk to him again when he wasn't in such a strange mood.

FINN FLEW UP to Seattle that afternoon and rented a car for the drive to Fairhaven. Time was running out and he had a lot of talking to do before he headed to the medical center. He was nervous about that, but he'd made a commitment to Carly. If he let her down again there would be no coming back from that. Nothing was more important to him than her, not even the concert. He had to prove to her he was serious about changing.

His first stop was Sam's Realty with a check for the deposit on the house. The money wasn't necessary until Carly accepted his offer but Finn wouldn't be available when—if—she did accept so he gave it to Sam to hold in trust. Finn signed some papers, shook hands and headed across town.

He parked in front of his parents' house. It was after 5:00 p.m.; his mom would be home from work. Still, he didn't move. He could feel the lick of fear breathing down his neck. Then he squared his shoulders. There was no going around this.

Slowly he got out of the car and walked up the path to the front steps. He knocked and waited, shifting from one croc-skin boot to the other.

The door opened. Nora crossed her arms over her chest. "What are you doing here?"

He cleared his throat. "I've come to ask your advice on the direction of my musical career."

"Why would you want my advice when you stopped listening to me years ago?"

"I can't guarantee I'll follow it," he conceded. "But I'd like to hear what you have to say." He paused. "And I want to apologize."

Nora's expression remained impassive and for one horrible moment he was afraid she would turn him away. Finally she said, "Come in."

She led the way into the living room where the TV was tuned to a sitcom. She switched it off in the midst of a burst of canned laughter. "Your father's bowling tonight. Do you want something to drink?"

"No, thanks." Instead of sitting Finn prowled

the room. Family photos were arranged on the top of the upright piano in the corner. Joe in his navy uniform, his mom and dad dressed up for some function—in recent years judging by his dad's gray hair. His aunt and uncle and their now adult children. The only photo of Finn was his high school graduation picture. Everyone had grown up, it seemed, except for him.

He turned to Nora, who stood, hands clasped, waiting for him to settle. Taking a deep breath, he said, "I'm sorry for all the worry I caused you." His voice broke. "For the embarrassment."

"Don't be silly," she said, almost crossly and touched a fingertip to her eye. "Dingo told us about your problem after the open mike. Oh, Finn, why didn't you ever say anything?"

He hunched one shoulder. "We weren't talking to each other."

"We're talking now. Sit down and tell me what's going on with you."

"I'm going to go for it, with the band." He leaned forward, elbows on knees. "Songwriting is satisfying, being a studio musician pays the bills, and the Molto gig—if I got it—would be a career highlight. But none of those things give me the excitement I get from performing. From what I remember of that, anyway."

Nora's brow wrinkled as she studied him. "I

take it you've figured out how to get over your stage fright?"

"Anxiety. Yes, I have," he said. "There's a guy in LA who cures some of the toughest cases using virtual reality therapy. I'm booked in for my first session with him tomorrow."

"I hope it works for you," Nora said. "Does Dingo even want you in his band after what happened at the café?"

"He's the next person I need to see, to find that out." Finn paused. This bit coming was the most important… "Back in high school, Dingo introduced me to rock music but I started our band. I want it back, to guide it, steer it to where I know it can go. What I can't decide is whether to tell Dingo before the RockAround gig or afterward."

"It's his band now," Nora said. "You can't dip out for twelve years and then expect him to just hand it over. At this point, you're riding on his coattails."

"I get that," Finn acknowledged. "But if I'm going to go into performing wholeheartedly then I want to start with a bang."

"I don't know what to tell you, Finn. This is something you've got to work out with Dingo."

"Let's look at it from another angle," Finn said. "Which makes a bigger splash on the show bill—Finn Farrell and band, or band with Finn Farrell?"

"What does your agent say?" Nora asked. "He's the expert."

"I'm asking what you think," he said. The dilemma was a no-brainer, really, and his mother would know that, but he was trying to include her in his process. Trying to show her he cared what she thought.

"You should have top billing," Nora said.

"That's what I think, too. I hope Dingo will agree." Finn rose. "Sorry to make this so brief but I don't have much time. I've got to go see him now."

Nora walked him to the door. "Let me know what happens."

"I will." Finn hesitated on the porch. "By the way, I'm buying Irene's house. Trying to, at least."

Nora's eyebrows rose. "Are you going to live there?"

"It depends," he said. "On Carly."

"Oh, Finn, don't get your hopes up," Nora began.

Finn held up a hand. "I don't want to hear about how I'm not good enough for her or that I can't give her the finer things in life. The finest thing in life is love. That, I can give her plenty of."

"I believe you. But she's made a life in New York. She's worked hard and is climbing the ranks in her company. Or so I gather from what she said at dinner at her house. Giving all that up would be a big sacrifice."

"I know," he said. "I'll be sacrificing my comfort zone. I might crash and burn, but at least I'll know what I'm made of. I want to prove myself worthy of her."

"Oh, Finn. Of course you're worthy." She hugged him, her eyes moist. "I'm sorry, too, honey. I know I was hard on you growing up but I only wanted the best for you. I should have backed off, should have listened to you more."

He hugged her back. "I'll make you proud, you'll see."

She eased away and smiled through her tears. "I'm already proud."

How long had he waited to hear that from his mother? Funny. Now that he had, it almost wasn't important anymore. Oh, he was glad she felt that way and it made him feel good to hear her say it, but the person he was trying to prove himself to was himself. "Thank you."

"Let me get this straight," Dingo said, hands on hips, an incredulous look on his long face. "You want to take over leadership of the band, renaming it Finn Farrell and the Dingo Pack."

"Or something better," Finn said. "Let's toss

around ideas. I thought it would be good to have your name in there, too."

Dingo continued to give him a hard stare. "That's not the issue."

"I know." Finn raised his hands, palms out. "I have no right to ask for so much. But it was my band originally," he reminded him.

"Until you abandoned it and me."

Finn winced. "Fair enough. But times have changed. I've changed."

"Have you though?" Dingo demanded. "How can I be sure you'll be onstage when the curtain goes up?"

"All I can say is I'm taking serious steps to work on my issues," Finn said. "This time I'm not giving up till I'm over it."

"So the rest of us are what? Your backup group?" Dingo said. "That's not going to sit well with the guys."

"You'd all be integral to the sound," Finn said. "Yes, I'd be the creative driving force but without you all I'm just a guy with a piano who sings."

"Like Elton John?" Dingo said sardonically. "Because he never made it big."

"I could go it alone and I will if I have to. But remember what we dreamed of back in high school, you and I fronting a band? I want you as my bandmate. You're not only the best undiscovered lead guitarist I know, but my oldest friend. Leroy and Billy are both terrific musicians, too. Leith, as well. And Annie…we'll be lucky to hang on to her once she gets known."

"Speaking of Annie," Finn went on before his friend could respond. "I want her to have a bigger role. You have to admit she's got a unique voice."

"She does," Dingo conceded. "As for Leith, he's been wavering about joining the band. If you're back, I reckon he'll bow out."

"That would be too bad but I understand." Finn paused before moving on. "I also want the band to play original music. No group makes it big unless they've got their own sound. I've got a backlog of my songs we can start with, but I'm open to collaborating."

Dingo paced away and back, head down. "Anything else?"

Finn had asked Tom's advice on the business angle. "I want to rebrand, get professional marketing and publicity, update our sound and look."

"Sounds expensive," Dingo said. "We're not making the bucks to warrant that kind of outlay."

"We will," Finn said. "I'm positive we'll recoup our costs and more."

"All that—if it happens—is in the future," Dingo said. "We don't have time to do all that marketing let alone learn new numbers before the RockAround concert."

"No, we'll still have to do some covers and the marketing push will have to wait a bit," Finn conceded. "There's one song of mine I'd particularly like to do, though. We'll work on that and as many others as we can nail before the gig."

"I don't know," Dingo said. "Even if we do start making a living from our music down the track, right now the guys can't afford to quit their day jobs. Leroy and I have families."

"It's a risk, no question," Finn said. "But I'm willing to throw everything I've got into this. I'll use my savings to finance the band for the rest of the summer. I'll sell my house in LA if I have to." Dingo's eyebrows rose and Finn went on, "I'm serious. We'll record, we'll tour, we'll work our butts off. There are no guarantees but I'm willing to back myself. And us."

Dingo stood with his hands on his hips, shaking his head as if trying to absorb everything. "Just to be absolutely clear, you're asking me to give up leadership of my band. And to hand over creative control and play second fiddle to get you onboard?"

"I admit, it's a lot to ask." Some of the fizz went out of his enthusiasm. Dingo had lost trust in him and he could hardly blame him. Still he gave it one last pitch. "I'm in this for the long haul, not just for the RockAround gig or other one-off events. What do you say? Take this leap of faith with me?"

There was a long silence. Then Dingo threw up his hands. "Why not? Let someone else carry the can for a while."

"Is that a yes?" Finn said, not quite believing.

"I can't speak for the other guys. I reckon they'll want to wait and see how the Rock-Around gig goes," Dingo said. "They don't know you and your music the way I do. But…" He shrugged. "We've been struggling for years, eking out a living and frustrated because we know we could do better. If we do all right in Seattle I think they'll go for it."

"Sure you're not upset at me getting top billing?" Finn said.

"I'll be upset if you're a no-show in two weeks time. As to the other…" Dingo shrugged. "You have a higher profile, a platform, if you like. And there's something different about you now. I don't quite know what it is but I'm willing to go out on a limb for you. Who knows, with you headlining the band we might go all the way to the top."

"That," Finn said, embracing his friend, "is my master plan."

CHAPTER EIGHTEEN

CARLY LISTENED TO the phone ring and ring before she hung up in frustration. Finn had been incommunicado for two weeks. How could she make up her mind whether to sell him the house if she couldn't talk to him about it?

That aside, the RockAround concert was tonight and she wanted to wish him luck.

Nearly 4:00 p.m. and almost everyone had left the office, slipping away carly to start the Memorial Day long weekend. Not Carly. She was working. As usual.

Not totally incommunicado. A letter had arrived from Finn a few days ago. It contained a ticket to the RockAround concert, an airline ticket and a heart-shaped slip of paper with the words *Marry Me* scrawled across it. Her heart leaped every time she saw the message in his loopy handwriting. She beat down the flutter— she really couldn't take his proposal seriously.

Althea and Erica were probably halfway to the beach right now. They'd asked her to go but she'd declined. She hardly saw them these days because her hours were so long. Everyone she knew was going out of town for the long weekend. Even her father, although his engagement was mainly business combined with a little socializing in the evening. But then, he was a workaholic.

Restless, she rose and went to the window. Thick dark rain clouds were building above the high-rise canyon. She sighed, thinking about the sunset on Teddy Bear Beach. That would be a great place for a picnic and to watch the fireworks. Would Finn be in Fairhaven tomorrow? Might depend on how his concert went. She should be there to support him. Whatever else had gone down, they were still friends.

Sam said Finn's offer was serious; he'd paid a deposit already. Should she accept? The other buyer had dropped out and no one else had come along. Part of her wanted to keep the home. She loved so many things about the town, the sense of community, the slower pace. She could see herself getting into growing vegetables and having the time to bake bread.

But moving there would mean giving up her whole life. Why would she throw away the job she'd worked so hard for within a few months of achieving it?

Because the achievement hadn't transformed her, or made her complete, the way she'd been subconsciously expecting it to? Because work alone wasn't enough to fill the hole in her heart left by Finn's absence?

He'd broken her heart. Twice. Only a fool would give him an opportunity to do it a third time. Only a fool would chuck in her good job and apartment to marry a man who'd belatedly decided he was going to live out his teenage dream of being a rock-and-roll star. And she was no fool.

Carly went back to her desk but the words on her computer monitor were a blur. She wrapped her arms around herself against a sudden stab of fear on Finn's behalf. He was exposing himself, risking his equilibrium for the slim chance that he would be a star. What if he failed? What would that do to him?

And yet, the last time they'd talked his optimism had had a larger-than-life quality. And that rash proposal…that wasn't like him. What if he truly was changing, not just on the surface but deep down, moving in some fundamental way toward the man he was destined to be?

Herb paused as he passed her office. He'd taken off his tie and rolled up his sleeves. "You're still here? I figured when I hired you that you'd be the dedicated type. Glad to see I was right. It's the only way to get ahead at Hamlin and Brand."

Carly smiled brightly, hoping her inner agonizing wasn't visible on her face. "Finishing up soon."

"If you don't have any plans for the weekend, you're welcome to join my wife and I at our place in the Hamptons," Herb went on. "We're hosting some of the firm's biggest clients for Memorial Day."

This must be how it had started for her father. After Carly's mother died, he hadn't remarried, instead throwing himself into his work. Gradually, he'd lost touch with anyone outside his professional sphere. Now he was a powerful wheeler and dealer, but he had no personal life. Carly had forgotten that fact in her desire to succeed. Top dogs might be top dogs, but they didn't have many friends.

The truth was, she needed Finn as much as he needed her. They needed each other. So what was she doing in New York when she could be with him?

"Thanks, Herb, but actually I do have plans." She didn't often act impulsively, but when her instincts were telling her something, she listened. "I'm flying to Seattle. A friend of mine is in a band and they've got a big concert tonight."

"I saw the Rolling Stones when I was twenty," Herb said wistfully.

"That must have been something." She shut down her computer and grabbed her purse. Muttering an apology for her abrupt departure, she added, "Have a wonderful weekend."

She hurried out to the elevator, pulling up the taxi app on her phone. Herb was in his sixties so he must have seen the Stones in their heyday. Would people still remember Finn so fondly forty years on? She could believe they would.

On the ground floor she pushed through the revolving glass doors and looked up and down the street for her ride. The afternoon was still and sticky and the black clouds hung ominously overhead.

She checked her watch again. She was cutting it fine but she could make her six thirty flight. Thanks to the time difference, if all went well, she would land in Seattle around nine thirty, and get to RockAround in time for Finn's concert.

A white compact pulled in to the curb. She checked the license number and hopped in. "JFK and hurry, please," she said to the driver, a guy in his thirties with a hipster beard and glasses. "I'm running late."

"No problem." The driver pulled into traffic just as another taxi headed for the curb. The two cars clipped each other with a clash of metal and her car spun around and faced the wrong way on the street.

Carly was flung against the side of the car

and her purse slid across the seat and fell to the floor. She straightened, shaken.

"You okay?" the driver asked, peering around the seat. A trickle of blood oozed from his forehead.

"Yeah, fine," she replied, dazed.

"You saw, didn't you, lady?" her driver said. "He was going too fast."

"Sorry, I wasn't paying attention." No one was hurt and she didn't have time to hang around. "I have to go."

Getting out of the car, she tossed a twenty at the driver and waved frantically at a passing taxi. To her huge relief, it stopped. "JFK," she told the cab driver. "Hurry but please drive carefully. I need to get there in one piece."

By now she was perspiring and flustered. Taking deep breaths she calmed herself down. Everything would be all right. One little accident wasn't going to stop her.

One little accident wouldn't have. But on the parkway a six-car pileup blocked traffic in both directions. After being stalled for half an hour Carly was ready to scream. She texted Finn to wish him luck and say she was on her way. No reply. Either he was busy with preshow sound checks or whatever bands did before a gig—or he'd bailed again.

No, she refused to think that.

Finally traffic started to move, and once past the accident scene, flowed smoothly again. Carly checked her watch. If nothing else went wrong she could still make her flight.

The universe, however, had other ideas. The heavens opened and rain poured down. Visibility was nil. Traffic slowed to a crawl. Carly shut her eyes as water drummed on the roof. Maybe it was an omen. She wasn't supposed to fly to Seattle tonight.

"What time is your flight?" the driver asked. His sympathetic gray eyes watched her in the rearview mirror.

"Six thirty." She checked her watch again and groaned. Whether Finn was in trouble or whether he aced it, she wanted to be at his side. "I'll never make it now."

"I can get you there, miss," the driver said. "But it'll cost you an extra twenty dollars."

She threw up her hands. "Okay."

"Hold on." The driver accelerated into the next lane, slipping into an impossibly narrow space between a semi truck and a 4X4.

Carly's stomach dipped. Eyes scrunched, she held on with both hands and braced her feet. The car swayed with the force of sudden changes of direction, and skidded sideways on the rain-slick streets. Her eyes flew open to see them barely miss sideswiping a truck. A horn blared. She shut her eyes hard again and concentrated on breathing exercises.

Her life as it could have been flashed before her eyes. She and Finn, living in the house on the hill, surrounded by kids and dogs. He was the man she was meant to be with. He was annoying, exasperating and frustrating. Kind and generous and sexy. He might screw things up sometimes, but he had more talent than anyone she'd ever known. Her head said, *forget about him*. Her heart said, *never let him go*.

She sent a quick text to Annie. Good luck! No reply. She texted Nora. Is the concert going ahead? The reply came back within seconds. As far as I know. Why? Have you heard differently?

That was Nora, anxious and suspicious. No, just checking. I'm on my way to the airport.

We're in the car, driving to Seattle.

Save me a seat? I might be late.

Nora replied with a thumbs-up emoji.

"What airline, ma'am?" The driver slowed at the departures level. They'd made it, and in one piece.

She told him, put away her phone, and buttoned her trench coat. The rain had eased but was still splashing down.

Five forty five. She didn't have checked bags.

If she ran… If there was no lineup… If her gate wasn't at the far end of the terminal…

She paid the driver, remembering at the last minute to peel off an extra twenty. "Thanks."

"You will make it, miss," he called as she ran inside.

Of course her gate was at the far end of the terminal. She started to jog.

"Last call for Flight 73 to SeaTac Airport. Will all passengers make their way to the boarding lounge. The gate will be closing in five minutes."

The overhead board told her she had twelve minutes travel time. She took her heels off and sprinted. No way was she going to miss this plane after everything she'd been through just to get to the airport on time.

At the gate she thrust her e-ticket at the attendant and waited panting while the woman scanned the barcode. On the tarmac, workers were removing the chocks from behind the airplane's wheels.

The attendant handed back her ticket, spoke into her intercom and then said to Carly, "Hurry."

Carly was the last person on the flight. She slowed in the aisle, aware her hair was all over the place, she was in her stocking feet and she was breathing hard. She slipped into her business-class seat.

"A big, big glass of chardonnay, please," she

said to the flight attendant, indicating a glass roughly the size of a whole bottle.

Her problems hadn't ended, naturally. Due to weather delays, planes were banked up in the queue to take off. Her flight didn't leave until nearly forty minutes after scheduled departure. There was nothing she could do about this, she told herself, sipping her wine. No way to make the plane go faster. Relax. Even if she missed the concert Finn would still be in Seattle or Fairhaven. She would find him.

"More wine, ma'am?" The flight attendant held the bottle over her glass.

"No, thanks. Could I get a coffee?" She needed to wake up. She felt as if she'd been sleeping nearly all her adult life.

Sleep working. Was that a thing? If so, it's what she'd been doing. There was nothing wrong with working hard, she believed in it. But she'd been working to cover up the fact that she had no life. No love. For a moment she felt as if she were suffocating. Was this what Finn's panic attacks felt like?

Suddenly it was imperative that she tell him how she felt about him. She didn't want to spend the next twelve years wondering what would have happened if only she'd had enough courage to say what was in her heart. She would find a job with another firm on the west coast. Or she could strike out on her own. What mattered was to be with Finn. She didn't care what he did for a living whether it was writing songs or working in a record store.

By her calculations, the plane would touch down at 10:15 p.m. She would be lucky to catch the last half hour of his performance.

FROM BACKSTAGE, FINN peered through a crack in the black velvet curtains at the nightclub. The enormous room was only half full. Enough house lights were on that he could see his mother and father sitting at a table near the front, nursing a couple of drinks. A coat was slung over a third chair but there was no sign of Carly.

He reached for his cell to check if she'd sent a message, but his phone wasn't in his jacket pocket. Then he made a face as a clear image came to him of leaving it on the passenger seat of his car. Of all the times…

She hadn't said she would come. But she hadn't said she wouldn't, either. He loved her, though, and he believed she loved him. He had to have faith that what they meant to each other would outweigh all the obstacles.

He also had to have faith that when he went out on that stage tonight his case of nerves wouldn't escalate to panic. The virtual reality therapy had left him feeling like a new man.

However, nothing was certain until he was put to the test.

Leroy and Billy had been surprised and disgruntled when Finn took over as band leader but they'd accepted the change after Dingo admitted he was relieved to relinquish the reins. As Dingo had predicted, Leith had left the band with no hard feelings on either side.

From the beginning Finn showed himself to be decisive and firm. Discipline was key to any kind of success and a band was no exception. He'd given them music to learn while he was at the clinic and they'd rehearsed hard with the result that half their short playlist would be his original songs.

"Everyone ready?" he said, turning back to the guys and Annie. He got a thumbs-up from Leroy and Dingo as they moved into their positions. Billy nodded and kicked an electrical lead out of his way. Annie hummed scales under her breath. She'd toned down her makeup and dyed her hair a rich auburn instead of black. Her clothes weren't as tight or else she'd lost a little weight. Either way, she looked terrific.

"Here's the final playlist," Finn said, handing out slips of paper. "We've only got an hour to make an impression. Let's rock this joint."

"There's hardly anybody here," Billy said.

"We're the warm-up act," Leroy explained. "The place won't fill up till just before the main event."

"People will filter in over the next hour," Finn said. "We give it our all whether there's ten people in the audience or ten thousand." He walked around the stage, giving them each a high five. "Years from now you'll remember that this was the night your life changed forever."

He heard the MC introduce them and stepped behind the keyboard, one of a bank of three keyboards.

The curtain rose. The lights came on.

"One, two, one, two, three, four..." Finn nodded the beats, checking the guys were with him. Then he brought his splayed hands down on the resounding opening chord.

CARLY TEXTED FRANTICALLY all the way to the RockAround. No one was answering her texts now, not even Nora. That could be good, or bad.

When the taxi dropped her off out front, she joined the lineup to get in. These people had arrived late like her although probably they'd only come to hear the headline act. Carly caught a riff of exuberant piano music and she realized it was coming from people's phones. Was it being transmitted by friends inside? The crowd was restless at the slowness of the bouncers and wanted in. Clearly whatever was going on in there had caught their interest.

Once inside, she moved with the stream of concertgoers through the outer corridor toward the main room. The buzz of noise grew as she got closer and she was propelled inside by the jostling crowd during the lull between songs. When her eyes adjusted to the dark room she saw that people were crammed in, standing between the tables and along the walls.

Under a blazing spotlight Finn stood front and center, surrounded by banks of keyboards. He lifted his hands and then brought them crashing down, signaling the beginning of the next song. A roar went up from the crowd.

Carly felt a visceral thrill run through her at the first sound of his deep and powerful voice. He stood tall and broad-shouldered, legs braced as he pounded out the music, his wild black hair haloed by the klieg lights. One by one, the other band members joined in, adding their instruments to the growing power of the music.

Then another spotlight came on and Annie stepped to the microphone. Carly barely recognized the teenager with her auburn hair and sexy, confident movements. And those weren't the clothes she'd picked out with Carly. They were more refined. The other band members, too, had stepped up their look with more fashionable jeans and shirts.

Finn looked every inch the rock star in a black, fitted shirt with the sleeves rolled up over muscular forearms roped with leather and silver, his long legs encased in ripped black skinny jeans. Tall leather boots completed his pirate look. His racing hands chased rippling chords over the keys. The music was energetic, almost muscular but also melodic and catchy. It fell somewhere between pop and rock and classical, embodying the best elements of all three. Carly's heart swelled with pride. It was unique. It was Finn.

There was no hope of finding Nora and Bob's table so she stayed where she was and let the music roll through her. Tears spilled down her cheeks. If Finn never did anything else, this performance would be remembered forever by every single person in this room.

The crowd went wild when the song ended and the curtain fell, stamping and shouting and whistling their approval. The curtain rose again on an empty stage. Still the cheering went on and on. One by one, the band came back on. First Leroy sat at his drums and beat out a rolling tap tap tap to usher in Billy, who picked up his bass guitar and plucked out a melody that sounded vaguely familiar. Then Dingo loped on and picked up his guitar, spraying the room with a virtuoso guitar lick that had the audience cheering. Annie slipped in to a burst of applause, shaking a tambourine and grinning from ear to ear.

The tempo built during the instrumental introduction. She couldn't quite identify the song even though she recognized Finn's stamp all over it. The audience was clapping and swaying in time to the beat. Finn strode onstage, arms upraised, bathed in lights, and the audience raised the roof with rapturous applause. Carly pressed a hand to her chest. She'd never experienced anything like this in her life.

Finn leaned across the keyboard to speak into the microphone and the room fell silent. He introduced the band one by one, pausing for appreciative applause. Then told the audience that their encore was a cover of a current hit on the charts. Carly's outgoing breath joined the general murmur of disappointment. If she only got to hear a couple songs she would have preferred to hear his originals.

Finn hit the keyboard and her disappointment was forgotten as the band broke into a joyous and uplifting number. The room pulsed with the music and everyone was dancing on the spot. The beat was infectious, impossible to hear without wanting to move and shout and sing.

A full minute into the song she realized that

he was playing the hit by Screaming Reindeer. It was Finn's song, played his way. The other band had done a great rendition but this was on another level entirely, light-years better. Wow. So that's what he meant when he said they had the tempo wrong. It wasn't supposed to be a quiet song. It was supposed to be raucous and merry, to raise the spirits along with the roof. Now she understood the extent of his genius. Soon the world would know, too.

When it was over, the band left the stage in reverse order, leaving Finn alone at the end, playing the keyboard in an improvised jazzy finish that trailed away to a tinkle of notes echoing the dominant melody until it became softer and softer and softer. The audience held their collective breath until it was so quiet you could have heard a pin drop. Then the lights went out. Silence.

The room erupted in sustained applause that went on and on. Eventually the house lights came on for the intermission. Everyone groaned but no one was unhappy. Smiles abounded and everyone was talking about the band and especially about Finn, and wondering who he was. Canned music played over the speakers. People headed for the bar.

Carly found Nora and Bob near the front

of the room, hugging each other and smiling and crying.

"Finn was awesome," Carly shouted over the noise. She hugged them both. "Can we go backstage?"

Nora showed her a pass on a lanyard and pointed to a door to the right of the stage. A bouncer with a shaved head and multiple piercings stood guard. "Sorry folks, the exit is that way."

"We're with the band," Bob said. "Finn Farrell is our son."

The bouncer inspected the pass and waved Bob and Nora through. "Not you, ma'am," he said to Carly. "Not without a pass."

"I'm his girlfriend," she pleaded.

"That's what they all say," the burly man said, crossing his arms over his massive chest. "If you don't leave I'll have to escort you outside."

"She's with me." Finn's voice was hoarse and he looked like he'd run a marathon. He held out a hand to Carly. She slipped past the bouncer and into Finn's arms. The door shut behind her.

"Oh, Finn." In the dim passageway he held her tightly. His shirt was drenched in perspiration and he radiated body heat like a minor sun. "You did it. You were amazing. All of Seattle is going to be talking about you. Actually, the world is going to be talking about you."

"I'm so glad you came." He kissed her cheeks, her eyes, her mouth. "I didn't know if you were out there but I sang to you anyway." He put an arm around her and started walking her down the hall. "Come on. We've got champagne on ice."

In the dressing room, Carly melted into the background as Finn collected accolades and backslaps from his bandmates. Nora and Bob stood in a corner drinking champagne and beaming.

Annie handed Carly a glass of bubby, her eyes shining. "We killed it."

Carly hugged her. "You sure did. Girl, get ready because you are going places. I love your hair by the way."

"Thanks. I feel more like myself." She glanced across the room. Taylor waved. "I'd better go get him."

Carly laughed. She felt a hand on her back and turned to see Finn.

"The guys are going to grab something to eat and keep the party going," he said. "We're all staying at the Marriott tonight. Figured win or lose, we would celebrate our big night in the city. My parents will be there and Joe flew up from San Diego. Will you come?"

It was the early hours of the morning New York time after a very long work week. What she should do was get some rest so they could talk tomorrow. But never mind that. This was Finn's night and she wanted to celebrate with him, to savor the first of what she was sure would be many successes.

"Absolutely, I'm coming," she said. "I can sleep anytime but it's not every day I get to hang with a rock star."

CHAPTER NINETEEN

THE RESTAURANT AT the Marriott had been about to close when the band walked in along with their entourage of around fifteen people. But when Finn ordered a dozen bottles of Dom Perignon and share platters of food, the maître d' told waiters to pull three tables together. The party was on.

Marla had left Tyler with her mother for the night, and Leroy's wife Latisha was there, too. Billy was flanked by his girlfriend. Tom had flown up from LA for the night. Joe, with his short back and sides, polo shirt and dress pants, couldn't have looked more different from Finn but the brothers were clearly good friends judging by the warmth with which they joked with each other. Taylor's friends had left but Taylor had stayed to be with Annie. He had his arm around the back of her chair and her hand was on his knee.

The group feasted and drank, riding the high on the success of their show. Tom fielded text messages from promoters who wanted to book the band and everyone was buzzing about a possible tour of the west coast in the fall. They all agreed they would take every decent gig that came their way to build a following.

Around 1:00 a.m. Nora and Bob went up to their room, pleading fatigue. Before they left Nora hugged Finn hard and Carly heard her whisper, "I love your music. I had no idea."

When Finn eased out of her embrace, there were tears in his eyes. "Thanks, Mom," he said, his voice breaking. "That means the world to me."

Joe left around 3:00 a.m., explaining he was used to getting up at five every morning. Shortly after that, Carly noticed that Annie and Taylor had quietly disappeared.

"I'm hitting the wall," Carly said, leaning on Finn's shoulder. "Can I have your key card?"

"I'm too wired to sleep. Tell you the truth, I'd rather go home," he said. "To Fairhaven."

"Now?" she said, blinking. "There's no way I could drive. Can you? This is no time to get a DUI."

"I've only had one glass since we got to the restaurant." Sure enough, he reached for the water glass from which he'd been sipping the whole evening.

"Turning over a new leaf?" she asked.

"I've got my sights on big things. I need to stay focused."

She pushed a straggling lock of hair off his forehead. "Your life is going to change dramatically."

"I'm kinda counting on that," he said with a small smile. "I'm under no illusions that the path will be smooth but I'm ready to walk the walk."

Finn got his bags from the room and checked out while the valet brought around his rental car.

"Tell me about this intense therapy," Carly said as they drove through the empty streets of downtown Seattle. "Clearly it did the job."

Finn made a turn, heading for the freeway entrance and explained. "By the last day I almost didn't want to leave, the techniques were working so well."

"It's mind-boggling that it worked so fast," Carly said.

"You're partly responsible for my quick progress," Finn said. "The therapist reckons that your idea to get me onstage at the RockAround and turn on the klieg lights jolted free suppressed memories. In between virtual reality sessions he did more traditional therapy, talking through issues and digging into my relationship with my mother."

"That must have been painful," Carly said. "Anytime you combine love and guilt the result isn't pretty."

"I'm going to ask Nora to come with me to a session," Finn said. "Our fight might have left her with issues, too. The main thing I've learned so far is to stop blaming both her and myself for what happened."

"I could have told you that. Oh wait, I did." She smiled and touched his arm to show she was teasing. "I know that's something a person has to figure out for themselves." Then she yawned and blinked. "Sorry, I'm so tired."

"Sleep if you want," Finn said.

"I might do that." Carly put her seat back and closed her eyes.

The next thing she knew it was an hour later and they were cruising down Chuckanut Drive. Sleepily, she raised her seat. "You've been up all night and you're taking the long way?"

"It's such a pretty drive," he said. "I wanted to remind you of the beauty of the Pacific Northwest."

"I don't need reminding. I love it." The endless evergreens, blue water and log-strewn beaches set against a backdrop of snow-capped mountains had gotten into her blood as a child and would always be a part of her. To the west, the soaring Olympic Mountains blushed pink with sunrise. Even though she'd been raised on the east coast, this felt like home.

"So…" he said, touching her hand. "Are you going to accept my offer?"

"Which one?" Carly replied. "The house or…"

"Both, I hope." He glanced at her and added softly, "We could have it all, you and I, if we gave up our lives in Los Angeles and New York." He winked. "But we have to want to change."

She smiled and looked into his warm, dark eyes. Eyes that had always seen inside her to the person she really was. That, she realized, was why she loved him. Not the romance and excitement he brought to her life although those were wonderful, but the fact that he got her, deep down. He saw the woman who was looking for a home but didn't want to be confined to it. The woman who drew satisfaction from helping others but didn't know when she needed help herself. She opened her mouth to speak and he held up a hand.

"Don't answer yet," he said suddenly. "Wait until you see what I've done with the place."

Carly laughed. "I've been away a month and you've already changed it? It's not yours yet, bucko."

A thick black eyebrow rose. "Bucko?"

"Short for buccaneer." She shrugged. "Well, possibly not but it's nautical in origin."

"Now I'm even more confused," Finn said.

"Inside joke. Never mind." She wondered if he would consider dressing as a pirate this Hal-

loween. Thinking of him in a white shirt showing a bare chest and breeches and boots with a
big black hat made her want to fan herself.

A few minutes later they were driving up
South Hill and turning onto their street. Finn
pulled into the driveway and cut the engine.

Carly got out of the car and started up the
path. She was halfway to the steps when she
stopped dead. There on the porch were two
hand-carved rocking chairs. "Finn Farrell, no
fair. You're playing hardball."

"Come and sit down before we go inside," he
coaxed. "You like?"

She nodded because her throat was too full to
speak. Reaching out, she took his hand and they
sat quietly and looked at the town below and the
bay glowing with sunrise. She could imagine
them still here in another forty years with their
grandchildren playing at their feet. What was
harder was reconciling Finn's coming rock star
life with that vision of home and hearth.

"Are you sure you want to settle down?" she
asked. "You're going to be touring most of the
time. Don't you want to enjoy the moment?" She
held her breath, waiting for his answer.

"There's only one woman I want to be with,
Carly, and that's you," he said, answering her
unspoken question. Finn brought her hand to his
lips and kissed her palm. "My biggest regret for

those lost years is that I didn't try hard enough for you. When I lost faith in myself I thought you were lost to me, too. Now I've found you again. You gave me the impetus I needed to change. Sure, I want to ride the whirlwind as long as possible but I want—need—you by my side."

"Oh, Finn." She squeezed his hand. "I'll be here, beside you all the way."

"You know, none of the good stuff may come to pass," he warned. "The music industry is notoriously fickle. We might be getting excited about what will turn out to be a flash in the pan."

"I don't believe that but even if that happens, it doesn't matter."

"What I can guarantee will last is my love for you," he went on. "We're meant to be together. You're my anchor, my true north. You were the one to guide me home and always will be. Please say you'll share your life with me."

"I will." Tears blurred her vision and she dashed them away, saying fiercely, "Rich or poor, it doesn't matter. I love you. I always have and I always will. Whether you're working in a record store or playing Carnegie Hall."

She got out of her chair and climbed on his lap. His hands framed her face as she lowered her mouth to kiss him. Then she buried her face in his neck and breathed in his musky scent while he held her, stroking her back.

"What about you?" he said, brushing her hair off her wet face. "How are we going to make this work for you? I know your job is important."

"I'll look around for something else or go out on my own," she said. "Getting the job and winning the big account gave me confidence. If I move west I'd like to make Fairhaven our base and live here, in this house."

"That's what I want, too," Finn said. "The whole band is here so it only makes sense. And life will be hectic on the road. It will be good to come home to peace and quiet. To you."

Carly looked up at the house. "It's going to be both strange and wonderful to live here. What room will we use? Mine would be cramped with a queen-sized bed but I can't imagine sleeping in Irene's room."

"As I said, let me show you what I've done." Finn gently set her on her feet and rose. "If you don't like it, we'll think of something else."

As they climbed the stairs Carly thought back to the night of Irene's funeral and how Finn had taken care of her when she'd fallen apart. How could she ever have accused him of screwing things up? He was a man who could be relied on. He'd saved her house and handed her his heart. What more could she ask for?

Finn opened the door to the master bedroom and Carly stepped inside. It was unrecognizable as her aunt's room. In place of the old white-painted bedstead was a king-sized, hand-carved rosewood bed with matching nightstands. The charcoal duvet, snowy white linens and plump colorful pillows were also brand-new.

Dragging her gaze away from the bed, she took one look at the walls and laughed. Finn had salvaged her old posters and decorated the room with Savage Garden, NSYNC and a new picture of a prancing Lipizzaner stallion. Her music box and cat figurine stood on the dresser. "You are too much."

"We'll tweak it," Finn said. "What do you think?"

"I love it. And I love you." Carly pulled him down onto the bed. Sinking into the comfy mattress, she was suddenly too tired to think about home decor or anything but sleep.

Finn wound his arms and legs around her and touched his nose to hers. "I love you, too."

They twined together, his voice rumbling softly in her ear. "We're going to live together in this beautiful house and make music and babies and bake loaves of sourdough and grow vegetables…"

"Sounds perfect," she mumbled, dragging the quilt over them both.

Finn yawned and snuggled in more comfortably. "This might be the only time for a while that we get the house all to ourselves. We should make the most of it."

"Mmm-hmm." Carly's eyes fluttered shut and she started to drift off.

Curled up in bed with Finn, knowing that their whole future lay ahead of them was all she needed at the moment. As Finn's breath deepened, the birds in the big maple tree started chirping in the dawn. Carly smiled. She'd missed the little rascals.

* * * * *

Be sure to check out these terrific Harlequin Superromance novels from acclaimed author Joan Kilby:

HOME TO HOPE MOUNTAIN
MAYBE THIS TIME
TO BE A FAMILY
PROTECTING HER SON
IN HIS GOOD HANDS
TWO AGAINST THE ODDS
HER GREAT EXPECTATIONS
HOW TO TRAP A PARENT

Available now at www.Harlequin.com!